CHARLIE'S WORLD

Patti Hales

Pen Press Publishers Ltd

Published in Great Britain by
Pen Press Publishers Ltd
39–41, North Road
Islington
London N7 9DP

ISBN 1-905203-40-3

Cover Illustration by Kaye Hodges
Cover design by Jacqueline Abromeit

Dedication

To Mark Fennell... the original Charlie... Thank you, darling. I will never forget when, aged 5 and around the table on a Sunday teatime, you told us, so sincerely, that you wanted 'an axe' for your birthday. Not for any evil purpose; just to cut down things which got in the way and to let the sun shine through.

Thanks, also, to all you other marvellous grandchildren, who shared with me your hopes, dreams and fears. Giggles, too. I love each and every one of you. You are very precious and special.

To Ian Sommerville, the late Fiction Editor of My Weekly magazine. You saw the potential of Charlie'sWorld. You suggested that, after the first little tale proved so popular with your readers, a series of six might be a good idea...then another...and another... You encouraged me every step of the way. I miss you, Ian, but I know that you are still cheering me on.

To Edward Gunn...my wonderful business manager. Without you, this book would not have happened. You have worked so hard on my behalf. You believe in me. You raise me up...

About the Author

 Patti Hales' first interest in writing occurred when she joined creative writing classes in Margate in 1991. Her first story was published in 1993, and since then she has been a regular short story contributor to various best-selling magazines. She occasionally writes topical and informative feature articles. Her stories have also been published under the names of Tricia Holden and Helen Tyndall.

The author gained an Adult Education Teaching Diploma with a view to teaching for the University of Kent, and still tutors private groups when her time allows.

Patti is a mother of four and has thirteen grandchildren, so is well versed in the antics of youngsters growing up – the basis for her successful *Charlie's World* stories. She lives and writes from her study overlooking the sea on the coast of Kent.

For more information on Charlie, visit his website www.charliesworld.pattihales.co.uk

Acknowledgement

Sincere thanks to the marvellous Kaye Hodges for allowing me to use her wonderful illustration on the cover of Charlie's World.

Kaye can be contacted via chris@artistspartners.demon.co.uk

Contents

A Hard Act to Follow

Jean, Dr Gilbert's receptionist, looked distinctly harassed: strands of her greying hair had escaped the confines of its usual severe knot at the nape of her neck and her ice-blue eyes, instead of flashing no-nonsense efficiency, were filled with a plea for understanding.

Cheeks flushed, she thrust her head through the hatch which divided the surgery office from the waiting-room.

"I'm terribly sorry," she told the assembled patients, who included Tessa and Charlie Harper, "but Dr Gilbert has been unavoidably detained by an emergency. There could be a considerable delay.

"I've rung Nurse to see if she can help out and she'll be here as soon as possible, but I honestly can't say how long... just... well... I'm sorry and if anyone would like to make an alternative appointment..."

"What does delay mean, Mum?" Charlie's voice soared above the muted groans. "And 'mergency. What's a mergency? Does it hurt? Is it like when Dr Gilbert sticks a needle in you, so you don't get measles and things and you have to be very brave?"

Tessa shook her head.

Mentally she flicked through all the things she'd planned to do after she'd had her check-up... tea with her Mum... call into the School Shop to see if Charlie's new grey and red blazer was in yet... get something quick for supper.

If the delay was too long...

Maybe, she thought, it could be a good idea to call it a day and join the impatient-looking, smart-suited chap with the briefcase and the tight-lipped woman in the tweed outfit and brown brogues, who'd complained louder than anyone else.

Through the glass-topped door she could see the pair jostle for pride of place at the reception desk. And Jean, looking very fed up!

Tessa glanced up at the clock on the wall. 2:15. She'd give it a quarter of an hour, she decided, or until Charlie got too boisterous. He was a good little soul, but there wasn't a lot here to hold his attention. Anyone feeling a bit under the weather might just find him a bit *too much* to cope with.

Besides, her own appointment wasn't that urgent. It was just that her blood pressure had been up a bit and Doctor Gilbert, aware of her history, had advised a regular check.

"Just to be on the safe side," he'd said, when he'd given Charlie his pre-school booster injections the month before.

"Mum," Charlie nudged her, "you still haven't told me what a delay is. Don't you know? Shall I ask that man over there, the one with the patch on his eye, like a pirate?" He'd lowered his voice, but it still held an echoing clarity, which seemed to bounce off the peach-painted walls.

Blushing, Tessa scooped him onto her lap. She rested her chin against his soft chestnut hair. It smelled of last night's shampoo and this morning's outdoors.

"A delay," she began to explain, "is when somebody can't do something, because a problem has cropped up and they've got to see to that first. A very important problem, like-"

"A 'mergency!" Charlie interrupted, his voice wobbly with excitement. "I've just remembered what a 'mergency is. Granny told me." He wriggled himself into the crook of Tessa's arm.

"If your house goes on fire, that's one. So is if a bad robber climbs through the window to steal your television and if the man next door falls out of a tree."

Tessa swallowed a giggle.

Their own man-next-door – a kindly widower in his early seventies, Hector Smythe – was around the sixteen stone mark. She couldn't imagine his dumpy legs getting anywhere near even the lowest branch of the old horse chestnut at the bottom of his typically English country garden.

Charlie's voice broke into her thoughts. "Nine, nine, nine," he said. "You pick up the phone and you dial number nine, three times. Then when somebody answers, you say 'Charlie Harper, 79 Broom Crescent, Eddingfield and I need a fire engine, please and an ambulance, please and... and..."

"A policeman?" Before Tessa could supply the missing word the suggestion came from the man with the cotton-wool pad, taped across his left eye.

Her arms felt suddenly empty. She watched as Charlie crossed the tiled floor like a whirlwind, watched as he perched himself between the man and an old lady with heavily bandaged legs, felt her mouth drop open as he gently patted the woman's knee.

"Oh dear, did you fall off your bike?"

The tired face which, Tessa had thought earlier, exactly matched the beige of the warm wool coat, was treated to a colour wash of pastel pink. Behind nondescript spectacles, faded blue eyes crinkled at the corners and lips, with blurred edges, tilted, showing too white, too perfect false teeth.

"I wish I had, ducks," she said.

Charlie seemed to be locked in a mental battle with himself. A deep frown creased his smooth forehead and his dark brows drew together in a straight line. Tessa wondered what was going through his mind.

She didn't have long to wait.

"I'll push you off," he offered, shaking his head, "but I don't think you'd really like it. It hurts. Look." He shrugged out of his jacket and rolled up the sleeves of his red jumper. Both elbows were peppered with remnants of scratches and bruises.

"I got this one – and this one, when I fell off mine. And this huge one... Mum, where did I get this huge one?"

Tessa winced. She could still hear the sickening thud as he'd toppled, sideways, off the trampoline at a friend's birthday party. For a horrible moment, she'd thought he'd done real damage, but, being Charlie, he'd bounced straight back again, performing somersaults with more confidence than skill, enjoying every second of yet another new experience.

"At Daisy's," she reminded him.

"Daisy Johnson's. Oh, yeah. That was brilliant!" Charlie slid off the polished bench. He stood in the middle of the floor, arms rigid by his side. "I can't actually do it now," he explained to his new friends, "because the floor is all hard and a trampoline is all springy, but this is how you start. You jump up and down, as quick as you can, faster and faster and faster, then—"

"Charlie!" Tessa shook her head. She patted the space beside her. There was a *Thomas the Tank Engine* comic on the table. If she could interest him in that...

"I won't be long," Charlie panted. "I just want to talk to this pirate first. I've never met a real live one before." He grinned, then turned his small back on her.

Enough, Tessa decided. She could easily come back tomorrow. Or the next day, for that matter. Either morning would do nicely. And with Charlie safely occupied by his pre-school classes, her blood pressure should reach a nice safe low.

But as she stooped to pick up her bag, the first flutterings of her new baby rippled under her outdoor coat, causing her to catch her breath. She folded her arms, protectively, round her expanding waist; felt a surge of love fill her heart.

Her last two pregnancies hadn't reached this stage, but she grieved for her lost children every time she looked at Charlie.

Taking any kind of a risk would be madness. Really, she ought to wait. Quickly she took stock of the situation.

The pirate – *stop it*, she scolded herself – the man wasn't looking the least bit put out by the attention Charlie was inflicting on him. He didn't seem to mind in the slightest that a faintly-grubby finger was circling the cotton wool pad and that the questions as to how he'd received his injury were flowing, thick and fast.

Also, she noted, several other patients – a teenage lad with dreadful acne, the elegantly-dressed woman who managed the town's newest jewellery shop and a couple of genteel-looking ladies in matching felt hats and grey gloves – had inched their way round and seemed totally engrossed in simple explanations about cataracts being like an unwanted overcoat on a warm day and how a magic operation meant that the person could see again. Ending with: "I'm what you call a new man... or rather I will be, when this patch comes off!"

"Well I never!" she heard Charlie say, sounding a dead ringer for his paternal grandpa.

"I had that operation ten years ago," one of the women said, "and I've never looked back since."

"I 'xpect you only look forward now, don't you?" Charlie's innocent question brought a guffaw from the spotty youth and muted chuckles all round.

"She didn't mean it that way, ducks," Charlie's bandaged friend told him. "What the lady meant was that she could do anything she wanted to do, now that she could see properly again."

"What? Like riding her bike and *not* falling off? Is that why you're here?" He stopped and frowned. "No... you want to fall off yours, don't you?"

As more laughter rang out, Jean's head appeared through the hatch. She glanced at the merry gathering in the corner, then met Tessa's eyes and smiled... a *real* smile, instead of the token gesture to which everyone had become accustomed.

"Thank you," she mouthed silently. Then, in her normal concise tones: "Nurse is here and Doctor is on his way. Thank you for your patience," she informed everyone.

"I'm not a patience today, Jean," Charlie called out, cheerfully. "I'm just here looking after my mum. She's pregnant, you know." The murmur of approval changed to laughter as he folded his arms and added, very seriously, "Does anyone know what pregnant means?"

Now, Tessa thought, she'd find out whether or not she and Martin had done a good job when they'd answered Charlie's constant stream of questions.

He knew that the foetus – Martin had insisted on the correct terminology and on sharing the charts in the book, which the hospital had supplied, with his son – was inside her, but, fortunately, he hadn't yet got round to asking how it happened to be in there in the first place.

That one might be a bit more tricky! The baby nudged her softly, like a whispering breeze, as she waited.

"Edward Forbes, Nurse is ready for you." Charlie's pirate looked put out as his name was called. He rose, reluctantly.

"Back in a minute," he said.

"It means that she's going to have a baby," Charlie yelled at his retreating back. "It means," he said, turning his wide-eyed gaze on the rest of what Tessa was beginning to think of as his adoring fans, "that inside her tummy… right now… is my brother, Wilfred Harper."

The lady from the jewellery shop was looking at her, a bit oddly, Tessa felt. In fact, everyone was looking a bit surprised.

Not that she could blame them. She wriggled in her seat. *Wilfred!* Where on earth had Charlie dug that one up from? They'd discussed several names… Callum, Max, Rhys… and for a girl… Laura, Lyndsey and Amy.

She had to ask.

"Charlie, who's Wilfred?"

"My friend, Tom Patterson's rabbit. It's a great name, isn't it?"

Tessa nodded, struggling to keep a straight face. "But what if it's a little girl?"

"Can't girls be called Wilfred?"

She didn't have a chance to say "No." Everyone else beat her to it.

"Oh, well... I suppose..." Charlie didn't look the least convinced, but he did cast a sympathetic eye over the layers of bandages. "What's *your* name, lady?"

Dolly, Tessa thought, instantly. On second thoughts, she could be a Queenie. Queenie Harper! No... they couldn't... not in the nineties. Any more than they could consider a twenty-first century Wilfred.

"Katherine Mary. After my two grandmothers."

Katherine Mary. Katy Harper. Not bad. In fact, rather lovely. Tessa mentally added the names to her list as the door swung open and the tall man, minus his patch, green eyes twinkling, joined the others, sitting down again in the seat he'd so recently vacated.

Perhaps, Tessa thought, he had to see the doctor, too, before he got the all clear.

"You don't look like a pirate any more," Charlie told him, sadly.

"Katherine Downs? Nurse is ready for you," Jean announced, crisply.

With surprising agility, the old lady rose and padded across the floor. "Don't go away," she said, winking at Charlie.

"And, Mrs Harper. Doctor will see you now."

Tessa stood up. "Charlie. Come on."

"Can't I stay here with my friends?" He tilted his head on one side and treated her to a full beam gaze from his round greeny-blue eyes. "Please, Mum."

Saying no, wasn't going to be easy. This was neither the time nor the place to remind Charlie about strangers and safety. Of course she knew, instinctively, that her son was in no danger, but still, she didn't want to send out the wrong messages.

"Mrs Harper…"

Tessa turned. Jean was beckoning her. She walked over to the hatch.

"I'll take personal responsibility for the boy," Jean said. "I know all these people and," she puffed out her thin chest, "no one gets past me without being seen!

"Besides," the receptionist carried on, "if Dr Gilbert wants to discuss anything a bit – well, you know – personal, then it might be easier if you were on your own."

Tessa nodded. Jean was right, of course. It *would* be so much easier. She turned slowly. Everyone was watching… waiting, it seemed…

"Okay," she said, "but don't be a nuisance, Charlie, will you? Promise?"

"I won't be a nuisance. Cross my heart. I love you, Mum. One hundred and two."

Tessa blew him a kiss. "Love you back. Same amount!"

"What are we going to talk about now?" she heard him say as she left the waiting room and crossed the corridor into Dr Gilbert's surgery.

Her blood pressure was fine. And, when she mentioned the baby's first flutterings, was subjected to a gentle examination, then rewarded by a wide grin from the elderly GP.

"Everything seems to be going according to how it should do. I can't see any cause for worry, In fact, I reckon you've got another Charlie in there," he said, watching as her pale stomach moved the merest fraction.

Another Charlie! Tessa gave a mock groan. "Charlie wants to call the baby Wilfred. Even if it's a girl."

"Dare I ask why?"

"Would you believe it's because it's the name of his best friend's rabbit?"

Laughter filled the small room. "When it comes to that boy, I'd believe anything," Dr Gilbert said, wiping his eyes with the back of his hand. He relaxed back in his chair. "I get so many brats in here," he confided.

"Absolute little monsters, if I'm really honest. Whereas when I see your name on my list it… well… it brightens my whole day. You're doing a good job." He stood up and helped Tessa back on with her coat.

"Jean told me to ask you if you'd mind renting Charlie out for emergencies. Like today." He walked with her back to the door to the waiting room.

"A 'mergency," Tessa said solemnly, "according to my son, is when the man next door falls out of a tree."

Dr Gilbert struggled to keep a straight face and failed. "I'll see you in a couple of weeks."

The first thing that struck her as she went to rejoin Charlie was the noise. It was more like a party than a gathering of sick people. Even Jean was in on things – elbows on the hatch, looking years younger and nothing like her usual sombre self. Her eyes were pure sapphire, instead of pale ice.

She straightened up when she saw Tessa. "I think I'm in love," she said, flashing Charlie, now perched on the ex-pirate's lap and being shown how to make paper versions of Concorde from old magazines, an adoring glance.

And apart from the lad with the bad skin, who'd just been called in to see Dr Gilbert, the semi-circle Tessa had left behind was still intact. No, she realised, doing a mental head-count… there were now two more men and three more women, one hardly more than a schoolgirl with braces on her teeth and a high pony-tail which swung as she laughed.

Charlie looked up. "Hi, Mum. Watch this." The swallow-like plane did a couple of perfect circles before landing at her feet. "Brilliant, eh?"

Tessa nodded. "Fantastic. You'll have to show Dad how to do it." She fished in her bag for her diary. "I have to come back in a couple of weeks," she told Jean.

She was suddenly aware that a silence, as thick as a sheepskin blanket, had settled itself over the waiting room. After several breathless moments, Charlie's voice rang out.

"What day are we coming again? My friends want to know, so they can come too." He slid to the floor. "I've told them I'm going to school – all day – after Summer, but it's not Summer yet, is it?"

Thankfully not. Tessa shook her head and a lump formed in her throat. Life without Charlie. It wasn't going to be the same. "You've a hard act to follow, Wilfred Harper," she muttered to the child growing inside her.

In the meantime...

Clearing her throat she pretended to give the matter of her next appointment some consideration.

"I was thinking of two weeks tomorrow. Tuesday afternoon. Around..." she looked at Jean for guidance.

Jean flicked through the pages. She chewed thoughtfully on the end of her pencil. "Right. How does this sound? Mrs Downes at two, Mr Forbes, two fifteen – the Misses Sommerville to see nurse at two ten." She scribbled furiously, "Mrs Harper – and Charlie – at two thirty, Ms Brewster..." Stopping, she tossed the pencil aside.

"I tell you what... why doesn't *everyone* come at two o'clock and we'll go from there...?"

Charlie's Dilemma

"He looks as if he's about to explode!" Molly said. Tessa grinned and nodded.

Charlie's face was crimson, his cap was balanced at a precarious angle on top of his thick chestnut hair and the tail of his grey shirt fluttered under the hem of his new school blazer as he sped towards her.

As he got closer, she could see a banana-shaped smudge of bright yellow on his left cheek. And that his shoes were on the wrong feet. As usual.

She held her arms out. Charlie, panting like a steam train, ran into them.

"Hi, Mum," he said, accepting her kiss and eagerly returning it. "Did you miss me?"

Tessa assured him that she had and was rewarded with a beaming grin and his arms reaching as far round her middle as they could, given the circumstances.

A second infant hadn't been discovered until a later scan.

"Hello, babies," Charlie shouted, burying his face into her huge stomach. "And how are you today? I'm very well, thank you. I had a great dinner. Tuna pasta, then some barbecue and custard. It was brilliant."

Over his head, Tessa met Molly's eyes. "*Barbecue* and custard?" her friend mouthed.

"He means rhubarb," Tessa mouthed back, causing Molly to collapse into giggles, made worse by the little boy's further revelations.

"Jodie Peters had an accident. She wet her knickers! Miss Herbert gave her some of her own dry ones. She keeps them in a big cupboard. Hundreds of pairs. And I got a gold star for spelling!"

"Well done," Tessa murmured, not sure whether she ought to explain that she was referring to the star and not her son's teacher's seemingly endless supply of underwear.

Molly saved her from having to make a decision.

"Ah, here's Chloe," she said, recovering herself and spying her daughter strolling casually across the playground, deep in conversation with a circle of friends. "At last!"

Charlie looked up thoughtfully. "Girls always have something to talk about, don't they?" He shook his head. "Even when we're doing music and movement, they're talking all the time. Talk, talk, talk.

"Miss Herbert calls them Chatterboxes, but I think they do it because they're very good at it. I expect it's because they don't like interesting things like football and that they're practising to be ladies.

"Actually," he stared into space for several moments, "Miss Herbert is a bit of a chatterbox too. I must remember to tell her that on Monday. She likes us to tell her interesting things."

Tessa struggled to keep a straight face as Chloe bounced up to them, her blonde ponytail swinging.

"Well? Did she like it?" she asked Charlie, her blue eyes sparkling in an angelic, heart-shaped face.

"Oh, I forgot. I was busy talking to the babies. Hold on a minute."

"Charlie Harper! Honestly!" Chloe heaved an exaggerated sigh as he dug into his satchel and pulled out a sheet of paper, which he thrust at Tessa.

She studied the still-tacky painting, not sure, at first, whether she had it the right way up.

But judging by the position of the boot-black eyes, she decided that she probably had.

"It's them," Charlie said, his voice rising in excitement. "The twins. Now we know what they really look like. Miss Herbert said it was very good. She's seen twins before, you see. She had three lots last year."

"Amazing," Molly murmured to no one in particular. "Congratulations," she whispered into Tessa's ear. "You're about to give birth to Mr and Mrs Blobby!"

Don't laugh, Tessa told herself, biting hard on her lower lip.

The two figures were very round and very pink. One had a mop of yellow ringlets, while the other sported something which vaguely resembled a bowler hat.

Both were grinning, revealing rows of huge white teeth.

"Imagine breast-feeding *them*," Molly gasped.

That was exactly what Tessa had been imagining. She pulled a wry face.

"It's beautiful, sweetheart," she assured her beaming son, who was scrambling into the back seat of the car and carefully belting himself in.

"Have you had any more twinges?" Molly had finally stopped laughing and was now casting an experienced eye over her.

Not exactly twinges. More a sensation of her body becoming more and more crowded by the second. Tessa shook her head.

"What did the hospital say?"

"That I probably won't last out until next week."

Molly nodded knowingly. "I'll be amazed if you make it until *tomorrow*." She kissed Tessa on the cheek and gave Charlie's work of art a final lingering glance.

"Ouch," she said.

* * *

"So which one is which one?" Charlie asked the following afternoon, scratching his head and clearly confused.

Tessa's heart went out to him.

There was no doubt about it. Her gorgeous twin daughters were identical from the tops of their bronze-gold hair to the tips of their miniature toes.

How she was ever going to tell them apart, she couldn't imagine.

She also wondered what else might be going on inside Charlie's head.

Until now, the babies had been something to be talked about and looked forward to. Having to share his life with them was a totally different thing.

There was only one thing for it – to play it cool.

Stooping over the first of the two clear plastic cribs, Tessa casually lifted a tiny wrist and checked the pink name tag. She resisted the urge to pick up the slumbering tot.

If Charlie asked her to then she would, but for now…

"This one is Georgia. She's quite nice, isn't she?"

Charlie nodded thoughtfully. Then he peered into the second crib and sighed loudly.

"So this one *isn't* Georgia, but she *looks* like Georgia."

"This is Beth."

Charlie didn't respond. He shifted his weight from one foot to the other, his expression unfathomable. Lowering herself to his level, Tessa wrapped her arms round his sturdy little frame and gently hugged him.

She longed to scoop him up into her arms, kiss away the doubts and fears which might be lingering in his mind, but she couldn't.

The past 12 hours had really taken it out of her. Her body felt as though it had gone six rounds with Frank Bruno.

Everything had happened so quickly…

Teatime; Charlie's hilarious bath routine, sinking into bed just before 11 only to be wide awake again in the early hours.

Then Hector, their elderly next-door-neighbour and Charlie's bosom friend, being called on to babysit until Martin's parents arrived from thirty miles away.

"Have a nice time," Hector had called from the doorstep, wearing a tartan dressing gown and waving them off as if they were going on holiday.

"Hurry," she'd shrieked at Martin as they'd made a mad dash to the hospital.

"You're cutting it a bit fine," the smiling nurse had teased, pushing Tessa into a wheelchair and speeding along the corridor to the delivery suite, taking the corners like Damon Hill on a Grand Prix quest.

Then, with hardly a pause to allow their exhausted mother to draw a decent breath, the twins had sped into the world as though they couldn't bear to be parted, even for a few seconds...

Charlie's sudden shriek startled her.

"She knows me, Mum." Tearing himself from Tessa's arms, he spun round and grinned at Martin. "Beth knows me, Dad. Look, she's waving."

Clever little girl, Tessa thought, gazing at the minute fist, punching the air. Great sense of timing!

Charlie waved back, using both arms. Then he turned his attention to Georgia.

As if on cue, she gave a tremulous windy smile.

Charlie clapped his hands and danced a little jig. He grinned at his sister, stretching his mouth wide to show off his small white teeth.

"Wow! So does she. So does Georgia."

He looked at Tessa. "Do they know *my* name?"

She pretended to think about it.

A "Yes" might steal Charlie's thunder; a "No" and he might just feel as if he didn't matter.

She glanced over at Martin for help. He blew her a kiss and gave her a 'you're better at this kind of thing' look.

She stuck her tongue out at him, but at the same time accepted that he was probably right.

As Charlie had pointed out, just the day before, girls were very good at talking.

"What we did, Charlie," she said, "was to tell the babies that they were the luckiest little people in the whole wide world. Do you know why we did that?"

Charlie puzzled over the question. Then he grinned. "Because it was getting a bit crowded inside your tummy and they were fed up with having to eat yukky Brussels sprouts just because *you* like them."

Tessa struggled not to laugh out loud. She could see a small nerve twitch on Martin's cheek too.

"No. That wasn't the reason," she went on seriously. "We told them that they were lucky, because they had the best big brother in the whole world. We nearly told them his name, then we decided that *you* would like to do that yourself."

"I see," Charlie said. Then, "What *is* his name?"

Tessa and Martin exchanged a smile. "Charlie Harper," they said in perfect unison.

"Oh, yes. Me." Charlie positioned himself between the cribs and took a deep breath. "My name is Charles Edward Harper. I'm five and a bit and I go to school. It's great – you'll like it.

"My teacher's name is…" he stopped and looked at Tessa, his eyes wistful. "Mum, could I *touch* Georgia and Beth?"

"You can *hold* them."

"What… with my own arms?"

Tessa nodded. "Take your shoes off and climb onto the bed."

Two blue trainers skidded across the polished floor.

"Sit right back," she instructed. Charlie wriggled himself against the heap of pillows.

She gave him Beth first. The baby stirred and opened one sleepy eye. Charlie winked back at her. "She's got a real nose," he said happily.

Ignoring Martin's muttered, "Thank heavens for that," Tessa lowered Georgia into the crook of his other arm.

The tot gave a small sigh and snuggled against Charlie's striped shirt.

"I think she really, really likes me," he whispered, his cheeks bright pink.

"They both do. They love you," Tessa told him as Martin captured the scene, over and over again, on film. "And just to show you how much, they've brought you a couple of presents."

The carefully-wrapped gifts were the first items she'd packed in her suitcase. Before the essential nighties and toiletries. Now they were stowed away in her bedside locker.

Charlie would adore them. A book on dinosaurs – his absolute passion – and a huge painting set.

Tessa put them on the bed beside him. "Shall I hold the girls while you open them?"

He gave the packages a cursory glance and shook his head. "I'll look at them when my sisters have their tea." He turned his attention back to the now wriggling bundles.

"Thank you very much, Beth and Georgia. That was very kind of you. I've brought you a present too. Dad and I bought them this morning."

He looked over at Martin. Tessa followed his gaze. Of course.

When they'd been shopping she'd seen two identical traditional bears. The old fashioned type, with longish fur and moveable limbs, golden brown and sporting tartan ribbons.

She'd opened her purse, but Martin had stopped her.

"Why don't we let Charlie choose when the time comes?" he'd said and Tessa had accepted the wisdom behind his suggestion.

Selecting his sibling's first toys would make him feel important. Besides that, he had extremely good taste for a little boy. A great eye for colour and style.

So in the bag, nestling between Martin's jean-clad legs, would be two pink creations, Tessa reckoned. Not necessarily bears either.

They could be fluffy mice, wearing pretty dresses, topped with cream lace aprons. Real little cuties.

Or even plump piglets, crowned with flowers. Silky rabbits, holding red hearts.

Her eyes widened as they settled on the bright purple giraffe which Martin placed on the white bedspread. It had thick black eyelashes and was wearing a green felt hat. Pretty was the last word she'd have chosen to describe it.

Charlie looked from one twin to the other, back and forward, several times.

"This is yours, Georgia," he said eventually. "I've called him Gary, because I sit next to Gary at school, but you can change it if you like. I won't mind and neither will he."

Tessa gulped. Not Teddy the Bear, but Gary the Giraffe! She watched, open-mouthed, as Martin produced a second toy with a flourish.

This time it was a fat orange and navy blue spotted monkey.

"She's yours, Beth. Her name is Pizza, because I love pizzas.

"Dad said you were idic... indent... that you were just the same," Charlie carried on, "and I thought so too, when I first saw you. But you're not, are you? You're different."

Tessa couldn't imagine what lay behind that statement. She'd studied them endlessly. Each was a mirror image of the other, she'd decided.

One of the nurses had even joked that it mightn't be a bad idea to leave the identity bracelets on for as long as possible, then after that to make sure that one always wore pink socks, the other yellow.

She lowered herself onto the bed beside the trio. The girls were now wide awake and seemed mesmerised by their brother's voice.

"Charlie, can you really tell them apart?"

"Easy, Mum," Charlie said. "Georgia has got wiggly eyebrows, like Granny Allen's. They go up at the corners. Look."

Tessa obeyed. Yes, there was a distinct flick, like a little tick. They did look just like her mother's. How she had missed it, she couldn't imagine.

"Beth's got a curly bit at the front of her hair. Just there." Charlie pointed. "And her nose is the same as mine. Georgia's is a bit more flatter…"

Again he was right.

"You're a genius, Charlie," she said.

"So are you," he replied cheerfully, then he pulled a face as first Georgia, immediately followed by her sister, began to cry. "What's wrong with them?" he asked anxiously.

"They're hungry. And it's the only way they know how to tell me that their tummies are empty." Tessa picked up Beth and rocked her gently. Immediately the howls ceased. Charlie did the same with Georgia.

"Wow," he said. "It works. I'll help you do this when you come home. Until they learn how to talk." He looked up at Tessa. "When *are* you coming home?"

"The day after tomorrow. You can't be missing me already," Tessa teased.

"I am. And I want to ask you something important. Something very, very important. About making babies. I need to know so I can write it in my news book. I write *everything* in my news book. Even what Daddy said when he fell off the ladder when he was painting the kitchen. Miss Herbert said it was very interesting."

From the other side of the bed came a muttered "Oh, no." Tessa glanced at Martin and grinned.

"Why don't you talk to *Daddy* about your problem Charlie?" she asked, her eyes dancing with mischief.

"I didn't think he'd know the answer. Chloe says boys are a bit silly."

"She's absolutely right," Martin confirmed. Tessa took no notice.

"Daddies know as much about making babies as Mummies do."

Charlie thought about it for several moments. Then, "We've got two girl babies and no boy babies. I mean, there aren't any more waiting inside your tummy to get born, are there?"

"No," Tessa said, adding a silent, "Thank heavens."

Charlie nodded. "Well, Chloe told me that mothers make girl babies and fathers make boy ones, so you must have worked very hard."

Tessa confirmed that she had done. Charlie looked at Martin, who was now muttering something about strangling Chloe when he got his hands on her.

"So what did *you* have to do, Dad?"

"He made me a bacon sandwich," Tessa murmured, but her words were drowned out as both twins made their presence felt in the loudest possible fashion. Skilfully, as though she'd been doing it for ages instead of just few hours, she reunited Georgia with her sister.

It didn't help.

Charlie put his fingers in his ears. "They've got very loud voices," he shouted over the din.

"They'll be fine after they've had their tea," Tessa assured him.

Charlie slid off the bed. He danced across the floor, found his shoes, thought about it for a moment, then slid them on. The right way, this time, she noted with pride.

"So will I," he said. "My tummy is making lots of noise." He caught hold of Martin and pulled him to his feet. "Can we go for a burger or a pizza, Dad?"

"Great idea," Martin said, clearly relieved that the delicate matter of conception had been replaced with something as nicely basic as ordinary hunger.

"Your Mum will answer all your questions when she comes home on Monday," he told Charlie. "She's *much* better at these things than I am."

"Is that because she's a girl and very good at talking?" Charlie asked, shrugging into his jacket.

"Absolutely," Martin confirmed, grinning smugly at Tessa.

"Chicken!" she accused as she kissed him goodbye.

"No. Pizza," Martin said, his lips leaving hers and gently touching each of his daughter's smooth foreheads. "A large cheese and onion, with garlic bread and double chips…"

Stealer of Hearts

The programme had immediately followed Charlie's favourite lunchtime viewing. The singing and word games had suddenly stopped, the screen being filled instead with eager-looking, blue-clad young men talking about the whys and wherefores of their chosen careers.

Normally, Tessa tried to limit the amount of television her son watched during the school holidays, but he had seemed keen to see what went on in "*A day in the life of a community policeman*" and she'd been struggling to count the rows in a complicated cable twist pattern...

So, "Just this once," she'd murmured.

"Wow!" Charlie had said several times. His eyes had widened as he'd witnessed two lads, accompanied by their worried parents, being shown the cells in a police station as a warning to mend their ways.

"Is that a real live burglar?" he'd asked, watching a shabbily-dressed woman being caught on camera, shop-lifting groceries. "Poor lady, poor little children," he'd murmured, hearing her defence that she was only doing it because her family were hungry and her husband was ill and she had no money to buy food.

Tessa had quickly and firmly told him that stealing wasn't the answer. To anything! Then she'd found herself questioning what she'd do under the same circumstances.

And had been unable to come up with a truthful answer.

"That was great, wasn't it?" The programme finished. Charlie rolled across the carpet and switched off the television. "I like things about cops and robbers. I think *I* might be a policeman when I grow up."

"Great idea." Tessa looked up. Deciding to knit Martin a cricket sweater had been a big mistake. The sleeves seemed to go on for ever. She smiled, glad of the interruption.

"That man – the one in the big fast red car – he was being bad, wasn't he?" Not waiting for her response, Charlie carried on. "He could have knocked someone over. A boy on a bike. Or a hedgehog. And a poor old lady with bandages on her legs and a walking stick, like Mrs Patterson down the road.

"He could have done, couldn't he? And if that had happened, he'd have been put in prison, wouldn't he? For ever and ever or…" Charlie puffed out his cheeks, "for a whole month."

A month! That about summed up modern justice, Tessa thought, groaning as one of her needles slid down the side of the chair. She abandoned her immediate thought – not fishing it out until later.

The twins would be wakening soon from their nap and, now they were mobile, well, probing little fingers sought out the most unlikely places.

It was a risk she wasn't prepared to take.

"Can you give me a hand, Charlie?" Carefully she lifted the sea of creamy wool from her lap and placed it on the carpet. Immediately half a dozen stitches leapt off the end of the remaining needle.

"Oh—" Tessa stifled a curse. Just in time, she congratulated herself. Already she'd had to explain to her son about a couple of distinctly dodgy words he'd picked up at school. It wouldn't be setting much of an example if she came out with one herself.

Hauling back the springy cushion she peered into the narrow gap. Charlie joined her.

"You nearly said a bad word, didn't you, Mum? I think you *nearly* said—"

"Look! There it is. See that little red tip," Tessa interrupted brightly. "Your fingers are just the right size to get hold of it and pull it out. That's the way... do it very slowly... keep it away from your face..."

The long pin was produced with a flourish and a very loud, "Charlie Harper to the rescue! Three cheers for the brave boy who fights off dragons and pirates and bad people."

Tessa seized it before Charlie had a chance to turn it into an imaginary sword.

"Thanks, sweetheart, I don't know what I'd do without you," she said.

He suddenly frowned, his smooth forehead creasing into neat little pleats. His round greeny-blue eyes became troubled.

"Should I not go to Hector's then?"

Whoops, Tessa thought. Wrong choice of words. Charlie was at the stage where he took everything literally. "Of course you should go to Hector's," she told him. "You're going to help him today, aren't you?"

"Yes, but what if *you* need my help and I'm not here? That policeman told these bad boys that they should never, ever, upset their mothers and fathers. He said they should listen to them and help them.

"So what if... what if... if a burglar should come or if the phone rings when you're in the loo and I'm not here to chase him away or say 'Hello? Who is it, please?'"

Tessa pulled him into her arms and hugged him. "I promise to keep the doors locked and if the phone rings... well, they'll just have to call back again when you *are* here.

"Anyway," she grinned, "I can always call out of the window if I need you, can't I?"

Her words didn't instantly placate him. She could sense rather than see Charlie mull the situation over in his mind. Planting a kiss on his soft cheek, she briskly stood up.

"My goodness, look at the time. You should be off by now. Hector will be thinking you've got lost. He'll be wondering what he's going to do without his workmate."

Just for a moment Charlie still seemed unsure of where his priorities lay. Then he grinned and shot out of the door, returning seconds later clutching something.

"Right, Mum. I've had a very good idea. I won't *be* in Hector's garden. Not today. Remember? We've got to go and get Mrs Patterson's sunshine back for her?"

Bristling with importance, he thrust a small object into Tessa's hand.

"But if your knitting thing falls down the chair again, then just blow that three times and we'll hear you. Right? Do you understand? Three times or else we won't know it's you."

Chuckling, Tessa watched Charlie race down the garden path to the gap in the hedge. Her fingers closed round the small whistle. Three blasts or they wouldn't know it was her?

Just how many of their neighbours actually *owned* a whistle, she wondered.

* * *

Hector Smythe was balanced on the top of a sturdy pair of stepladders. Hands on hips, Charlie watched him saw through one of the straggling branches which were blocking out a great deal of sunlight.

He'd had a go at tugging out some weeds and there were a couple of dusty streaks decorating his pink cheeks.

"What should I do now?" he called out. "Do you want me to catch it when it falls, Hector? I could, you know. I'm an excellent catcher. You ask my Dad."

The elderly man shook his head. "Not this one, mate. It's going to be on the heavy side. But you could put these small twigs in—"

His suggestion was interrupted by a soft voice coming from the other end of the overgrown garden.

"Would the workmen like a nice cup of tea? Or maybe some orange squash?"

"A cuppa would go down very nicely, Mrs P," Hector said.

"So would some orange," Charlie agreed. He looked up again. "Will you be all right on your own if I go and help Mrs Patterson? She's a bit wobbly? Her legs aren't what they used to be. I know that, because she told me."

He paused thoughtfully, then, "What did they used to be? Longer? Or fatter?"

Hector chuckled. "Young and strong. Like your mum's."

"Oh," was Charlie's parting comment as he sped towards the house, his own robust little limbs pounding like pistons.

Inside, the kitchen was dark and gloomy; the walls coated in a flaking layer of old dark green emulsion, the ceiling a grimy, mud-coloured brown. Charlie's sharp gaze took in the shabby scene.

He frowned. "I don't think a burglar would come in here, Mrs Patterson," he said, matter-of-factly. "You don't really have a lot for him to steal, do you?"

Edna Patterson smothered a sigh. The lad wasn't being rude. Just horribly honest.

The best she could say about her house was that it was as clean as she could manage, but the place was falling down round her ears and she was just too proud to ask for – or even accept – help.

So much so, that she'd almost refused Hector's kind offer when he'd called round, the other day, with a bag of tomatoes, a crisp lettuce and a couple of pounds of new potatoes from his own fertile and well-cared for garden.

Now she was glad she hadn't. Besides the weak rays of newly-freed sunshine which were trickling weakly through her dusty windows, it was so wonderful to have a bit of company.

Little Charlie Harper was a delight. A beautiful child. Just like his pretty twin baby sisters. The kind she and Joe had always hoped they'd have; only their prayers had fallen on deaf ears.

Having satisfied herself that the kettle was firmly placed on the gas ring to boil, she limped across the worn lino to the big old dresser.

"Would you like a biscuit, love?"

"Yellow!" Charlie replied.

Edna looked down at him, puzzled. "I think I've only got ordinary rich tea."

"And a blue roof, like the sky," he went on dreamily. "And I could draw you some very nice pictures and you could put them on your fridge and Mum could help you make some nice new curtains…" his voice tailed away and he was silent for several moments.

Then, "So what I think we need is a good burglar to take away all the bad things and bring you some nice new ones!"

Edna began to laugh. What a boy! Good burglar indeed! Then she stopped.

There had been a lot of break-ins recently, one of them just two doors away and in broad daylight, while the young couple had been at work.

What a mess the intruders had made. Losing your precious possessions was bad enough, but the sheer, mindless vandalism…

There were no such things as *good* burglars. She told Charlie just that, not going into too many details. No point in frightening the child unnecessarily, but best get the idea out of his head right now.

"They're *all* very bad people, love," she finished, turning away and spooning tea in a big brown pot.

Behind her, Charlie chewed thoughtfully on his lower lip.

* * *

Tessa wakened with a start. The pale green light on her radio alarm showed 2.35. Propping herself on one elbow, she listened. The house was eerily silent, yet something had roused her.

Probably one of the girls, she told herself, sliding out of bed and into her towelling robe. The poor little souls were teething.

But a quick glance showed only two peaceful tots, deep in slumber, their red curls standing out like halos in the dim glow of their nightlight. Satisfied, Tessa crossed the landing.

Her hand was on the door to Charlie's room when she heard a noise. A creaking sound. Coming from somewhere downstairs. For a moment she stood there, telling herself it was probably only the wind, then it happened again. Only this time she recognised the distinct tug of a drawer being pulled out.

Heart thudding, she sped back to her own room.

"You... what... ?" A bleary-eyed Martin stared at her stupidly.

"Downstairs," Tessa spluttered. "We – I mean, I think – for heaven's sake move yourself, Martin. We've got burglars!"

This time, he sprung into action. "Have you checked the kids?"

"The twins, but not Charlie. I was just about to when—"

"Do that first, then ring the police." His gaze frantically searched the room, eventually settling on Tessa's favourite vase, a solid lead crystal which had been her grandmother's.

Tessa dashed off. Seconds later she was back. "He's not there!" Her voice was high-pitched with terror. From downstairs came the sounds of light, but very rapid footsteps and a scraping noise as if something was being dragged across the floor.

"Ring the—" fingering the heavy glass Martin stopped suddenly. He frowned. "I wonder... did Charlie say anything to you about Mrs Patterson's house?"

Tessa couldn't believe what she was hearing. Her precious son was missing, someone was downstairs rifling through their belongings – even now she could hear her fridge door being opened – and Martin wanted to discuss the old lady who lived down the road!

He must still be half-asleep. He hadn't yet grasped the severity of the situation. Her hand shot out to grab the phone. Martin stopped her. He kept his voice low.

"The reason *real* criminals succeed is partly down to their skill at being carefully silent, therefore allowing them an undisturbed orgy of thieving!

"You, my darling, have been pounding back and forward across the landing like a baby elephant! Any experienced lag would have cut his losses by now. He'd have been back out of the window like a rocket and settled for number 93 – or wherever – instead."

Pulling Tessa towards him, he whispered, "I'd put money on it that *our* burglar is a member of this family. Charlie 'Robin Hood' Harper! Takes from the rich to help out the poor, especially ones with dark horrible kitchens, sore legs and nobody to draw them nice pictures.

"Follow me." He replaced the vase.

Dazed, Tessa obeyed without question. Together they crept down the stairs. The kitchen door was ajar; the lights blazing. And the shadow, silhouetted now and again on the pale-painted walls, a very small one.

Tessa moved to get a better view. One of Charlie's large toy boxes – the blue one which usually housed his large collection of plastic dinosaurs – sat in the middle of the floor.

Already it was filled with an assortment of brightly-coloured tea towels and a motley collection of crockery, the stuff from the very back of the cupboard. Perfectly serviceable, really rather nice, but odds and ends she hardly used because they didn't match with anything.

She gasped. Louder than she'd intended. A pyjama-clad Charlie, scarlet cheeked from his exertions, spun round from his position in front of the fridge where he was removing some of his gaudy paintings from their magnetic traps.

He met Tessa's eyes. For a moment she thought he was going to cry. He didn't. His expression was very calm and quietly determined.

"Don't worry, Mum, I'll do you some new ones. I'm burgling these for Mrs Patterson. You know her, don't you, Dad? I told you about her at teatime." The paintings fluttered into the piled-up toy box.

"We're very rich, you see," he carried on. "We're not like that poor lady on the television who had to steal so that her children could have some beans on toast. I don't think *she* was a bad person. I do think there are *good* burglars.

"People like us who have got nice things they never use and pretty curtains and each other."

Taking a deep breath and fighting back the tears which had sprung into her own eyes, Tessa approached her son. "I understand what you mean, but you don't have to *steal* anything, Charlie. It's wrong. You can *give* them away instead."

Charlie stood his ground.

"No, I can't! Hector says Mrs Patterson is very proud. He says that means she doesn't want people to know that she's all alone and that she hasn't got any family and nice friends to help her.

"Except Hector and me, of course. We're her friends now.

"That's why I thought that when we went back tomorrow to finish giving her back her sunshine, I would put the new things in her house when she wasn't looking and she would just think that a good burglar had given them to her and be very happy and proud."

Martin and Tessa exchanged a glance. Martin nodded.

"Your heart's in the right place, Charlie, but I'm afraid your mum's correct. Stealing is *always* wrong. Let's think about this," he said, ruffling his son's chestnut hair. Lifting Tessa's shopping notepad off the shelf, he sat down at the table.

"Tell me what you think Mrs Patterson needs most?"

Over his shoulder, Tessa watched as the scribbled list grew longer and longer: curtains, paint, grandchildren, new cups, pictures, strong legs, more friends…

Strong legs! Sadly, there was nothing she could do about that. But as for the other things on the list… yes, as a family they could certainly help out.

The last thing she wanted was for Charlie to think that caring for others wasn't a good idea, in spite of his confused methods.

"Tell you what, I could call in and see Mrs Patterson tomorrow," she suggested. "Take the girls with me. See if she needs anything at the shops."

Charlie whooped with glee. "I've got *another* great idea. *We'll* be her grandchildren, me and Beth and Georgia! We'll send her cards on her birthday and at Christmas and she can come to tea and…" he stopped suddenly and yawned.

"It was very hard work being a burglar, you know," he said, scampering over to his basket of booty and lifting out the gaudily-coloured drawings.

He handed them to Tessa.

"These are yours, Mum. I shouldn't have burgled them, because I made them for *only* you. I'll do Mrs Patterson some beautiful ones tomorrow. Special. Just for her." He yawned again. "I'm going back to bed to get some energy."

"I'll be up in a minute to tuck you in," Tessa called softly, feeling Martin's arm slide round her waist. "Did we handle that one right?" she asked, resting her weary head against his chest.

Martin chuckled. "I think so." He turned out the lights. "Charlie 'Robin Hood' Harper – don't you just love him?"

Tessa nodded. As a stealer of hearts her son was in the master criminal category…

Bless Us All

The noise was deafening. Mary Allen, clutching the large cardboard box which held the precious pink and cream coloured cake, winced as she let herself in through the back door.

She pulled a comical face at the scene in front of her.

All three of her grandchildren seemed to be having a marvellous time.

"Hello, my darlings," she called out.

Nothing. Absolutely no response at all. Hardly surprising, she thought, shaking her head.

The radio was pumping out pop music. The identical seven-month-old twins, side by side and securely strapped in their high chairs, screamed with glee and banged wooden spoons on their plastic trays.

As for Charlie – he was involved in some kind of war dance; one which seemed to involve every high-pitched shriek and wail known to modern civilisation.

He turned suddenly. His face lit up as he bopped his way towards her. Mary clutched the cake to her chest.

Besides the baking, it had taken her a whole week to create the icing rosebuds, the butter-cream daisies with the pink tips and the piped, intertwined names: *Beth and Georgia.*

"Hi, Granny," Charlie yelled, waving his arms like, she thought, a demented Al Jolson. "I'm being a big help. I'm keeping the girls happy, so Mum can have a bit of peace and quiet to get on with dusting the dining room."

Stooping, Mary kissed his upturned face. *Peace and quiet?*

Crossing the kitchen to hug each of the curly red-headed babies, she gulped as she digested that little gem, storing it in her memory bank to pass on to Gordon later.

He already had two notebooks filled with what he fondly referred to as The Thoughts of Chairman Charlie.

"Oh, hello, Mum," Tessa, looking exhausted and clutching a can of furniture polish, appeared at the kitchen door. Her face was the colour of parchment and there were dark smudges under her grey eyes.

"I noticed things had gone a bit quiet," she said, with a wry grin. "So I guessed you'd arrived."

Mary supposed the racket had decreased by a couple of decibels. To help things even further, she switched off the radio.

"Oooh," Beth and Georgia cooed, in perfect unison.

"They like music. Shall I sing to them?" Charlie suggested.

"Later, darling," Mary said, ruffling his chestnut hair. "Is there anything I can do for you, love?" she asked Tessa. "A cup of tea? Some ironing? And where can I put this?"

Tessa immediately perked up. Crossing the floor in long strides, she opened the lid of the box.

"Mum! That is *gorgeous*. Look, Charlie."

On tiptoe, Charlie obliged. "That is excellent, Granny. This is the best cake in the whole wide world. You are a very excellent cooker."

"Excellent is his new word," Tessa mouthed over her son's head. "Put it in the dining room," she said out loud. "On the sideboard."

The job done, Mary returned to the kitchen.

"There must be something I can do," she said firmly.

Tessa opened her mouth. Charlie got in first. "You could take me home with you. I could sleep at your house tonight. I'd like that."

Mary wasn't quite sure how to respond. The twins' christening was tomorrow. Tessa had been adamant in ensuring that her son didn't feel left out, so surely she'd want them all to leave for the church together.

"I'd like it too – I'd love it, in fact – only I'm not sure if…" she began slowly.

Tessa dropped to her knees. She held her arms out. Charlie nudged himself into them.

"Would you really like to go home with Granny?" Mary heard her ask.

She didn't hear his response, because first Beth, closely followed by her sister, began to wail loudly. But she did see Tessa nod and rise to her feet.

"He says he wants to make sure you and Grandad don't get lost on the way to church tomorrow," she told her mother, winking.

"Go and get your pyjamas and slippers," she instructed Charlie, who sped off as if he was being chased. She called after him. "And your new clothes. Bring them down and I'll put them in a bag."

"You really don't mind, dear?" Mary asked, delighted. Having Charlie to stay was something she and Gordon always looked forward to.

Tessa shook her head, opened the biscuit barrel and gave each of the twins a finger of rusk. Like magic, their howls ceased.

"He's been so good, but I think he's probably had enough. A little bit of spoiling won't do him any harm at all." She grinned and gestured at her daughters. "I don't suppose you'd fancy taking these two as well?"

* * *

Charlie's bath time had taken well over half an hour and the room was hazy with steam. Wrapped in a thick warm towel, he sat on the green mat, carefully drying between each of his small toes.

Mary, perched on the edge of the tub, watched fondly.

Bless him, she thought as his round face grew pinker and pinker. "Let me help you, sweetheart," she offered for the second time.

Charlie looked up, his expression very serious. "No thank you, Granny. It's kind of you, but I have to learn to do this by myself.

"We all have to learn to look after our feet, you know. Even the Queen and her children! Miss Herbert, my teacher, says they are very important and useful things because they lead us through the path of life."

Mary smothered a giggle as his mouth twisted and his nose wrinkled, then he carried on.

"I'm just trying to remember the next bit.

"Oh, yes, if we don't take proper care of them, then we won't be able to play football or wear smart shoes and all our insides might slide down our legs and fall out on the floor.

"You wouldn't like that to happen to you, would you?" he asked solemnly.

"Absolutely not," Mary spluttered, turning away and taking her time retrieving a Diving Dolphin from the cooling suds. To allow herself a bit longer to straighten her face, she removed the plug.

The water began to eddy away.

"It goes down different in Africa." Charlie, his task apparently completed to his satisfaction, knelt up and rested his elbows on the edge of the bath. "Like this." He pointed his index finger down and circled it furiously, making loud slurping noises.

Mary knelt beside him and gave him a hug. He smelled, she thought, not just of soap and shampoo, but of everything that was good in this uncertain world.

"It goes down the other way in *Australia*," she gently pointed out, checking the rest of him was completely dry.

It was. She reached for the talcum and dusted him lightly with it.

"Australia *and* Africa? My goodness," Charlie said.

"No, not Africa. That's the same as here."

"How about China? I know a Chinese boy. He's nice. His name's Li and he's in my class at school. His Dad," Charlie continued, raising his arms to allow Mary to ease on his pyjama top, "makes excellent food. Really excellent!"

"So, you like Chinese food?" she asked, relieved that, for the moment anyway, the subject of draining bathwater seemed to have been forgotten and that she wouldn't have to decide which countries fell into which hemisphere.

Geography had never been her strong point. Gordon was much more knowledgeable on the subject; he could tell Charlie all about it later, over a bedtime cup of hot chocolate and a plate of ginger biscuits.

Charlie slid his chubby legs into the soft red trousers, then his feet into his slippers. "Well, not the stringy bits or the green things, but I like the rice and chicken. Oh yes… and the pizza.

"They come from China, you know."

"Italy, actually, sweetheart," Mary said, scooping up the sea of damp towels and stuffing in them the laundry basket.

Charlie puffed out his cheeks. "Do they? Well, you must be right because you're bigger than me and you know more things, but," his face was filled with confusion, "they've got eyes like this."

Putting his hands on each temple, he stretched his smooth skin until his own round greeny-blue eyes became narrow slits.

"Do I look like an Italy person now?" he asked.

Oh heavens, Mary thought. Talk about getting in deeper and deeper. And she'd have to explain. Or at least try to! Charlie soaked up information like a sponge and never, ever, seemed to forget anything he'd been told.

"What I meant was that pizza comes from…" she began, then stopped suddenly, hearing the sound of car tyres crunching on the gravel outside.

Charlie clearly heard it too. His face broke into a wide grin.

"Wow! Grandad's home with the fish and chips. I'm starving. Please may I go down and see him? Right now?"

Mary nodded and a blur of red sped past her.

Later that evening, with the geography problem sorted out and Charlie safely tucked in and fast asleep, she relaxed on the settee, snuggling against Gordon.

The television was on, but she was too weary to concentrate.

"Imagine, it won't be that long until we'll be having all three of them to stay!" she murmured.

Gordon chuckled. "D'you know, I was just thinking exactly the same thing. Beth and Georgia… two more Charlies! I'm going to need a lot of notebooks, aren't I…"

* * *

Camera at the ready to capture every moment, Mary circled the family gathering, determined not to miss a single moment of the happy occasion.

Gordon had his notebooks; she had her precious photo albums. Together, they would supply a perfect record for future generations.

And holding court – in the centre of the group she'd just captured on film – was Charlie. He looked so grown-up, she thought, watching as he greeted his assembled relatives.

Not quite six, yet he exuded confidence.

"Thank you for coming. It is very excellent to see you," she heard him say, over and over again, shaking hands and allowing himself to be kissed by various great aunts.

And in their palest pink and ivory dresses, the twins – in the arms of their paternal grandparents – looked like two fresh little flowers.

Tessa, too, she was relieved to see, seemed to have made a miraculous recovery.

The harassed Mum from the day before had been replaced by a calm, proud young woman, elegant in a cream suit and matching, wide-brimmed hat, with a single deep pink rose tucked into the ribbon band.

Only Martin appeared uncomfortable as he approached her.

"Mary," he said, planting a firm kiss on her cheek. "Help! I think Georgia has either spat or thrown up on my tie. Look!"

Mary obliged. There certainly was something… a greasy blob, slap bang in the middle of the pale yellow fabric. Taking a tissue from her bag she dabbed at it.

All that happened was that the stain managed to double in size.

"Oh, heavens," Martin said, running a hand through his dark hair until it stood on end. He glanced at his watch. "I haven't got time to go home for another one. What on earth am I going to do?"

Mary undid the neat knot, slid the strip of silk around, and retied it. No good. The stain still shone out, but in a different position.

She tried again. And again.

Neither had noticed that someone else was showing an interest in the proceedings.

"Yuck! But don't worry, you can borrow mine, Dad," Charlie's voice rang out. "It's itching my neck anyway."

Hooking a finger under his collar, he gave a couple of firm tugs. The bow tie, attached to a circlet of elastic, slid over his head. He handed it to Martin, who stared in dismay at the gaudy-coloured Disney characters.

"Mickey Mouse! I can't…" he began.

Seeing the Vicar at the old oak door of the church, and Tessa approaching, Mary made a snap decision.

"You can," she said firmly, trying desperately not to laugh.

"It looks really cool," Charlie assured his father's retreating back as he followed him into the old building.

The ceremony went without a hitch. Charlie sang '*All things bright and beautiful*' very loudly, holding his hymn book upside down; the girls behaved angelically, even when their fiery curls were doused in the sacred water from the font.

"My goodness! Did he do that to me?" Charlie asked so loudly that his voice echoed off the cream stone walls.

Gordon grinned. Mary nodded.

"And was I happy about it?" Charlie's smooth brow creased in a puzzled frown.

"Yes, you were," Mary whispered, smiling as she remembered how her grandson had actually chuckled out loud at his own christening.

"Where is big brother Charlie?" the vicar's deep voice rang out. "The original owner of this lovely tie." He gestured at Martin, whose blush exactly matched the scarlet of the famous mouse's waistcoat.

"I'm here," Charlie shrieked, jumping up and down and waving both arms in the air. "With Granny and Grandad Allen. Mum's mum and dad. I stayed with them last night. I had an excellent bath, we all had fish and chips, then Grandad and me watched *Jungle Book*.

"I think Granny was in the kitchen washing up and doing girl's things."

Laughter rang out round the church.

"It sounds as though you had a wonderful time. Why don't you come and join your sisters and tell them all about it?" the vicar suggested, immediately inviting the congregation to take as many photos as they wished now that the solemnities were over.

"Thanks very much. I will."

Mary watched his sturdy little frame skip towards the font area. She saw him say something to Martin, who shook his head. Then he turned to Tessa – and her reaction seemed to back up her husband's gesture.

The flower on her hat wobbled.

Seemingly undaunted, Charlie sidled over to the vicar and tugged on his flowing robe. Immediately the tall figure gave the little boy his full attention, nodding thoughtfully as he listened.

"What's he up to now?" Gordon asked.

Mary shrugged. "Goodness only knows," although she did wonder if it might have something to do with the font, plugs and which way the water would circle away.

Then the vicar rose and held his arms up to attract the congregation's attention.

"It seems," he said, "that this ceremony is not quite complete. Charlie has made a… shall we say a… rather unusual request, but the reasoning behind it makes very good sense and I can't think of one good reason to refuse.

"In fact I feel it's an *excellent* idea.

"So if you would bear with me a moment…" He moved towards Tessa and Martin. A quick discussion followed, then, open-mouthed, Mary watched as the twin's frilly socks were removed.

Solemnly, the vicar scooped up a trickle of water and made the sign of the cross on the four bare little feet. "May these lead them safely through the path of life." He turned and smiled gently. "Was that what you wanted, Charlie?"

"Oh, yes, sir, Mr Vicar." His lips clamped together for a second, then, "I was just wondering…"

A second quick exchange of words then a beaming Charlie sat down on the purple carpet. His shoes and socks were rapidly discarded.

Easily supported in the cleric's strong arms, his sighed with pleasure as his own feet were solemnly blessed.

"Now my insides will never trickle down my legs and land on the floor," he announced blissfully.

Giggling, Mary turned to Gordon, to share the moment. She'd been so whacked the night before that she'd completely forgotten to tell him about Charlie's sudden interest in feet.

He didn't return her grin. He was totally engrossed, scribbling in his notebook...

Charlie's Darling

While Tessa tried to settle her recently-fed, freshly-bathed, but still fretful twin daughters down for the night, in the living room, Martin Harper listened to his son, Charlie, reading from his new school book.

It was only on Fridays that he was home early enough to take part in the homework business and he was, he admitted to himself, highly impressed.

In just a week the little boy seemed to have come on by leaps and bounds.

Charlie had clearly inherited his mother's passion for the written word. He'd read almost the whole story, his voice filled with expression and hardly faltering, only occasionally stopping to sound out a word.

"'Tom hugged his Mum. 'I'm sorry I was rude to you,' Tom said. His Mum said, 'You are a good boy. I love you.' Tom was happy'," Charlie finished.

He looked at Martin, who clapped his hands.

"That was great," he said, proudly. "You're getting *really* good. Perhaps tomorrow we'll get some new bookshelves for your bedroom. Those blue ones we saw at the DIY shop. You'd like that, wouldn't you?"

Charlie's reaction surprised him. He didn't look particularly thrilled with the suggestion. Quite the reverse, judging by the way his forehead had creased into a deep frown.

Then, "I don't think that was a very good story, you know."

"Why?" Martin asked, curious. "You understood it all, didn't you? Tom hadn't been very nice to his mother and he was worried that she wouldn't love him, but of course she did, because mums always love their children, even when they've been a bit naughty.

"And Tom was happy when she told him. What's wrong with that?"

Charlie closed the book thoughtfully. He drew his knees up to his chest and rested his chin on them.

"Yes, but Tom's mum didn't say 'I love you... anything... why didn't she say I love you... sweetheart? *My* mum always does.

"Sometimes she says 'Darling'. That's what I call Daisy Pollock. I always say to her 'Hello, darling.' Daisy Pollock really likes it. She's made me promise I'll call her that for ever and ever and ever.

"And I will. All the time. Even if she is a bit bad."

Daisy Pollock? Darling? Now the confused expression was Martin's.

"Is Daisy your, er, girlfriend?" he asked gently, not wanting to embarrass the child.

Charlie shook his head firmly. "Daisy Pollock is my... what do you call the lady you're going to get married to, Dad?"

"Fiancée."

"Yes... she's my... one of these things you just said." His gaze became dreamy and faraway. "She's very beautiful. She's got hair like this," Charlie raised both hands and made wild squiggly shapes all round his own head, "and it's exactly the same colour as Hector-next-door's cat."

Martin's mind spun. The cat in question was a tortoiseshell; her glossy coat a mixture of white, orange, a sort of muddy mole and pure black.

He was still debating what colour his future daughter-in-law's locks might be, when he realised that Charlie was speaking again.

"Daisy Pollock sort of talks English… sort of. Chloe," he went on, referring to his friend, who was the daughter of Tessa's closest friend, Molly, "says it sounds a bit French or Japanese, but I understand her all right.

"I think Daisy Pollock's got a lovely voice. She sometimes sounds like she's singing.

"And she's got eyes… two eyes… round ones, with spots on them. And a nose and a mouth and some teeth. Oh yes, and she's got legs and arms, too."

Martin struggled with the laughter which was threatening to choke him. Apart from the lurid picture Charlie was painting, it also struck him as hilarious that his son only ever used both his intended's names.

Not once had he referred to her as just Daisy.

"She sounds lovely," he eventually managed, his voice sounding to his own ears, as though he was being slowly strangled.

"Daisy Pollock *is* lovely!" Charlie confirmed. "And do you know, she's got new sandals for the class trip next week, red ones with holes in them? I 'spect I'll love her another bit more when she wears them.

"Maybe," he paused thoughtfully for a moment, then a small smile lifted the corners of his mouth, "maybe I'll ask her to wear them when we get married. That would be a great idea, wouldn't it, Dad? Red sandals?"

This time Martin could only nod furiously. He desperately wished Tessa would come down and take some of the heat off him. She was much better than he was at hiding her amusement.

Practice, he supposed. Six years of the hilarious *Thoughts of Chairman Charlie*, as her father fondly referred to them.

Besides that, he wanted to share with her this particular little gem.

But he could still hear her soothing voice drifting from upstairs. And an occasional restless cry. The twins were teething. She could be ages yet.

He was well and truly on his own with this one!

Suddenly, and to his great relief, Charlie changed the subject.

"Do you know what, Dad, if you were to say to me 'Do you fancy a strawberry milkshake and a biscuit, Charlie?' I'd say, 'Yes, please, that would be great.'"

Martin grinned. If his son had suggested a three-course meal, he'd have given the matter serious consideration.

"I've got a terrific idea," he said. "Charlie, is there any chance you might just fancy a strawberry milkshake and a biscuit?"

"My goodness," the little boy's greeny-blue eyes widened in what looked like genuine amazement. "What a brilliant idea. Yes, please. All that reading has made my throat tickle."

Later that evening, all three children fast asleep and feeling like a wrung-out rag herself, Tessa listened, open-mouthed, as Martin relayed the conversation.

Then, "Daisy Pollock?" she murmured thoughtfully, shaking her head. "I know most of Charlie's friends, but I've never heard of this one. Are you sure you've got the name right?"

Martin groaned. Got it right? It was etched into his brain. Raising an eyebrow, he studied his wife's tired face.

Then, "Even if I have got it wrong, Tess – which I sincerely assure you I most definitely have not – how many little girls do you know who have corkscrew hair the same colour as Hector's cat, eyes – two of them – with spots, some teeth, the usual amount of limbs and who speaks sort-of English with a Japanesey, French accent?"

* * *

The following morning Charlie seemed to have forgotten the great love in his life. Throughout breakfast – Tessa always insisted on cooking something at the weekend, along with the usual cereal and toast – he chattered on about anything and everything.

Having exhausted the subject of whether goats really did eat *everything* off people's washing lines, he turned his attention to the twins.

"You can say 'No', can't you, Georgia?" he asked his sister.

"No," the tot responded obligingly, adding a ferocious scowl.

Charlie chuckled. He turned to the other tiny girl. "Can you say it, Beth?"

The toddler looked thoughtful for a moment, then shook her head firmly.

"I bet she can really," Charlie said. "I bet they talk about all sorts of things when we're not there. Things like… what their favourite colour is… and if they like potatoes or pasta best.

"I bet they talk, talk, talk all the time."

"I wonder who they take after," Martin murmured, reaching out for another slice of toast and a couple of rashers of the crispy bacon from the warming tray on the centre of the table.

"Anyone want any more scrambled eggs?" he asked.

"No! No!" Georgia shrieked, nodding furiously.

Martin scooped a small portion into her bowl and was rewarded by a wide beam, which was distinctly gummy in places.

Some teeth! Something along the lines of Daisy Pollock, he supposed, suppressing the laughter which began to bubble in the back of his throat.

"Yes!"

For a second there was silence. Charlie broke it, whooping gleefully.

"Beth said that. I *told* you she could." Leaping from his chair he dashed round the table. "Say it again, Beth. Say 'Yes'. Say… 'Charlie Harper is cool'."

"Yes," Beth repeated.

"Oh, wow! This is great." Charlie danced a wild jig. "Do you want some more eggs, little darling?" he asked, echoing one of Tessa's endearments.

The rosebud mouth clamped together.

"How about some toast?" Charlie suggested.

"Yes!"

His chestnut head swivelled. "Did *you* just say that, Georgia."

"No!"

"I don't know if I can stand all this intoxicating chit chat so early in the day," Martin told a giggling Tessa, who was squirting washing-up liquid into a sinkful of hot water.

Satisfied with his sisters' progress, Charlie went back to his place, picked up his own used cereal bowl and plate and took them to Tessa.

"There's an awful lot of washing up to do when a girl is a mother, isn't there?" he said thoughtfully.

Tessa agreed. She flashed Martin a sideways glance. "Unless, of course, the girl just happens to have a dishwasher!"

Before Martin had a chance to respond, Charlie was off again. This time, on a familiar subject...

"Daisy Pollock and I are not going to have any children!"

"Wise decision," Martin muttered. Tessa flicked a fingerful of suds at him. Charlie appeared not to have heard the interjection.

"It's not because we don't like them," he carried on, "but Daisy Pollock and I only want to cook *two* dinners, you see. Just *two*. And we only want to cook *two* breakfasts and *two* lunches and make *two* milkshakes and—"

"Do I know Daisy?" Tessa interrupted, keeping her voice deliberately casual.

Charlie pulled several thoughtful faces. He scratched his head.

"I don't think so, Mum. She's only been in our class for… oh… about a week… or two weeks… or a month…

"She used to go to a different school. A faraway one. I think it might have been in India or somewhere like that…"

His mouth filled with the last morsels of his breakfast, Martin choked. Tessa thumped him on the back with her soggy, rubber-gloved hand.

"Serves you right," she told him. "India? My goodness," she said to Charlie.

"Or it could have been Cornwall. I'm not very sure, but I'll ask her. She's beautiful, Mum. Really, *really* beautiful. Nearly as pretty as you and her nose has got brown dots on it. Big splodgy ones."

Coughing and wiping his eyes, Martin sprang to his feet. His voice was tinged with desperation.

"If we're going shopping we ought to make tracks soon. Before everywhere closes."

Elbow-deep in washing up, Tessa glanced at the clock on the wall.

It wasn't yet 8:30.

* * *

Inside the vast DIY store, Tessa stopped, for the umpteenth time, to allow someone to admire her little girls.

"Yes, it is hard to tell them apart," she confirmed, parrot-fashion, her eyes scanning the packed aisles.

Charlie and Martin were probably in the Shelving section, she decided. That, or Ready-To-Construct furniture.

On the journey she'd suggested that a bookcase might be better than shelving; would allow easier access for short legs. There was plenty of room and it could still be painted blue, she'd pointed out, reasonably, she'd thought.

But, "This is boy's stuff," Charlie had assured her as they had all got out of the car. His sturdy little frame had bristled with self-importance.

"Dad and I will decide. You and the girls can just have a lovely time looking at the pretty things."

With that, the pair had strutted off.

Pretty things like what? Tessa had wondered, strapping the wriggling twins into their double buggy.

Batteries for the doorbell, which had recently lost half its chime, yet only she had noticed?

"Your brother is in danger of becoming a bit of a chauvinist," she'd warned her daughters, negotiating the automatic doors and wondering for a moment if the mysterious Daisy Pollock realised just what she was letting herself in for, "but we'll soon sort that out, won't we?"

"Yes!" Both twins had come out with the same word at exactly the same moment.

Suddenly, Tessa caught a glimpse of Charlie's distinctive purple and black T-shirt, the one her mother had brought back from America and which bore the slogan 'Cool Guy'.

"Excuse me," she told the two elderly ladies who were oohing and aahing into the buggy. The girls showed off their skill at waving goodbye. As Tessa approached, she realised that her husband and son had also been sidetracked in their quest.

Martin was shaking hands with a huge fair-haired man; as for Charlie – he didn't look the least bit cool. His cheeks were bright pink and his eyes round and adoring.

He spun round when Tessa said, "Found you at last," looking, she thought, as though he might explode with pride.

Then, "Mum, this is my darling Daisy Pollock. My darling Daisy Pollock and her dad. His name's Mr Pollock."

Tessa accepted a handshake which threatened to crush her bones.

But all her brain really registered was a wild head of tight mouse-brown curls; flecked hazel eyes peering at her curiously from behind a pair of thick glasses; and more freckles than she'd ever seen on any single human being.

Her throat went dry. She tried to tell herself that the apparent love of her son's life was pleasantly plump, but she knew it wasn't true.

Charlie's darling was a fat little butterball. Her arms and legs were wreathed by pleated layers of pale flesh.

Beautiful, Charlie had said. Telling herself that appearances didn't matter, it was lay behind the outer skin that really counted, Tessa struggled to see what it was that she might have missed.

Then Daisy smiled; an endearing, infectious grin which perfectly displayed her missing front teeth, but lit up her plain little face.

In that split second, Tessa realised, she was gorgeous. Not only that, but lively and confident. The perfect match for her precious son.

"Hello, Mrs Harper. Nice to meet you. How are you? Charlie and me – we're going to get married," Daisy said confidently, in a heavily-accented, sing-song voice.

Her hand reached out and grasped Charlie's. "Aren't we, pet?"

Charlie just nodded, seemingly lost in his own blissful little world.

"They've recently moved here from Gateshead," Martin's voice reached Tessa as though it had travelled through a long tunnel as she remembered her own first love…

Melvin Pugh. Chronic acne, hay fever and a dictatorial mother who had put the fear of God into every teacher in St Matthew's High School.

Almost everyone else in year one had cruelly shunned Melvin, but she had loved him, hopelessly and helplessly.

Now, face to face with someone else who might not exactly fit in with the modern ideal of beauty, Tessa prayed that Melvin had found the same kind of happiness that she had.

"It's lovely to meet you, Daisy," she said. "You must come to tea very soon."

Daisy looked at Charlie. He nodded and mouthed something.

"Right," she said. "I'll come tomorrow. Best tell you I don't like cauliflower. It stinks."

Tessa dealt with, she turned her attention to the twins, silent for once as though aware of the importance of this first time meeting.

"They're not bad, Charlie," Daisy said, matter-of-factly.

"No," Charlie agreed, nodding furiously. "Actually they're *very* nice."

Suddenly he looked up at Tessa.

"Mum, could I just take my darling Daisy over there?" He pointed towards the rear of the store, at the section bearing a scarlet banner .ELECTRICAL GOODS – HUGE REDUCTIONS.

"Just for one minute," he pleaded. "There's something very important I need to show her."

Tessa looked dubious. Charlie gave her an old-fashioned look.

"Don't worry," he assured her in a sing-song voice, "we won't let you get lost or anything.

"I'll keep turning round and waving, so I know you're all right."

Put like that, how could she refuse?

"Okay then, but *don't* touch anything and stay where I can see you."

"Daddy? Dear Daddy?" Wearing a quaintly comical expression, Daisy glanced up at her own parent, her lashes flickering furiously behind her glasses.

Steve Pollock's eyes creased with unconcealed mirth.

"Off you go," he said to Daisy. "They learn young these days, don't they?" he murmured to Martin and Tessa.

"What *is* he up to?" Martin asked, moments later, watching his son's arms waving around like windmills, while Daisy, her back to them, was almost doubled in half.

"Only one way to find out." Tessa released the brake on the pushchair.

"Looks like he's trying to sell her something," Steve said softly as they approached the duo, now huddled together and gazing into the gleaming, empty dishwasher.

Charlie's voice rang out.

"My Granny's got one. They're brilliant. You put the plates in here... and the knives and forks in that bit... and the pots go at the bottom... then you just press the button and," he shrugged, "that's it!"

"Mmm." Daisy's curls wobbled. "So what you're saying, Charlie, is that if we get one of them then we *could* have some children as well and not have to worry about doing the dishes afterwards?"

Charlie's arm shot out and slid round Daisy's middle.

"That's right. Every single mum must have a dishwasher. It should be the law! In fact, I think it is the law."

Tessa mimicked Charlie's action. She prodded Martin's ribs a couple of times.

"All very well for the *single* mums," she said, flashing him a wide grin and batting her eyelashes, Daisy fashion, "but what about the married ones?

"Tell you what," she went on, "while you're thinking about it, I'll find us a salesman to give us all the details.

"Charlie..."

Animal Instincts

Martin leaned over to call out of the car window.

"Have a good time, you two. Charlie, keep an eye on your Mum. We don't want her getting locked in with the gorillas just because someone thinks she looks exactly like a monkey's mother!"

Tessa pulled a face as her excited son giggled and pressed his snub nose against the rear window.

"'Bye, Beth. 'Bye, Georgia. We'll bring you back a lovely present. Be very very good for Daddy," Charlie said.

Strapped in their seats, the grinning twins, eyes dancing with mischief, shook their heads as Martin re-started the engine.

"That's my girls," Tessa muttered under her breath. "Give him hell! Show him it's not all lollipops and roses and sitting with your feet up watching afternoon telly."

"'Bye, Dad. You have a nice day, too." Charlie waved until the car turned the corner out of sight.

"I can hardly wait," he said, skipping along by Tessa's side as they headed for the crowd gathered outside the school gate. "I can hardly wait to see the lions and the tigers and especially the – Oh, Mum. Over there. It's my darling Daisy, with Mrs Pollock and Auntie Molly and Chloe."

Charlie sighed and shook his head. He puffed out his cheeks. His voice was filled with awe. "Doesn't my darling Daisy look just beautiful?"

Beautiful? *Colourful* was the first word which sprang into Tessa's mind. She chuckled softly as her son's sweetheart dashed towards them.

Daisy's floppy sunhat was striped in vivid lime green and fluorescent orange. Stitched to the crown, wobbling as she ran, were three bright pink flowers on padded stems. The whole thing clashed wonderfully with her red dress and matching sandals.

She insisted on keeping the hat on right through the coach journey in spite of being assured that no, the sun wouldn't burn her through the grey-tinted glass.

Except for a couple of minutes when, much to his obvious delight, it was transferred onto Charlie's chestnut locks.

"Very smart, pet," Daisy declared.

"It looks ridiculous on you," Chloe said slightly huffily and sounding older than her six and a bit years. She was instantly withered by a glare from Daisy.

"Take no notice," she told Charlie. "I think she's a bit jealous because we're getting married."

Charlie looked concerned for several moments. Then he flashed Chloe and Daisy, a bright smile. "Perhaps the three of us could get married," he suggested. "That would be nice and friendly, wouldn't it? We could—"

"No," Daisy interrupted firmly, snatching back her headgear, "we couldn't. It wouldn't be right! We're *not* like them people on the telly. We're *decent*!"

Tessa, Molly and Susie Pollock, their lips twitching, swallowed hard and looked everywhere except at each other.

But Tessa found it almost impossible to keep a straight face when, once inside the sprawling animal park, she watched Susie produce several tubes from her bag and Daisy's numerous freckles disappear under a series of stripes which exactly matched her hat.

"Oh, wow," Charlie said, gazing at the green nose, the pink cheeks and the orange mouth. "That is so cool!"

Chloe's face too showed signs of definite envy. "It's very nice," she murmured wistfully.

Daisy lifted her chin proudly. She tapped her chest. "It makes me look like a pop star, doesn't it? And it means I won't get sunburnt. It's dangerous to get sunburnt." She lowered her voice, confidentially, "If you do, your nose drops off when you get old... and other bits..."

Charlie took a step back. His mouth fell open. "What other bits?"

Daisy shrugged. "Just parts."

"What... like legs and arms and things?"

Chloe's lower lip wobbled. She flickered a tearful glance at Molly. "I don't want my bits to drop off, Mummy."

"And they won't," Daisy assured her with a generous gap-toothed grin, "because me mam will paint you if you want. Then we'll *all* look like pop stars!"

Susie was almost knocked off her feet as the eager pair jostled for pride of place.

She dug deep into her bag again. "I think there's blue in here somewhere..."

"Blue for boys. Charlie must have blue," Daisy stated.

Susie worked swiftly and skilfully. As a final touch, she rubbed six arms and six legs with high protection sun cream, which left the little limbs looking faintly chalky.

"They look like extras from *The Last of the Mohicans*," Molly muttered as the party eventually made their way to the centre of the park and the signpost which would help them select their particular preferences.

"Right," Tessa said when they arrived and she'd carefully studied the array of pointing arrows, "we can't do everything at once, so who wants to go where first?"

As soon as she'd said it, she knew she'd made a mistake.

The din was deafening. All she could pick out were a few words: lions, giraffes, crocodiles. Holding her hands up, she began again.

"One at a time. I'm afraid there aren't any crocodiles. Chloe, you go first. What's your favourite animal?"

"Gorillas!"

"Daisy?"

"Gorillas!"

"Charlie?"

"Goats!"

Chloe sighed loudly. Her shoulders went up, then sharply down. "I knew he'd say that! Charlie, I've told you before, goats aren't very exciting. In fact they're boring."

His indignance was almost tangible. "They are *not* boring. They're kind and... clever."

Daisy wrinkled her lime-coloured nose thoughtfully. She peered at Charlie over the top of her glasses.

"But goats aren't *real* animals, are they, pet? Not like tigers and elephants and dinosaurs."

Charlie tutted. "Dinosaurs are extinct. And of course goats are real animals. They're not people, are they? I mean they don't wear clothes and shoes and sleep in beds. They don't go to school or drive cars.

"Goats are," his bluey-green eyes became misty and faraway, "very cuddly and I love them."

"Cuddly?" Tessa heard Susie mutter and she sensed too that Molly was about to put in her own twopenny worth.

Not wanting Charlie upset, she reached a snap decision.

"Tell you what, the gorilla house is just over there," Tessa pointed, "past the lion enclosure. See these big railings? If we go there now, we'll have lots of time for a good look round before we eat our sandwiches.

"And we could eat those and watch the elephants at the same time. Now that'll be fun, won't it?

"Then, later," she carried on quickly, seeing Charlie's hurt expression, "we can visit the goats *and* the tigers *and* giraffes, who are," she double-checked the signpost, "on the other side of the park. How's that?"

Charlie's mouth twisted. He appeared to be giving the matter a lot of thought. Then he grinned.

"That's actually a brilliant idea, Mum. I can keep a bit of sandwich for the goats and some biscuits and crisps." He turned to the girls. "They're always hungry, you see. That's why they eat *everything*! Even clothes off people's washing lines!"

"They do not!" Chloe countered immediately.

"They might do," Daisy said thoughtfully. "We had a rabbit, once, who ate everything… even the knobs off the remote control and the back of Dad's chair.

"Mr Whitenose his name was. He had a wife and seventeen children."

"Did they live *inside* your house?" Charlie asked, his voice filled with amazement.

"No, but *he* came inside to watch telly now and again. To give his wife a bit of peace, I think. Anyway," Daisy shrugged matter-of-factly, "he's dead now, but he died happy, with a smile on his face, me dad said."

Sensing that Charlie wouldn't be satisfied with just that sparse bit of information, but not wanting the conversation to develop too much further at this stage, Tessa called out brightly. "Come on, you lot, otherwise we won't have time to see anything at all."

The lions worked their magic. The subject of Mr Whitenose was instantly dropped.

Charlie said, very seriously, "They've got lovely hair, haven't they? I like the one with the sticky-up bit round his neck. He's the husband one, isn't he?"

Tessa nodded. "His name's Rambo," she said, pointing at the sign on the wall.

"He reminds me of Martin," she joked to Molly and Susie, watching as the king of the beasts snoozed in the sunshine, totally oblivious to his harassed partner's struggle as she tried to keep three lively cubs under control.

Chloe let out a shriek of glee. "Look… his wife's name is Chloe… same as mine!"

"And the bairnies are called Annie, Duke and Sarah," Daisy slowly sounded out the three words.

"Bright little sparks, aren't they?" Susie's voice held more than a hint of pride.

Then it was on to the gorilla enclosure.

All three children watched, mesmerised, as the younger members of the colony played to the crowds, swinging on the long expanses of tree bark and perfectly mimicking the actions of their elders.

"I'm going to write about them in my news book," Chloe giggled as a particularly comical little fellow peered at her, then poked out his soft, pink tongue.

"And me," Daisy said, the flowers on top of her hat wobbling.

Tessa glanced down at Charlie. She noticed that his attention had wandered from the frolicking infants and now seemed to be entirely focused on a huge male, sprawled out on the straw-covered floor and wallowing in the loving care of the several smaller females, who were plucking at his dense dark coat.

"Enjoying yourself, sweetheart?" she asked, following Charlie's gaze.

"It's great, Mum. Are these his wives?"

"I expect one of them is. The others are probably his friends."

"Which one?" Charlie persisted, but before Tessa had time to make her selection, his voice rose shrilly. "Look! Look what he's doing. He's trying to get his wife to give him a piggy back!

"She doesn't seem to want to, does she? I expect she thinks he's too heavy. Oh, he's changed his mind. Now he wants his friend to give him one."

Someone at the back of the enclosure guffawed. Susie blushed and giggled nervously. Molly prodded Tessa in the ribs. "Many a true word," she began. Tessa silenced her with a stare.

"Mr Whitenose used to like piggybacks, didn't he, Mam?" Daisy suddenly piped up. "Every single day he—"

"Who fancies an ice cream?" Tessa butted in as the action behind the bars began to hot up and several families headed swiftly for the exit.

"What – *before lunch*?" Charlie's face registered his disbelief.

"Why not? We can call it our… er… backwards lunch. Pudding first, then sandwiches."

Relief filled her as all three children whooped their agreement and raced for the door, without a backwards glance.

"You were wonderful. I don't know what I'd have done if I'd been on my own," a still pink-faced Susie admitted to Tessa when they were back outside.

"She's right," Molly gave her friend's arm a quick squeeze. "Even I was getting a bit hot under the collar. You're a genius at handling embarrassing situations, Tess."

Tessa fished in her handbag for her purse.

"Embarrassing? It was nothing," she lied airily.

Later that afternoon, having seen all the other attractions and having purchased two identical little monkeys for the twins and a bookmark for Martin, Tessa watched as her son gently stroked the grey nanny goat and her kid.

The others were at the far side of the Pet Enclosure, the two girls oohing and aahing over a placid lop-eared rabbit called Pickles.

Wearing a blissful smile, Charlie read out the details which were pinned on the fence beside him. 'This is Ju-li-et and her daughter, May."

His smile widened into a grin as Tessa took a couple of photographs. As though aware of the importance of the moment, both animals snuggled themselves against the little boy.

His coo of pure pleasure matched that of the plump white doves in the nearby aviary.

"I love you," Charlie told the soft-coated pair. "I love you, Juliet and I love you, May. I'm going to write all about you in my..." he stopped and his brow wrinkled.

The words tumbled out in a torrent.

"Mum, I've been thinking, how did Juliet know her daughter's name was May? How did you know my name was Charlie or Beth and Georgia were Beth and Georgia?"

Tessa said the first thing that came into her head.

"Well, I expect this little creature," she pointed at the long-legged kid, "was born in May and so—"

Charlie's puzzled expression stopped her, mid-sentence. She guessed correctly at what was coming next.

"But there isn't a month called Juliet. Or Charlie. Or Beth or Georgia or Darling Daisy or Auntie—"

A voice rang out, interrupting the flow before it reached Granny and Grandad. Tessa didn't get the chance to point out that Juliet was probably for a July birthday and that the others were a matter of choice.

Out of the corner of her eye, she could see the unmistakable pink flowers and the war paint, slightly streaky now, like Charlie's and Chloe's, because of the heat.

"You're right, Charlie. Goats are quite nice." Daisy stroked the twosome with one hand and linked her other arm through his. "But we've got to go now, Mam says."

Checking her own watch, Tessa nodded.

"The coach will be here soon."

It was a much more silent return journey. Worn out by heat and excitement, several of the children nodded off, including Daisy – still decked out in her hat – and Chloe, whose long blonde waves had coiled themselves into tight ringlets.

Tucked in the crook of Tessa's arm, Charlie was obviously struggling to keep his own eyes open. His voice was hoarse with fatigue.

"I loved everything, but 'specially Juliet and May. Thank you very much for taking me. I've had a brilliant day, Mum."

Tessa dropped a kiss on his springy hair, which smelled of shampoo and outdoors. "So have I, sweetheart."

Charlie yawned. Three times in quick succession. His lashes flickered.

Then, "Daisy said you called me Charlie, because it was your favourite name for a little boy... is that right?"

"Our very favourite," Tessa assured him.

"So when you have another little boy, what will you call him? I think you can have two favourites. I mean, my favourite colours are blue and orange and that's all right, isn't it?

"And my favourite animals are goats and gorillas and Georgia and Beth must have been your two favourite girl's names and..."

Tessa let the rest of his words wash over her. Then she realised he'd finished and was waiting for an answer to his original question.

"I think we'd call him..." she stopped. No, she told herself. It wasn't even a possibility. She and Martin had both agreed that it was out of the question. Three children were enough.

There was no point in even considering any more names. Their family was complete.

But no matter how hard she tried to convince herself, Tessa felt a small pang of longing somewhere deep inside her.

Charlie, Beth and Georgia... the lights of her life, both their lives, hers and Martin's. Laughter and tears. Never a moment to really collect their thoughts. Hard slog – but worth every single second of it.

"Mum?" Charlie's elbow nudged her ribs. "We could call him Rambo, like that beautiful lion. That's a great name. Rambo Harper!"

Tessa smiled dreamily. "Or we could call him Sam..."

Language Difficulties - Summer Special

Martin had everything organised for the day trip in two days' time. The tickets were in his desk, he'd checked the car insurance would cover them on the other side of the Channel, and pounds had been exchanged for francs.

Only one thing was missing.

"I'm getting really worried now," he told Tessa. "If they don't turn up this morning, I'll give the passport office another ring. If necessary, I'll have to go there and queue…"

The words had barely left his lips when the doorbell pealed. Charlie pushed aside his breakfast cereal.

"I'll go. I want to thank Mr Brian Postie again for giving me the football stickers. They are very tremendous!"

As his son sped off, Martin raised an eyebrow.

"Tremendous? What happened to brilliant and cool?"

"Oh, they haven't gone away." Crossing the kitchen, Tessa put a hand on each of the backs of the two high chairs. "Beth, tell Daddy, what is Charlie Harper?"

Toast crumbs sprayed onto the tray as the little girl said "Cool."

Tessa didn't have to repeat the question.

"B'illiant!" Georgia offered, her small fist punching the air.

"And what is Daddy?" a chuckling Martin asked his daughters.

The twins exchanged a glance. Georgia's mouth twisted thoughtfully. Beth frowned. At that moment, Charlie returned carrying a thick envelope. He shook his head.

"You didn't ask them the question properly, Dad. They're only little. You need to say it right. Like this. Girls, what is Mar-tin Har-per?"

Two pairs of identical eyes sparkled.

"Ecslent!"

Charlie nodded approvingly.

"Correct! And what is Tes-sa Har-per?"

"Mummy!"

Charlie sidled over to Tessa and caught hold of her hand.

"Don't be too sad. I'm trying to teach them to say beautiful, but it's a bit of a hard word. I can't get them past the boo bit, you see. They keep on hiding their eyes and shouting 'Peep Boo'!"

He frowned thoughtfully.

"If you can think of an easier thing you'd like to be called, then just tell me."

Tessa ruffled Charlie's chestnut hair.

"Don't worry, Mummy's fine for now." She glanced at the package. "But it would be *beautiful* if these were our passports."

To a noisy chorus of "Peep Boo!" a relieved Martin left for work. Charlie studied the five documents.

"Dad looks a lot like Grandad. And Grandad says he's not old, just very extinguished. So Dad must have to be extinguished, too!" Oblivious to Tessa's giggles he carried on.

"Mum, you look nice, even though your hair's sticking out and your face is worried."

She did *not* look nice, Tessa decided. She looked like an anxious wreck!

Hardly surprising really…

The heavens had opened between the car park and the photographers. Her immediate task had been getting the children towelled off and spruced up.

There had been all sorts of problems trying to keep the small girls still for the camera, after which she'd concentrated on explaining to Charlie that this was one photo session when he mustn't smile too much.

As he'd asked, "So I can't say cheese or sausages?" the flashbulb had gone off, registering his puzzled expression.

By the time her turn had come…

Charlie's voice broke into Tessa's uncomfortable thoughts, that she'd be lumbered with this hideous image for the next ten years.

"I look… well… just like me, really… when I'm thinking about something."

But his main attention was focused elsewhere.

"If Beth got chickenpox or something and couldn't go to France, and if Georgia didn't have spots and could go, but had lost her passport, then she could just take Beth's, couldn't she?

"No one would know the difference."

He had a point, Tessa conceded silently, looking over his shoulder. No one looking at them could ever know how different the girls were when it came to personality.

Beth was placid and easy-going, a lot like Charlie; whereas Georgia's fiery temper underlined everything that had ever been said, or written, about flaming redheads.

Heaven only knew what might happen in the future if they ever decided to play on their identical looks…

"Beth won't get chickenpox," she said, firmly dismissing the notion from her mind. "We're *all* going to France. On Thursday. In a long tunnel, right under the sea. Imagine how exciting that'll be…"

* * *

It had been an early start, but for most of the first leg of the journey, all three children, securely belted in their safety seats, had slept. Charlie wakened first. He rubbed his eyes then peered out of the window.

"Mum, where are the tower things?"

"What tower things, sweetheart?"

"The Hefhel ones. Chloe said that in France there are all these towers. Hefhel ones. She said there are hundreds of them and if you go up to the top you can see the whole world. And America. And Mars!

"If you go to France and don't see a Hefhel tower, then you've probably gone to China instead, she told me."

Tessa ignored Martin's murmured comments about Charlie's best friend, Chloe, being a seven-year-old menace. "She never gets *anything* right," he grumbled.

Chloe was a dear little girl and as bright as a button. It was just, Tessa felt, that her husband wasn't used to pedantic young females who proclaimed to know *everything* about *everything*.

But, she thought, as first Georgia, immediately followed by Beth, stirred, he'd learn!

She swivelled round in her seat.

"We're not in France yet, Charlie. We've still got to go under the sea… remember? Through the long tunnel? In a train?"

Charlie raised his eyes.

"Silly me! I should have knew that. When I looked out the window. Everything's still a lot grey. In France, *all* the houses are painted orange and purple and they've *all* got green and yellow striped roofs.

"The people are very tall. Sort of like giants, I think. And they wear red jackets and blue trousers. Or skirts – if they're girls. I think they have hats, too, and they eat smelly food and insects and things which I don't think sounds very nice. But they do make very tremendous chips."

His declaration coincided with their arrival at the long queues to the ticket booths, which relieved Tessa no end.

Thank heavens they were off the busy motorway.

Martin's cheeks had taken on an unbecoming mauve hue. He looked as though he was about to explode as he muttered, "Ruddy Chloe!"

Resting her head on his shoulder, she whispered into his ear. "Lunch today, *mon amour*, will be stinky cheese, *sautéed* worms and French fries, eaten on the top of the nearest Hefhel tower!"

Her light-hearted teasing had the desired effect. Martin's shoulders dropped and his lips twitched. Tessa gave Charlie her full attention again.

"Chloe knows an awful lot about France, even though she hasn't ever been there. Auntie Molly was saying just the other day that they were planning a trip – just like this one – very soon.

"So how do you think," Tessa finished, "that Chloe found out all these things?"

Charlie puffed out his cheeks.

"No, Mum. Not Chloe. She only knows about the Hefhel towers, because her cousin sent her a postcard with one on it. It was my darling Daisy Pollock who told me the other bits.

"My darling Daisy went to France, you see, when she was just one. She saw everything because her mum and dad pushed her all round the town in her pram. Oh, yeah, and she ate frogs and slugs for tea."

"Dogs!" Georgia shrieked. "Woof woof!"

Not to be left out, Beth joined in the discussion.

"Lugs!"

Martin groaned as he inched the car forward. "Give me strength!"

* * *

Charlie's eyes were out on stalks when he caught his first glimpse of the train.

"My goodness, all the people in England could fit in that. At the same time.

"We're off! Here we come, France," he whooped minutes later. "*Bonjour*," he greeted the attendant who'd come to check that the car's handbrake was on and the windows open.

"*Bonjour, monsieur.*" The young woman grinned as she returned the greeting, before moving along the line. Charlie's cheeks turned bright pink with pleasure.

"Oh, wow! That nice lady knew what I said. I really can speak French! Mercy," he called out to her retreating back and was rewarded with a wave and a wink.

Martin had undone his seatbelt and opened the door. "I must stretch my legs. Fancy a little stroll, Charlie?"

He didn't have to ask twice.

"Yes, please, Dad. I want to be able to see out the window properly. The fish and things. And there might be a shipwreck with a pirate's flag, and an octopus, and a killer whale, a submarine, giant crabs and... all sorts of exciting things.

"When will we see them? In a minute?"

He should have thought of this, Martin mentally scolded himself. Poor little chap...

No Hefhel towers. No giants dressed in red and blue. As for marine life... the closest Charlie would get to that today would be by looking in a fishmonger's window in Calais.

Slowly, trying to make it sound exciting, Martin began to explain about all the complex digging and how long it had taken. Charlie nodded occasionally as he heard how important it was that the tunnel was made very strong and that meant tons and tons of metal and concrete, so it would never leak.

"I see," he said solemnly when Martin had finished, "but I still think they could have put in *some* bits of glass. The fish would have liked that too. It would have made their lives more interesting.

"Mr and Mrs Cod could have taken their children for a day out to see the people and the cars."

Charlie brightened suddenly.

"Dad, I have a tremendous idea! When we get home you could help me write a letter to the people who made the tunnel. We could tell them about the Cod family. Ask them to put in some nice big windows."

His greeny-blue eyes danced with enthusiasm.

"We can ask *all* the family to write polite letters. And Hector, next door. And his family. My darling Daisy. Chloe. Mr Brian Postie. Absolutely everyone we know.

"I even 'spect," he finished, confidently, "that Chloe will be able to tell them 'zactly how to do it!"

"I am sure you are 'zactly right about that," Martin agreed, raising his eyes at a grinning Tessa, who was mouthing "You got out of that one nicely. Let's hope you do as well with the Hefhel towers!" as she dispensed drinks to the twins.

In no time they were on French soil. Charlie was fascinated by the length of red ribbon Martin had tied round one side of the steering wheel.

"That's so you won't forget to drive on the right side of the road, is it, Dad?"

"It certainly is."

"But you always," Charlie sounded puzzled, "drive on the right side when you're at home and you don't use a ribbon then."

"We don't drive on the *right* side in England, we drive on the *left* side," Tessa said.

"But it must be the right side," Charlie persisted, "because if it was the wrong side then everyone would crash into each other."

There was no answer to that! Well, there was, but it could become complicated. Tessa decided that a change of subject might be preferable.

She pointed out of the window.

"Look, Charlie. Aren't these horses beautiful?"

"Heehaw!" Georgia screamed. "Heehaw! Heehaw!"

"Moo," Beth said deeply and solemnly.

"I taught them that," Charlie said proudly. He wrinkled his snub nose. "What's the French word for heehaw?"

"The same, I suppose," Tessa told him. "I think animals all over the world speak the same language."

"My goodness. How clever of them." Charlie sounded impressed. Then he let out a shriek and pointed.

"Coloured houses! Over there. A green one and a blue one. And in the corner there's a pink one. I bet you one hundred pounds we'll see orange and purple ones next, with green and yellow roofs."

Tessa decided to nip this one firmly in the bud. To save any further disappointments for her son. Even if it meant bending the truth a little…

"I've been thinking, Charlie… that Daisy must have been in a different part of France when she saw houses like that. It's quite a big country, you know?"

"I did not know. But it's very interesting. Thank you for telling me. I won't forget."

He wouldn't, Tessa knew. He never forgot anything he was told, sometimes with embarrassing consequences. But hopefully, she crossed her fingers, not today.

"And also," Charlie said, "I'm starving!"

* * *

Calais had a confusing abundance of eating places. With the twins wriggling restlessly in their buggy, Tessa looked at Martin and shrugged.

"Very French," he teased, "but I think we ought to settle for an 'English Spoken Here' establishment. My schoolboy stuff's a bit rusty."

Moments later, the girls strapped into high chairs, the family settled round a table near the window. An extremely tall – at least six feet six, Tessa reckoned – and well-built waiter handed them menus.

Charlie's jaw dropped as he looked up.

"*Bonjour*, Mr Giant," he said breathlessly. "You look very smart in your red jacket and blue trousers. I knew you'd be dressed like that. My darling Daisy told me. I 'spect your wife wears a skirt, doesn't she? And that you both have nice hats?"

Seeing the baffled expression on the Frenchman's face, Tessa stabbed a finger at the menu. She could hear panic in her voice.

"What would you like, Charlie? A burger? Or pizza? And fries – you'll definitely want fries, won't you? They're your favourite!"

Charlie's eyes were still fixed on the waiter.

"I don't want anything smelly, please. And I don't want slugs either."

Just as Tessa was wishing the floor would open up and swallow her whole, there was a chuckle from the big man.

"Smelly slugs? No, little man, you mean snails. With lots of beautiful garlic. Very tasty! *Magnifique*!"

Charlie looked dubious.

"Are they? Manny... what you said? Do I *have* to eat them? Is that the law in France? Like not driving on the right side of the road? Or is it the wrong side of the road? I'm mixed up!"

The chuckle became a deep rumble of laughter. The waiter's liquid dark eyes met Tessa's embarrassed grey ones.

"I have a son at home... just like him. Wonderful! We are very lucky, yes?"

"*Oui*," Charlie said. "I've just remembered. In France you don't say yes, you say *Oui*. Like not big, but you spell it different. I think. Can I have pizza and chips, please? How do you say please, Mr Giant?"

"*S'il vous plaît*."

"Pizza and chips on a silver plate. That would be tremendous! Mercy," Charlie declared. "And when I've finished my lunch, could you tell me, silver plate, where I can find some Hefhel towers?"

* * *

Fingers of pinks and mauves were trickling across the sky when the Harpers made their return journey. The twins, fingers linked loosely, copper heads almost touching, were sleeping peacefully.

Charlie, however, was still full of beans. And pizza. Ice cream and hot doughnuts.

"This has been one of the very best days in my whole life," he said happily. "I think France is very cool. In fact it's excellent and brilliant and tremendous! Mercy for taking me there, Mum and Dad."

He sighed with pleasure.

"I went under the sea in a train. Then I saw coloured houses, and horses who could speak English. I drove along a road back to front, I met a real giant called Henri, and he was wearing real French clothes.

"I went on a roundabout and paddled in a different sea and met a girl called Margarine and we had to talk with our fingers and make faces.

"But best of all, I have my very own Hefhel tower..."

Charlie fingered the small replica of the famous Paris landmark – a gift from the kindly waiter.

"Next time," he carried on happily, "we'll go and see it properly, won't we, Dad? When the girls are bigger? Or, we could drive to China. Chloe says it's great.

"There's a big enormous wall that reaches up to the sky... everyone carries paper umbrellas with funny writing on them and... guess what... the people in China don't have dogs and cats – they have elephants as pets. And ostriches..."

Fish and Vips

Shoeless, his earth-encrusted trainers discarded on the back doorstep, Charlie Harper bounced in from the garden. He'd been weeding his own small vegetable patch, with the help of his friend, Hector, the elderly bachelor who lived next door.

"Hector says my lettuces are brilliant," Charlie proudly announced to his mother, Tessa. "An' he thinks my carrots might be better than his ones when we pull 'em out, cos I'm a well good grower, he told me.

"But then *I* said that I'm only well good cos *he* showed me how to do it the right way round. An' how if he hadn't, then my carrots might have grew upside down."

Charlie flopped into a chair.

"Whew! I'm sweating loads! It's hot, outside. Actually, it's boiling in here, too, isn't it?"

Nodding wearily, Tessa pushed her hair back from her clammy forehead. Two hours of ironing yet the pile didn't appear to have diminished significantly.

But enough was enough, she decided, casting an experienced eye over the fruits of her labours: sufficient shirts for Martin's working week; dresses for the toddler twins, Beth and Georgia, who could easily get through three apiece in a single day, and who would soon be waking from their afternoon nap; jeans, shorts and T-shirts for Charlie.

Not much for herself, but she'd get by.

"What we both need, sweetheart," Tessa said, unplugging the iron and putting it out of harm's way, "is a nice cold drink. We could have juice or—"

"A fizzy one!" Charlie rolled his eyes comically. "Lemonade or cola would be brilliant. I've got this scratchy bit in my throat, but my finger's not long enough to itch it! Oh, yeah, an' then I need to talk to you about tremendously excellent people that live in Eddingfield. Or ones that used to, but don't now, cos they might have moved to Australia or London or be dead or something."

The child's logistics of upside down carrots, she understood. A scratchy throat – yes, she could empathise with that. But tremendously excellent people, dead or alive?

Where had that suddenly sprung from?

Tessa put the cola bottle on the work surface. She glanced over her shoulder. "Charlie, sweetheart, what are you on about?"

The response to her question was a warning wave of a distinctly grubby finger.

"You've forgot, haven't you, Mum? I told you last week that my teacher, Mrs Peters, who used to be Miss Willis, but got married and came back to the school as a new lady, wants us to think about… er, vips, I think she called them.

"An' then we have to make a list and say why we think they're special. D'you remember now?"

She didn't. But Tessa wasn't unduly worried. Charlie would soon put her straight. *He always did.*

She passed him his glass. He drained it vigorously.

"That was great! My throat's nice an' smooth again. Thanks, Mum. You know vips – well, I'm thinking that Mrs Peters might be one. If she's not, she must just be magic, cos when she was Miss Willis, she had plain brown hair and now she *isn't* Miss Willis, it's got stripes in it. Banana-coloured stripes an' snow-coloured stripes!"

Charlie puffed out his cheeks. "Thousands of them. All over the place. That's amazin', isn't it? My darling Daisy Pollock says it's a *big* miracle!"

His voice lowered, reverently. "Like in the Bible, when the whole world got fish sandwiches from hardly any bread and only four or five sardines! *An'* a tin of best red salmon, Daisy said. Her Mam *always* keeps tins of best red salmon in the fridge. In case people come and visit them and don't phone first.

"Do *you* think it's a miracle, Mum? Not the best red salmon or the Bible picnic – that *must* be true. I mean Mrs Peters's hair changing colour while she was away on her holidays. Or was it just magic?"

Time enough in the future, Tessa decided, to explain to a seven-year-old lad about feminine wiles; about how his own mother occasionally resorted to a brightening rinse to liven up her tawny hair and hide the odd grey strand.

He'd only broadcast it far and wide!

"I think," she quickly said, "that when Mrs Peters was talking about very important people – VIPs, Charlie, not vips – she probably meant someone who had done something *extra* special... like... a very brave deed. Perhaps saved a life, or even lots of lives.

"Or it could men or women who spent all their time helping other people and making the world a kinder, better, or safer place for everyone to live in.

"Mrs Peters might even have been thinking about a clever artist, who painted wonderful pictures that everyone would enjoy for hundreds of years; or a writer of marvellous stories; a wonderful singer..."

Replenishing both their glasses, she sat down.

"Sometimes, you see, we think of a VIP as being *only* someone we read about in the newspapers. The Queen, for instance. Our Prime Minister. Everyone knows them; who they are."

Charlie frowned.

"Yeah, but the Queen doesn't live in Eddingfield. The Queen doesn't really live *anywhere*," he stated matter-of-factly. "She's got loads of palaces and castles and boats and aeroplanes all over the universe!

"An' the prime man – Mr Bear – he lives in a clock in London. Big Ben! With his wife and his children. I saw them on the telly."

Not one of her best explanations! Tessa tried again.

"What I meant, Charlie, was that a VIP doesn't have to be a face we recognise straight away, because they're always on the television or in the newspapers. You see, all over the world, and right here in Eddingfield, there are others who quietly—"

The rest of her words were drowned out by her daughters, their high-pitched voices, in perfect unison, singing over the baby intercom: "Mummy, where are you?"

And her son, miraculously rejuvenated, speeding past in a blur, calling, "Wait a minute, I've got something brilliant in my satchel… a bit of paper with great ideas to help us think and places to go."

Later, when a heavily perspiring Martin arrived home from his regular Saturday afternoon game of golf, Charlie was entertaining his sisters in the garden, under the eagle eye of Hector who was watching their antics from over the hedge.

His, "You take a few minutes to yourself, love," had allowed Tessa enough time to treat herself to a quick shower and a squirt of refreshing body spray.

"You never fail to amaze me, darling," Martin murmured into her freshly-shampooed hair. "Cool as a cucumber *and* smelling delicious! The kids, happy as sandboys. And I bet you've got something mouth-watering simmering in the oven, too."

Tessa relaxed against him.

"Mmm, you're *sort* of right. The kids are fine. You'll be thrilled to learn that Charlie's carrots are growing the right way up. I'm cool, but only just."

She raised her face for his kiss. "It's the oven that's *tremendously* cool!

"I couldn't face cooking in this heat. Take-away time, Martin. Your choice. Pizza, fish, chicken – best red salmon sandwiches, if that's what you fancy!

"Just make sure it's accompanied by hefty portions of vips."

"Vips? You really are frazzled! You mean chips, don't you?" Martin said, grinning.

Tessa giggled. "No. I mean vips!"

* * *

"So much for the day of rest," Martin grumbled, good-naturedly, the following afternoon as the family left the old town cemetery. "So much for VIPs!" He nodded towards his son, who was clutching a notebook.

"The only thing that has really fascinated him here – apart from the bloke who was shipwrecked a couple of hundred years ago, and a woman who is now 'growing beautiful flowers in heaven' – are the amount of people who've been buried when they were just sleeping!"

Pushing the canopied, double buggy containing the snoozing twins, along the gravelled path, Tessa pulled a thoughtful face.

"I'm glad he came straight out with it, though. My grandpa used to bring me for walks here, when I was little. I loved it… the flowers and the birds… all the beautiful butterflies… until I was old enough to read the gravestones myself. Then I was terrified!

"Problem was, I didn't tell anyone. It was only when I started having nightmares about being buried alive, that Mum found out and explained what the words really meant!"

Martin patted her hand, consolingly. "Well, one thing we don't have to worry about is Charlie keeping quiet about *anything* that's going on in his head. And while we're on the subject of chatterboxes, here comes the greatest of them all!

"The north of England," Martin continued, wryly, "lost a potential world champion when Steve transferred to the southern branch of his company!"

Tessa followed his gaze. Steve and Susie Pollock, with their exuberant daughter, Daisy, who was clad in electric blue shorts, crimson T-shirt and a floppy denim hat, were just coming through the gates.

"Charlie! Pet!" Daisy shrieked, dashing forward. "We've been to the museum. I've got a dead lad called Joseph, who went to Africa and fought lions and giraffes and fish that eat you to teach people in sheds about Jesus. Another one – his name was Daniel – he wrote special poems for an old queen. And a live lady," Daisy glanced at her notebook, "Olive Blunt, who sewed a duvet.

"I even saw the duvet. It's fab! Tons of colours and pictures. I've asked me mam to sew me one for my bed. Tomorrow!"

Across the children's heads, Tessa's puzzled grey eyes met Susie's raised blue ones.

"A Millennium patchwork quilt," Susie mouthed. "On life in Eddingfield over the last hundred years. A masterpiece."

As Tessa smiled, Charlie's voice rang out.

"Well, I've got a very brave man who fell into a sea full of sharks and whales and octopuses when he was coming back, in a rowing boat, from China.

"His legs and arms got bit off, but he wriggled on his tummy *all* the way home to his family and brought them nice presents. He carried them with his teeth. Then he died."

Tessa couldn't believe what she was hearing.

The only details were that the deceased Seth Mason, husband and father, had been shipwrecked. And the date. 1792. Nothing more!

She gulped as Charlie continued, cheerfully.

"*An'* I've got a brilliant gardener lady, called Edith, who works for God. Right now! In heaven! That's well fab, isn't it? I bet she's got great wings."

Daisy's mouth twisted. "So she's dead, too, then?"

Charlie shook his head. "No, she was just tired doing all that diggin'. She fell asleep. It said so on the stone thing."

All four adults struggled frantically not to laugh as Daisy linked her arms through Charlie's. "That's just a decent way of saying dead, pet. Me dad told me that *ages* ago."

She glanced around. "If every one of the folk here are in heaven, then we can't really ask 'em any questions, can we? So," she carried on with a shrug, "I think we should all go and have some ice cream, then we can talk a bit more about what we're going to write down to tell Mrs Peters tomorrow…"

* * *

That evening, a pyjama-clad Charlie sat at the kitchen table, his small pink tongue poking out in concentration as he wrote slowly and steadily.

Also on the table, was the list of words he had asked Tessa to spell for him, before refusing any further offers of help with a "Thank you very much, but I can do this all by myself. I'm a well good writer. You ask Mrs Peters."

He coloured slightly. "An' anyway, it's *sort* of secret… just what *I* think…"

Half an hour later, when Martin went to check on his son's progress, he found the little boy slumped over his notebook. Scooping the sleeping child into his arms, he carried him up to bed.

"Charlie Shakespeare's candle has just snuffed itself out," he told Tessa on his return, holding up the notebook. "Let's have a look at what he's written."

Tessa gnawed on her lip. "We can't. Charlie said it was secret. It'd be like… like… reading someone's diaries. And I never want to be tempted to do that – to *any* of my children."

Exasperated, Martin pushed a hand through his hair.

"Tess! He's seven! We're not about to discover anything mind-blowing! So what if he's written his own theory about that shipwrecked chap and doesn't want us to know? Mrs Peters'll work it out for herself. Probably give her a good laugh and I, for one, don't begrudge her that!

"I'd need all the help I could get if I had to handle thirty or so kids every day. To hold their attention. Set them challenges."

Tessa struggled with her conscience. In all honesty, she was dying to have a peek, especially after witnessing, although not hearing, the in-depth conversation between her son and the love of his life, Daisy, in the ice cream shop.

The duo had insisted on sitting at a separate table. "It's not that we don't like you, it's just that me and Charlie have got important things to talk about," Daisy had declared.

Then there had been lots of mutterings; nods and shakings of heads; giggles and groans and sideways glances.

Maybe just a tiny look? No. Absolutely not, Tessa quickly decided.

"Martin, put that book in his satchel," she instructed firmly. "Right now! We don't *have* to read it. He'll *tell* us about it. When he's ready.

"You know what Charlie's like…"

* * *

"My goodness," Gale Peters said on Monday afternoon, gazing fondly at her little pupils, "you *have* worked extremely hard finding so many people who have made a big difference to all our lives!"

She scanned the long list in front of her, the one she had made as each child had offered their own ideas of Eddingfield's Very Important Persons: missionaries; painters; explorers; a poet; craftsmen and women.

But her favourites, she couldn't help thinking, had been the practical suggestions from Daisy Pollock, and Charlie

Harper's offerings – in spite of them being somewhat confusing and faintly embarrassing!

"I'm thinking," Daisy had said, "that it was very decent of all them dead folk to be so brave and kind. But I'm also thinking that my best VIPs are alive ones like Mario at the ice cream shop, cos he helps us stay nice and cool an' he sings a lot, to make people happy. An' Doctor Gilbert – he got rid of my wart, you know an' I'd had it for ages!

"Then I thought about Jim, our milkman, who brings yoghurt and juice, too, even on wet days, and Betty who helps us cross the road outside the school, so I wrote them down as well. An' Charlie Harper, cos we're going to get married. Oh, yeah, an' Olive Blunt who made the duvet in the museum," she'd added, almost as an afterthought.

Next, it had been Charlie's turn. The shipwrecked Seth got a vague mention, as did the heavenly gardener, then the little boy went into full flow.

"If we didn't have Mr Brian, the postman, then we wouldn't get letters and cards and stuff from our friends. That would be horrible, wouldn't it? Mr Brian is well cool.

"So is my friend, Hector. He helps everybody in our road. Young ones and old ones and people in the middle. I wouldn't know how to grow right-way-up vegetables if I didn't have Hector to show me how to do it. He's definitely a VIP.

"But the most tremendously excellent people in Eddingfield are my family an' all my friends, 'specially my darling Daisy. And you, Mrs Peters, for teaching us clever things and for making miracles happen.

"Your new, beautiful striped hair," he'd finished earnestly, "is the most brilliant miracle in the whole world... even better than fish sandwiches..."

Wedding Bells, Warning Bells

As usual, Charlie Harper had voluntarily interrupted his breakfast in order to retrieve the post from the doormat. "It's my very important job," the seven-year-old always insisted, "to make sure that everybody gets the right letter!"

Back in the kitchen, he carefully studied the morning's delivery.

"Sorry, nothing for you, Georgia," he told one of his little sisters. "Or you, Beth," he informed the other twin. "Oh, dear – there's nothing for me, either.

"But," Charlie brightened, "here's one for Mum." He handed it to Tessa. "It's from Uncle Ray, isn't it? I know, because it's like that on my birthday cards. Uncle Ray always writes in purple ink, doesn't he? That's because he's an artist, isn't it? And he's your little brother, isn't he?"

Without waiting for an answer to any of his questions, Charlie carried on, his voice filled with awe.

"Wow! Look at all these! There's one… two… three… four for Dad. Cool! People must really like him a lot. Dad's very lucky, isn't he?"

Tessa glanced, sideways, at the quartet of envelopes. All buff-coloured or official-looking. Bills, probably! She doubted that Martin would consider himself particularly fortunate when he came home this evening, probably exhausted after a three-day, business trip.

Charlie's voice broke into her thoughts.

"I've been thinking… why is Uncle Ray writing to you? Usually he just phones. Is his phone broken? Is it your birthday, Mum, or is it because Uncle Ray has some very tremendous news... like... he's going to paint a picture of the Queen or a famous pop star and he's too excited to say it out loud?

"That's what happens to me. When I get excited. My tongue gets caught up in my teeth and I can't say anything. Not even one word."

Charlie? Unable to talk? Suppressing a grin, Tessa pushed back her hair.

"No, it's not my birthday. And when I've read Uncle Ray's letter, I'll tell you all about it. Promise! Now, finish your breakfast, sweetheart. Auntie Molly'll be here soon, to take you to school."

As Charlie picked up his spoon, Tessa slid her finger along the sealed flap of the envelope.

"I don't believe it..." she murmured to herself moments later, "Ray's actually going to tie the knot. At last!"

His cereal finished, Charlie quickly drained his glass of orange juice.

"What don't you believe, Mum? That Uncle Ray can tie knots? He can, actually. He is brilliant at tying knots. He taught me what a reef one was. And a round turn and two half snitches.

"Oh, yeah, and a granny. Grannies are loose. They fall apart. Don't ever," Charlie waved a warning index finger, "tie a parcel with grannies. It will never get there... well, it might... but all the insides will have fallen out all over the country!"

This time, Tessa couldn't hide her laughter. The images of loose old women spilling their contents the length and breadth of Britain was just too much.

The letter in her hand vibrated in time with her helpless giggles. Charlie chuckled, too.

"I bet Uncle Ray has written you a good joke? He knows tons of jokes. Will you tell me it, Mum? Please?"

With difficulty, Tessa pulled herself together. She shook her head.

"No, darling, he didn't tell me a joke."

Charlie's smiles turned to puzzled frowns.

"So what were you laughing at? You were laughing. I saw you!"

Not wanting to confess to her lively son that it was his innocent remarks which had brought on her temporary hysteria, Tessa thought fast.

Then, "I was laughing because I am very happy. I've got you and Beth and Georgia. It's Friday, and Daddy will be home tonight, so we can all be together again.

"And tomorrow, remember, we're going to see Grandma and Grandad Harper's new house? I'm happy because it'll be nice to have them living a lot nearer to us, won't it?"

Immediately, the frown disappeared. Charlie whooped with delight.

"Yeah! It'll be great. Tremendously excellent! Grandad's going to get a new dog, you know? Well, not a brand new one.

"He's going to get a second-hand puppy from the kind people who look after dogs that nobody wants. Grandad said I could help him choose and I was thinking that maybe we"

The shrilling of the doorbell cut him off, mid-sentence.

"Oh, heavens, is that the time already?" Tessa sprang up. "Quick, Charlie, go and brush your teeth and get your blazer on."

Minutes later, she was waving him goodbye as he scampered up the path.

"Have a good day, sweetheart. Love you lots."

Charlie stopped at the gate. He turned.

"Mum, you still didn't tell me why Uncle Ray wrote you a letter. *Is* he going to paint a picture of a pop star?"

Tessa shook her head.

"He sent me a letter because he had some exciting news and he didn't want to forget a single thing. Sometimes that happens when you just phone someone."

Not exactly true. Ray's note had been sketchy. But, "Guess what, Charlie?" she carried on, brightly. "Uncle Ray and Katherine are getting married. They want you to be a *special* guest."

"Do they? My goodness!" Charlie said, thoughtfully. The gate swung shut behind his sturdy little body. Tessa quickly returned to the kitchen, where the twins, strapped into their high chairs, were finishing their own breakfasts.

At the sight of them, she groaned.

Georgia's flaming red curls were glued against her scalp, held tightly in place by the marmalade from the triangles of toast she'd decided to wear as an intricately-layered hat; Beth's creamy-skinned cheeks were thickly coated with her favourite yeast spread.

"Yukky!" Tessa grinned at her daughters.

"Yukky!" Beth repeated, wrinkling her nose, comically. "Yukky, yukky, yukky!"

"Baf!" her identical sister declared. "Now, Mum."

Although Tessa agreed that now would be ideal, it was almost ten minutes later when she lowered her sticky little girls into the suds.

"That was Granny on the telephone," she explained, gently trickling water over Georgia's head. "She wants to talk about Uncle Ray's wedding, so we're going to have lunch with her and Grandad today. After that, we'll go and get Charlie from school."

"Gary," Beth said, with a wide smile, her name for her maternal grandmother.

"Daddad!" Georgia offered, nodding.

"Charlie! Cool!" they shrieked, in unison.

* * *

The twins being happily entertained in the garden by their doting grandfather allowed Tessa and her mother the rare opportunity of an uninterrupted conversation.

"As soon as I saw his writing on the envelope I knew something was up. Of course it's good news, but four weeks' time. Seems a bit soon!" Mary Allen slowly voiced her doubts. "You don't think that Katherine's—"

"Not for one minute, Mum," Tessa interrupted, briskly. "Katherine's much too sensible for that. Trapping a free spirit like Ray is the very last thing she'd want to do.

"No, I reckon that your beautiful, talented, little boy, who has had girls swooning over him since he was fourteen, has finally realised that he's met the real love of his life and has wisely decided to snap her up before someone else does!

"For my part, I'm very glad it's Katherine. She's a sweetheart. The children adore her and you can't fool kids! When I think of some of Ray's lady friends…"

As Tessa's voice faded away, Mary nodded.

"I love Katherine, too. But," her mouth twisted, "that still doesn't explain why Ray didn't just phone? Like he always does? That's what's really worrying me."

Tessa chuckled. "In many ways, my brother and my son are kindred spirits! Ray draws constantly – so does Charlie. Both have the kind of smile which could melt a century old glacier.

"In general, they could enter a 'Talk for Britain' competition, but, when it comes to what they consider the really serious, very personal stuff, they prefer to put their thoughts into words!

"Like the note Charlie wrote me last week. It said *The handel fell of my Star Wars mug. I think it was because l bumped it agenst the tap. I am very sorry.*" Tessa propped one elbow on the table and rested her chin on her cupped hand.

"He signed it *Your friend Charles Edward Harper!*"

Mary's lips tilted. "Point taken." Reaching forward, she picked up her son's letter and scanned the closely-written lines, before looking up again. "Ray is the limit, though. He's getting married, he says. He wants us all to be there, he says. He's told us which weekend to keep free and plans, apparently, are well under way.

"But," frustrated she shook her head, "he's omitted to mention what *kind* of do it'll be! Registry office or church? Posh frocks or whatever happens to be lying around, because the bridal pair has nothing except paint-spattered jeans?

"All we really know," Mary finished, "is that he wants Charlie to play some kind of special role – but what?"

Tessa shrugged. "Haven't a clue. I'll ring Ray tonight." She grinned suddenly. "I've got this image in my mind of how it might be. Artistic. Romantic. The bridal pair dickied out in floppy velvet with lace collars and cuffs... and pageboy Charlie looking like Little Lord Fauntelroy!"

"Oh, surely not!" Mary's mouth twisted. "He would hate that!"

Tessa didn't entirely agree. Charlie adored dressing up. He loved being centre stage. Whatever was in Ray's mind, his nephew would likely look on as a very brilliant adventure!

She dragged herself from her thoughts as she realised her mother was talking again. In a very pensive tone.

"The little boy down the road – Robbie – he's the same age as Charlie. Well, his aunt wanted him to be a page boy at her posh wedding, last summer.

"Robbie wasn't having any of it! He promised his mother that if anyone made him wear light blue satin, he'd wet himself in church..."

* * *

The venue for the ceremony was an old manor house, newly granted a licence and set in the heart of magnificent countryside. Not in Cornwall, where the bridal couple had settled, but much closer to home.

"I got a nod from a friend of mine," Ray told Tessa, "that they'd be able to fit us in at short notice. Besides, Katherine and I knew how hard it would be for you to cart your lot all the way to St. Ives."

She'd been grateful for their consideration. And several of Tessa's suspicions had proved to be spot on. It was going to be a wonderfully romantic and arty occasion.

Katherine's dress was antique oyster lace; Ray's crushed velvet suit a rich burgundy colour. Their two witnesses – fellow artists – would complete the picture in rose madder and taupe. As for Charlie's outfit…

With the sun streaming through the window on the day of the wedding, the little boy trembled with excitement as he studied himself in the mirror.

"Oh, wow, Mum, I look like a real man!" He stroked the bronze brocade of the fitted waistcoat, which topped a long-sleeved cream silk shirt. "And these trousers aren't ord'nary boot cuts, you know. They're called flares! And they're 'zactly like people used to wear hundreds of years ago in a time called the sixties!

"Katherine's friend was very clever to make all these beautiful clothes for me, wasn't she? But," Charlie considered his reflection again, "really, it's my boots that I love best. Silver buckles! I have *always* wanted silver buckles. Ever since I was a baby!"

Tessa couldn't reply straight away. Suddenly, a lump had sprung into her throat. Charlie was right. He did look grown-up. Frighteningly so.

It was all happening much too quickly. Not just to Charlie, either. Each day, as their skills developed, the twins were becoming more and more independent.

When she'd zipped them into their matching Victorian-style dresses earlier, and twisted their bright red hair into curly topknots, it had struck her that the wobbly toddlers had almost gone.

She'd gazed at her two little girls. Soon, they wouldn't need her any more...

Charlie's voice reached her as though it had travelled down a very long tunnel. "Are you okay, Mum? You've gone a bit white. Do you feel a bit white? Or... what's that word Hector next door uses... er... woozy. D'you feel woozy?"

Tessa wasn't sure what 'white' felt like, but she definitely recognised 'woozy'. Lowering herself onto Charlie's bed, she smiled, shakily. "I'm fine, sweetheart. Just a bit—"

"Excited!" Charlie interrupted. "So am I, Mum. I've never hushed before, you see. And it's a very important job, being a husher, Uncle Ray said.

"But I know how to do it. He told me last night when we were all at Granny's. When people come, I have to go up to them and say, 'How nice to see you. I hope you are well. Isn't it a lovely day?' then I have to smile and hush them to their seats.

"If I didn't, well, I 'spect they'd have to stand all the time. For hours and hours. They wouldn't like that, would they?"

The room had stopped spinning. Tessa managed a grin. "They certainly would not," she agreed, "and now, Charlie, perhaps you'd like to *usher* me back to my bedroom. We'll have to be off soon. I've got to make myself look pretty."

"You look pretty, now," Charlie assured her, "and you're not all white any more. In fact, you're nice and very pink again. Like a red rose. Or a beetroot..."

* * *

That evening, Charlie was still up long after his usual bedtime, still dressed in his wedding finery, still nattering nineteen to the dozen.

"This has been a most tremendous day! It was a great wedding and it was also great being a hush – *usher*," he corrected himself. "Uncle Ray said I was excellent at it. Well excellent!

"So when I get married to my darling Daisy Pollock, I'll be the man who gets his wife and be an usher, too. My darling Daisy can help if she likes. Before I say a beautiful poem, pull back the curtain from her face, and give her a real golden ring."

Chuckling softly, Martin disappeared behind his newspaper as Charlie carried on.

"I liked the food! It was brilliant. Specially the yellow rice with the squiggly orangey things in it! I ate tons of that. Granny said I would burst, but I didn't. What were these squiggly things, Mum?"

"Prawns," a weary Tessa supplied from the comfort of her armchair.

"Oh, yeah, that's right. Auntie Katherine told me. She *is* my auntie now, isn't she? And when she and Uncle Ray have some children, they'll be my cousins, won't they? Mine and Georgia's and Beth's? And we'll be theirs, won't we?

"D'you think they'll have some children soon, Mum? Next week or something?"

If only! Smiling, Tessa shook her head.

"Remember, Charlie, how long it took when I had the twins? Nine whole months for the babies to grow big and strong enough to be born?"

Charlie pulled a thoughtful face. "Yes... but what if Auntie Katherine had only one baby at a time. Wouldn't it be a lot quicker?"

"I'm afraid not, sweetheart."

"Oh well," Charlie nodded philosophically, "I just hope it's not too long. A year or five years. I like babies. They are excellent."

Crossing the room, he perched on Tessa's lap. "Will we have another one, Mum? A boy called Rambo like that lion at the zoo, or Sam, like you said?"

Ignoring Martin's quickly lowered newspaper and the wary expression in his eyes, Tessa's arm curved protectively round her son. She buried her face into his silky chestnut hair.

"We'll just have to wait and see about that..." she murmured.

Secrets and Strangers

Charlie Harper, his best friend, Chloe, and the love of his life – his darling Daisy Pollock – were deeply involved in what they had mutually agreed was a top secret discussion and which had started earlier in the school playground.

After the visit from the Special Community policeman...

"Remember," Charlie instructed firmly as the trio of seven-year-olds huddled in the small tent in the Harper's back garden, "we must *not* say a single word to anyone. Not to *anyone* in the *whole world*. Until we're really sure that she *is* a stranger. Okay?"

Chloe tossed her blonde head. "For goodness sake, Charlie, I said that *ages* ago!" she told him, sniffily.

"So did I. And don't forget, it is *my* stranger. *You* haven't even seen her yet." Daisy shifted position. "I'm getting well squashed in here. Can you move back, Charlie, pet?"

Charlie obediently wriggled himself against the canvas wall. To allow his plump sweetheart more space, he drew his knees up. "This is tremendously exciting. Tell us about her again, please," he pleaded.

Daisy obliged in a hushed voice, heavy with drama, but not before she'd lifted the tent flap and peered outside. "There might be tons of spies out there, listening. I've seen things like that on the telly," she whispered before carrying on.

"No, it's okay. Your mam's not hanging out the washing or anything, Charlie, so I'll tell you. Well, she's old. Quite a lot old, I think. About... forty! She wears a strange coat and

92

she carries a strange bag and she wears strange shoes. Oh, yeah, and she's got a strange face!"

"What – a bit strange or tremendously strange?" Charlie asked, breathlessly. "I mean does she have two noses or a mouth on the top of her head? Is her skin green or purple?"

Daisy spent several minutes considering the question. She took off her glasses, cleaned them on the hem of her skirt, and then replaced them thoughtfully.

"I don't *think* so, pet, but I've still never seen a face like it before! Not in Gateshead, where I used to live. Not in Bradford – my nan lives in Bradford – and not down here!

"I never saw a face just the same as hers when we went to Spain for our holidays neither."

Chloe and Charlie silently digested the information, then exchanged a long, contemplative glance. "I think you're right, Daisy. She definitely *must* be a stranger," Chloe eventually said, nodding, "so you know what you've got to do if you ever see her again, don't you?"

Daisy's mouth twisted. "Do I?"

Charlie tutted. "Course you do. That nice policeman told us today." He began to count on his fingers. "You must *not* get into her car, no matter what she says. Er – does your stranger *have* a car?"

"Don't know." Daisy puffed out her cheeks. "I've only seen her walking along our road, sometimes. In her strange shoes. Oh, I've just remembered, she's got a strange hat, too. A bright green one, it is. Soft and sort of squidgy with a bit hanging over her face. I like it and—"

"You must *never* ask her if you can try it on," Charlie interrupted fiercely. "It would be very dangerous!"

"The policeman didn't actually say anything about hats; at least I don't think he did." Chloe's hesitant tone suggested her inner confusion. "You're right about cars, though, Charlie. We mustn't go off with *anyone* Even if they tell us that our mum said it would be okay.

"We shouldn't go even if they're walking and they look nice and kind and are carrying shopping bags and want to give us loads and loads of sweets. The policeman said that if anyone tries to catch hold of us, we must scream and scream and scream and run away fast."

Chloe's cheeks were bright pink when she finished.

"Or we could just *bite* them," Daisy suggested calmly. "Really hard. That'd likely make 'em shove off!"

Chloe shuddered. "They might be dirty. I wouldn't like to bite a dirty person."

"*Are* strangers dirty? Is that how we know they're strangers?"

Although Daisy had opened her mouth to respond, Charlie never received an answer to that question, because Tessa's voice rang out. "Come on, you lot. Tea's ready."

"Coming, Mum," Charlie called back.

Chloe seemed reluctant to let the matter drop just yet. "That policeman said you should *always* tell someone if you see a stranger," she said slowly, looking straight at Daisy, who shrugged.

"I *have* told someone. I've told you and I've told Charlie! And I don't think it'd be fair to tell anyone else. Not yet. 'Til we know."

Crawling out of the tent, Charlie turned. "Daisy's right! She might," he said, "not be strange at all, Chloe. She might be very nice, so… we've got to keep it really secret…"

* * *

Tessa was upstairs putting the two-year-old twins, Beth and Georgia, to bed when Martin walked into the living room. He was met with the sight of his son's back. Charlie had pulled a chair over to the window and, on his knees, was peering out into the quiet street.

He turned suddenly, his expression very serious. "I've been wondering, Dad, all day long, how many strangers do you know? Five? Or seven? Or even a hundred?"

His question rang a bell in Martin's head. Tessa had mentioned earlier that she suspected something was going on in Charlie's mind. "He was unusually quiet after Chloe and Daisy went home," she'd said.

Strangers! Could that be it? Martin flopped into his armchair.

"That's a tough one, Charlie," he admitted, frantically searching for the least complicated way to supply an answer and eventually settling on, "because, really, *everyone we don't know* is a stranger, which, I suppose, is most of the whole world.

"But… when we get to know someone… maybe at work… or at school… then they're *not* strangers any more. We can call them by their names. We can say, 'Hello, Jim.' Or 'How are you, Pete?'"

Charlie's russet-brown brows formed a straight line above his clear, greeny-blue eyes. He climbed off his chair and crossed the room, settling on the carpet at Martin's feet.

"But, Dad, we don't *have* anyone in our school called Jim or Pete. Or if we do have, I don't know them, so they must be strangers. And I wouldn't be able to talk to them even if they *were* called that," he carried on, "because the policeman said we shouldn't talk to strangers. *Not ever*."

Things began to slowly dawn on Martin.

He vaguely recalled seeing a slip which Charlie had brought home recently, informing parents that a specially-trained Community Policeman would be visiting all the local schools on a regular basis. Partly to encourage the children to think of the police as friends; but also to give informal talks on general safety.

He nodded thoughtfully, chose his words carefully. "I think the policeman was talking about *grown-up* strangers,

Charlie. I don't think he meant that you shouldn't make new friends at school.

"I mean, what about Daisy? She's not been in your class as long as most of your other friends, has she? She was a stranger when she arrived, you didn't know her, not even her name, but now she's your—"

"Darling!" Charlie quickly interrupted. "And we're going to get married and have a house in the country and lots of children and a dog, some cats, a goat and a thousand chickens.

"Daisy Pollock and I..." he stopped. And grinned. "I think I see what you mean, now, Dad. About strangers. Other children are all right, and so are... grown-ups that your family knows... and people like... your neighbours and your friends... and your friends' friends... and their families..."

Charlie paused for a moment. Then, "But not old people with strange faces, wearing strange coats and hats and shoes, and carrying strange bags.

"I'll tell my darling Daisy that tomorrow. That she must *not* go off with *her* stranger and that she must never, *ever* smile at her or want to try on her hat, even if it is a nice green one, because—"

It was Martin's turn to interrupt. "Hang on a minute, Charlie, what are you talking about?" he asked quickly, feeling a sudden sense of distinct unease.

Charlie sighed exaggeratedly. "My darling Daisy's stranger." He suddenly clapped his small hand to his mouth. "Oh, I wasn't s'posed to tell you about her. It was s'posed to be a secret."

A movement at the door distracted Martin from probing further. Tessa was standing there, her shoulders rigid. Quickly she covered the space between herself and Charlie, crouching on the floor beside him.

"Hi, Mum," Charlie said. "We've just had an excellent chat, me and Dad! He's told me a lot of well interesting things. About strangers. Don't worry about me going off with anyone. I never will. Cross my heart."

Tessa barely heard him. As she'd listened to the last part her son's revelations to his father, her throat had gone horribly dry. Seeing the exchanged, secretive glances between the children at teatime, listening to their muffled giggles and their whispered comments, she'd known *something was* going on.

But nothing as serious as this!

Although reluctant to frighten her son, she knew she had no choice but to get the truth out of Charlie. Steve and Susie Pollock, Daisy's parents, needed to know, as quickly as possible, the danger their gregarious little chatterbox daughter might be in.

Tessa cleared her throat several times. Charlie patted her hand, sympathetically.

"Oh, dear, have you got a frog in there, Mum?"

"Just a little one, sweetheart."

"Witches have frogs, you know," Charlie said. "They make spells with frogs. And *very* bad witches take little children away and put them in cages and give them tons of food to make them fat, then," his eyes danced with a mixture of excitement and horror, "they eat them!

"Chloe told us about it. She knew two children that nearly happened to. Or, anyway, her grandma did. Only it didn't happen, because a very brave woodcutter came along and chopped the bad witch's head right off and the children went home with a basket of goodies to their mum and dad and *everyone* lived happily ever after.

"That was lucky, wasn't it?"

Under normal circumstances, Tessa would have gently unravelled the combination of *Hansel and Gretel* and *Little Red Riding Hood*, but these weren't normal circumstances.

Her heart pounding against her ribs, she slid her arm round Charlie's shoulders.

"Sweetheart, if someone knows a secret that might be a bit dangerous, what do you think they should do?"

Charlie's mouth twisted. "I don't know. A secret's a very important thing. You only tell your *best* friends. That's why my darling Daisy only told me and Chloe about her one."

Tessa nodded. "I understand that. But... supposing Daisy's secret meant that she might get into some kind of trouble... wouldn't you want to stop that from happening?"

Charlie chewed on his lower lip. "I 'spect so." He snuggled against Tessa. "Yes, I would. So... I'll tell you... and Dad... but you mustn't say a single thing to anyone else. Not even one word..."

When she finally fell into bed that night, after umpteen telephone conversations between herself and Susie Pollock, Tessa felt like a washed-out rag, albeit an extremely relieved one.

"At least that's sorted out. Thank heavens Susie recognised her new neighbour's description," she murmured sleepily.

Martin thumped his pillows into shape. "It was the hat that did it, I reckon. Good job Charlie's a stickler for remembering every little detail."

"Mmm, but it doesn't get any easier, bringing up children, does it? All you can do is your best and hope it's enough to keep them safe."

"I don't know, Tess, I think we're doing pretty well under the circumstances. Look at it this way, in one evening, we've sorted out strangers – who is and who isn't – and secrets – which should and which shouldn't be kept!

"I reckon we can both sleep peacefully tonight, safe in the knowledge that no one in this house is keeping anything earth-shattering or life-changing to themselves."

In the dark, with Martin's kiss warm on her lips, Tessa felt her face grow uncomfortably, guiltily hot.

Tomorrow. First thing, she promised herself...

* * *

The following day, at playtime, Daisy's cheeks were crimson, too. "Guess what," she told Charlie and Chloe, hopping from one foot to the other, "I've got *another* secret. A *really* great one, this time.

"My stranger... you know, the one with the hat and the shoes and the bag... well, she," Daisy stopped jiggling and glanced over her shoulder, "came into my house, last night, *and* I tried her hat on!"

Chloe narrowed her eyes. "That's not a secret – that's a big fib!"

"It is *not* a fib!" Daisy replied indignantly. "She came into my house and she sat down, on the settee, and then she had a cup of tea and two of me mam's home-made coconut buns."

"Did she come into your house because she tried to run away with you and your dad came out with a big axe and stopped her, like the brave woodcutter in Chloe's grandma's story?" Charlie asked.

"Course she didn't, pet. Me mam wouldn't have given her two buns, would she, now? Me mam would likely have walloped her if she'd tried that!"

"So," Chloe still looked unconvinced, "why *did* she come into your house, then?"

"Because Mam invited her to," Daisy responded, patiently. "So's I could get to know her properly. I heard the phone ring, when I was watching the telly. I 'spect it was her. The stranger. Asking to come round and visit us."

Chloe's jaw dropped. "*My* mum wouldn't invite a stranger into our house. My mum – and my dad – would bolt the door and shout 'Go away, stranger.' Then they would dial nine nine nine."

Daisy's glasses had slid down her nose. Over the top of them, she met Chloe's horrified stare.

"Ah, but she's *not* a stranger, you see. I was wrong about that. She's very decent, Mam says, and she's just moved in.

Down the road. Number 11. Her name's really Miss Jackson, but *she* says I can call her Eliza."

"That's a very nice name," Charlie murmured. "If our new baby's a girl, I think my mum might want to call her Eliza. If it's a boy, she's going to call him Sam and – oh, dear," he pulled a guilty face, "I wasn't supposed to tell you!

"Well, not yet. Mum and Dad only found out today. I don't know *who* told them, but they said that cos I like secrets, I should keep this one for a bit longer." Charlie grinned suddenly. "But I don't 'spect they'll mind if I only tell you two!"

"Course they won't mind, pet," Daisy grinned, linking one arm through Charlie's, the other through Chloe's. "We're your friends. It's only *strangers* they won't want knowing…"

A Piece of Cake

Tessa Harper often accused her husband, Martin, of being a master of the understatement.

When a violent storm had caused one neighbour's chimney to crash, spectacularly, through another's roof, he'd surveyed the chaos and murmured, "Got a spot of bother there."

On viewing the annihilated remains of a friend's car, after it had been reversed over by an articulated lorry which had taken a wrong turning into a cul-de-sac, his opinion had been, "Doesn't look too good."

But, Tessa decided, this morning Martin had excelled himself.

"Touch of the sniffles?" he'd asked.

Not a word about her scarlet nose. Hoarse voice. The fact that her hair was glued to her clammy forehead. No, "Poor love, ten weeks pregnant and now this!"

Tessa had half-wondered if she was imagining the whole thing, that, really, she appeared her normal healthy self. But when he arrived in the kitchen, a bare-footed Charlie immediately confirmed what she already knew.

His concerned, greeny-blue eyes swept over her face. He tutted. "Oh, dear, Mum, you've caught a very bad cold. That's a shame, isn't it? Do you feel not well? Oh, and my slippers won't go on. They went on yesterday. I think my feet must have grew a lot when I was sleeping.

"Can we get me some bigger ones today, please? When we go shopping?"

Shopping! Tessa winced. Crawling back under the duvet… that's all she fancied doing.

"And can my darling Daisy Pollock come into town with you and me?" Charlie spread a slice of bread with his newest passion – peanut butter. "I said I'd ask you, an' then phone her.

"She got this vulture for her birthday, you see, and she wants me to help her swap it for something she *really* wants. It's quite a big vulture, Daisy says. She thinks she might be able to get a cat… or a computer or… something great… for it!"

Martin halted mid-task – cutting toast soldiers to accompany his two year-old-twin daughters, Beth and Georgia's, boiled eggs. "Charlie, did you just say that Daisy got a *vulture* for her birthday?" he asked.

Charlie nodded. "From her nan and grandpa. In Bradford. That's a different country, hundreds of miles away. You have to drive over lots of seas and rivers and things. But you *can* go in an aeroplane, if you're in a hurry.

"It only takes about a week." He looked momentarily thoughtful. "I wonder how the vulture got here…"

"I'm 'ungy! Bef's 'ungy!" Georgia's screech was ear-splitting. Martin had no choice except to quickly resume cutting.

"Charlie," Tessa croaked, "do you *know* what a vulture is?"

"Course I do! It's like real money, but not real money. My darling Daisy's was in a pink envelope with beautiful flowers on it. She said she'd rather have had a green envelope with a ogre on it.

"She likes ogres, like the one in Jack and the beanstalk… or was that a giant… I can't remember. But Chloe said that maybe the shop didn't have any ogre envelopes and vultures were terrific anyway.

"*She's* going to ask her grandma for one when it's *her* birthday, then she can go to the shops and choose something she likes."

The penny suddenly dropped. Tessa grinned weakly. "It's not a *vulture*, Charlie – it's a—" She got no further. All three children watched in alarm as she was racked with a bout of harsh coughing, which left her gasping for breath.

"All better now," Beth soothed as Martin pressed Tessa into a chair.

"It was very kind of you to cover your mouth with your hand, Mum," Charlie declared. "That stops germs flying round the room and landing on other people.

"Now you have to drink a spoon of that cough stuff, then go to bed and keep nice and warm."

If only! Tessa picked up the cup of tea which Martin had placed in front of her. She winced as the hot liquid hit a throat that already felt as if it was on fire.

A huge shop was needed today. She'd let the freezer contents run down, in order to defrost it. Because of that, there was now no ice cream, none of the usual joints of meat and chicken. Not a single pizza or fish finger.

They were also almost out of tea bags, biscuits, cheese and orange squash; also on her scribbled list was washing powder, fruit, stock cubes and peanut butter…

Martin's voice broke into her thoughts. "Sweetheart, Doctor Charlie's right. You *do* look a bit out of sorts. Off you go. Back to bed."

Tessa shook her head. Martin loathed food shopping. She wasn't exactly crazy about it herself, but had got it down to a fine art, even accompanied by three lively children.

It was only when an *extra-large* haul was necessary, like today, that she found it much easier to leave the mischievous twins with their Dad and just take Charlie, who seemed to look on the experience more as an adventure than a chore.

"Too much to do," she said, dabbing at her watering eyes with a soggy tissue. "Can't ask my mum and dad for help – they're away this weekend. Yours have friends staying.

"Unless… Molly… no… It's the dress rehearsal for Chloe's dancing school show. Molly'll be up to her eyes in it.

"I'll be all right once I've got myself going." Taking a deep breath which failed to fully inflate her lungs, Tessa struggled to her feet. Then promptly sat down again. "I can't," she wheezed.

"I've got a brilliant idea, Mum," Charlie whooped. "Dad and me and Beth and Georgia and my darling Daisy can get the shopping. It's easy-peasy, lemon-squeezy! I've seen you do it *millions* of times.

"You put everything in the trolley – even Beth and Georgia – then when you've found enough things to buy, you take it all out again and give the lady the money.

"Not for the twins, though. They're free. Sort of like… carrier bags!"

He glanced at his sisters. "You *love* shopping, don't you?"

Georgia grinned. "Chomping! Yeah!"

"Goody!" Beth agreed.

"So does my darling Daisy," Charlie carried on. "She likes *bargains*. When we were at the school fete, she wanted to buy a present for her mam. It was a nice purple dish and it cost seventy-five pence, but Daisy told the man who was selling it that it was too dear and she got it for fifty pence instead!"

Chuckling, Martin gently squeezed Tessa's shoulder. "Problem solved. I've got *two* experts on hand. Now let's get you upstairs. Don't worry about a thing. Believe me, it'll be a piece of cake!"

Piece of cake? Another little understatement? Tessa couldn't help wondering.

"There's a list on the pegboard. Add Charlie's slippers to it. And perhaps," she said when they were out of their son's hearing range, "you could suggest that maybe taking *Daisy* along with you today isn't a great idea. Explain to him that you've an awful lot to do. He's usually pretty reasonable."

Martin looked comically appalled. "And miss out on the bartering? The bargains? Not on your life! Besides, Tess, I'm curious. I've never actually *seen* anyone swap a birthday vulture, from an overseas country called Bradford, for a cat or a computer…

* * *

Charlie sat in the front passenger seat. His chubby sweetheart, her wild, brown curls scooped into a topknot on the crown of her head – reminding Martin of a nuclear explosion – was in the back. Strapped in between the twins.

Waiting at the traffic lights, Daisy's voice rang out. "If Mrs Harper didn't have the flu, you couldn't have taken me, today, could you, Mr Harper? We wouldn't all have fitted in.

"Me mam," she continued, "was just saying to me dad, last night, that you'll be needing a new car soon. When the baby comes. A big, huge one, with—"

"Perhaps you could buy a *bus*, Dad," Charlie butted in. "Not one with two floors and stairs… just a ord'nary flat one. Then when you and Mum have some *more* children, there'll be loads and loads of room.

"Even if she has three or four at the same time! Tripelets… I think that's what you call them."

Martin shuddered as the lights turned green. Although thrilled, now he'd got used to the idea, this baby – this hopefully *single* baby – was going to be the last.

Tessa had agreed on that, too.

Still, he mused, turning into the car park of the shopping precinct, he *would* have to start seriously looking for a bigger car – one with a third row of seats.

Daisy's grinning, freckled face filled his driving mirror as Martin pulled into a vacant spot.

"Me dad says you've to give him a ring, Mr Harper. Me dad's brother, that's me Uncle Trevor, he's a car man. He'll get you a bargain, me dad says."

"Is *everyone* in your family good at getting bargains, Daisy?" Charlie asked as Martin released the little girls from their safety seats.

She nodded, dug into the pocket of her purple dungarees and pulled out a battered, floral envelope.

"I'm the best, though. But me mam says I can't swap this vulture for a cat. She's says the dog'll sulk and might wee on the new carpet. And there won't be enough for a computer, neither. I'll have to think of something else.

So," she grasped Beth firmly with one hand, Georgia with the other, "let's find a trolley and bung them twins in it…"

* * *

Not needing any tea, because they'd been stuffing themselves with what Martin considered might be classed as 'junk food' but was still 'blooming tasty', the drowsy toddlers went willingly to bed that evening, without their usual bath – only a quick wipe with the flannel to get the worse off.

The mountain of shopping had been found a home.

"Now can we go and tell Mum *properly* about our tremendous day and show her my new Star Wars slippers?" Charlie glanced down at his feet. "My darling Daisy is *great* at choosing brilliant things, isn't she?"

"This," Martin told a still-flushed, but less feverish Tessa, who agreed with her son that, yes, the slippers were extremely excellent, "has been an experience I will *never* forget!"

Propped against her pillows, she smiled sympathetically. "That bad?"

He didn't answer immediately, then, "If anyone had ever told me that I'd actually enjoy myself shopping, accompanied by four children, I'd have said—"

"The best bit, Mum," Charlie interrupted, gleefully, "was when Georgia took a packet of chocolate biscuits off a shelf when no one was looking. She ate loads of them!

"Then Dad saw what she was doing and took them from her. She went mad! But my darling Daisy told her to 'Belt up!' and, guess what, Georgia did…!"

While Tessa was digesting that little miracle – her fiery daughter usually fought it out to the bitter end – Charlie carried on.

"An' Beth stole a strawberry yoghurt out of someone else's trolley and she poked her finger in the lid and ate it through the hole!" His eyes widened. "It was *all* over her T-shirt *and* up her nose!"

Tessa grimaced. "Beth's a messy little monkey. Martin, I *should* have reminded you to take a change of clothes with you. Sorry!"

"But there wasn't a problem, Tess. A certain Miss Pollock herded us to the Baby Care aisle, grabbed the wipes, which were on your list – only this box had 50% free – and cleaned her up. Perfectly.

"She did the same thing when we had lunch and Georgia decided that tomato ketchup made ideal face paint!"

Charlie hooted with laughter. "Yeah, her and Beth looked like real Red Indians. Everybody was looking at them. We didn't have the wipes with us, so my darling Daisy asked the burger-waitress lady for a big pile of the free lemon-smelly cloths you wash your hands with, and made the twins all pink and white again.

"When Georgia wanted to have another go with the ketchup, Daisy told her to 'Cut it out!' Georgia didn't even scream!

"But she did poke her tongue out a *tiny* bit…"

Tessa giggled. "My goodness, you have had an exciting day. And did you manage to get *all* the things on my shopping list, too?" she teased, not minding if they hadn't.

Just as long as there were enough basics to tide them over 'til she was back on her feet again.

Martin opened his mouth – Charlie got in first.

"Every single thing you wanted. And my darling Daisy bought you *two* bags of washing powder and got one of them for nothing. Free!

"She got loads of free things. When she swapped her vulture, I mean *voucher*, for a big box of colouring things, two books and a beautiful half crown tralala, it cost a bit over twenty whole pounds and Daisy only had twenty ordinary pounds, but the lady in the shop let her have them anyway.

"Because Daisy said the tralala box was broken and one of the books had a dirty mark on the cover, so it was only decent that she got a bargain.

"She looks lovely in her tralala. It's got jewels on it." Charlie yawned widely. "I'm a bit tired. I think I'll go to bed. I don't want any tea, because I'm still full up. Right down to my toes.

"Oh, and Dad, don't forget to tell Mum about you getting a new car from Uncle Trevor. Or did you say we'd get a bus instead?"

Not waiting for a response, he padded across the room, stopping at the door. "Open your hand, Mum. I'm going to *blow* you a kiss, so I don't get your cold. Catch it and blow me one back. Okay?"

When Charlie had gone, Tessa stared at Martin blankly. "I'll ask about Uncle Trevor and the bus when I'm feeling stronger, but a half crown tralala… with *jewels* on it?"

"Come on, Tess, think about it. What glittery thing does the queen wear on her head?"

"A crown?"

"Yes, but what about when she goes out in the evening? Somewhere posh?"

Moments later, Tessa chuckled hoarsely. "*Half* a crown… a *tiara*! But for the rest of my life, it'll always be a *tralala*! Same with *vultures*!"

She stroked Martin's hand. "I'm so relieved it wasn't *too* bad for you, darling!"

"Easy peasy, lemon-squeezy! Told you it would be a piece of cake." Martin rose. "I'm going to make us a cup of tea. Fancy a bite to eat to with it? Scrambled eggs? Peanut butter sandwich?"

"No, thanks, my throat's still dodgy. I expect the kids are full up, because, apart from lunch, they've been gorging on crisps and things. Don't feel guilty, *I* let them get away with it, too. Now and again. When I'm frazzled.

"But *you* must be starving. I hope you've treated yourself to a big juicy steak. After all, we must have saved an *absolute* fortune today, getting all these bargains and *free* things!"

Martin nodded vaguely.

As he went back downstairs, his conscience nagged at him. He wasn't at all hungry. And it hadn't been *quite* as simple as he'd made out. Nor as inexpensive!

Not being familiar with ordering economical child meals – usually Tessa organised that – the lunch bill had been enormous. Then, on the way home, exhausted and almost at the end of his tether listening to the horrendous racket inside the car, to save the last threads of his sanity he'd made an impromptu stop-off.

Not for just a simple piece of cake. For five chocolate milkshakes, five ice creams and probably what would amount to several full-sized gateaux…

Nicely in Perspective

Beaming hugely, Charlie Harper nodded into the telephone. "I've been very good, cross my heart, an' I'm having a well excellent time. Guess what – Auntie Katherine and me made a pizza yesterday – with our very own hands. We used real flour and stuff, then we put seven different things on the top of it.

"Cheese, tomatoes onions… green crunchy things called peppers. They're wicked. I love 'em."

Barely pausing for breath, he carried on. "An' ham, bits of real pineapple – do you know, Mum and Dad, an amazing thing? Pineapples doesn't grow in square shapes! They are big lumpy things with spiky leaves coming out of the top. A bit like my darling Daisy's hair when she wears it in a pony tail.

"Did you know they live in a hot country, where it *never* snows? Pineapple, I mean. My darling Daisy's hairs lives on her head. On *my* head, I've got a new baseball cap. It's green and black and I'm wearing it backwards. Brilliant, eh?"

Neither Tessa nor an audibly-chuckling Martin was given the chance to respond as Charlie quickly returned, momentarily, to his original subject.

"Then Auntie Katherine cut up some other green stuff and *I* made the pizza into a beautiful picture. She said it was great an' p'rhaps I'll be an artist one day. Just like her and Uncle Ray. They're teaching me loads of interesting things about how to be good at drawing…

"An' we *all* hope you have a happy annivers'ry today. An' *I* hope that Beth and Georgia will be good for Granny and Grandad and Grandma and Grandad. I told Georgia *not* to spit at anybody. I said it wasn't a nice thing to do, but I don't think she knew what I meant, cos she just spitted at me again.

"I'll see you tomorrow, Mum. You, too, Dad. Bye..."

After a quick word with her sister-in-law, Tessa replaced the receiver, her expression thoughtful.

Martin, who'd joined in the conversation on the bedroom telephone extension, returned to the living room. Seeing his wife's pensive face, he moved quickly to her side and slid his arm round her expanding waistline.

"Stop fretting," he scolded gently. "Charlie sounds like he's having the time of his life."

Of course he was, Tessa thought. His uncle Ray and his new auntie, Katherine, doted on him. He'd have been spoiled rotten!

And St. Ives, with its bustling cobbled lanes and riots of colour spilling from window boxes and floral hanging baskets, was as lively as Charlie himself. He'd be in his element in that environment.

Gnawing on her lip, she nodded. "I'm being daft! But I've been feeling a bit like I did when he started school. I know I've had the girls to keep me on the go, this time, but life's... well, it's not the same without him."

She pulled a guilty face. "I've never told you this before, but that first week, mine was the first car outside the school gates every afternoon. At least half an hour early!

"I found it hard to believe that Charlie could do without me. He seemed so little... so vulnerable... and now..."

Martin's hold on her tightened. Placing a finger under her chin, he tilted her face and kissed the tip of her nose.

"And now there are three... soon to be four... this will probably be the last time, for many years, that we'll have the house completely to ourselves," he pointed out.

"The last time we'll be able to have a slap-up meal, see a show and spend the night in a hotel. The last tomorrow morning…

"Imagine, Tess… no beds to make… no cereal up noses or wriggling twin octopuses to get dressed… no in-depth, Charlie-style discussions about whether today will be the red-letter one when the girls decide that potties are for sitting on and not wearing on heads!

"Absolutely no grim and graphic details as to what the outcome of that minor miracle might be!"

Tessa couldn't help giggling. "You win!" She snuggled against Martin and rested her head on his chest. "Really, I always knew Charlie would be fine spending this week's half-term holiday with Ray and Katherine, that they'd all enjoy it," she murmured. "But, I *was* concerned about leaving Beth and Georgia, overnight, with my mum and dad.

"Okay, they'd have coped, they're terrific with the twins, loads of patience and lots of cuddles, but I still couldn't help thinking that it would likely take them a week to recover from our two-girl, mini-demolition derby!

"It was such a relief when your parents were so keen to share the load. Between the four of them, they'll manage fine…"

"Of course they will. And tomorrow evening, we'll all be back together again. The usual chaos will reign supreme. So," Martin's mouth moved down to hers, "let's make the most of our equally precious time alone. Happy anniversary, sweetheart. Ten years. Where *has* the time gone?"

Later, the pair enjoyed a lazy lunch, eaten off trays balanced on their laps.

"Listen!" Martin said suddenly.

Tessa stared at him, blankly. "I can't hear anything."

He grinned. "I know. Wonderful, isn't it?"

While Martin washed up, Tessa packed, reminding herself how fortunate they were in having caring families who had suggested – no, insisted – that a special wedding anniversary, such as this one, should be celebrated with more than an Indian takeaway after the children had gone to bed.

But, "D'you think I should ring Mum again... to make sure that everything's still okay?" she asked as he was putting their overnight bag in the car. "It's just – well, you know what Georgia can be like..."

Martin shook his head firmly. "If Georgia spits, Georgia spits!"

* * *

Early the following morning, long before his parents would enjoy a leisurely breakfast in bed, Charlie and his uncle sat, side by side, in canvas chairs, on a cliff top a few miles out of St. Ives, sketching in companionable silence.

Ray smiled as the little boy suddenly thrust his pencil at arm's length and narrowed his greeny-blue eyes.

"Oh, dear," Charlie muttered.

"Problems, mate?" Ray asked.

Charlie sighed. "You know what we were talking about last night? About looking at things that are far away and not drawing them too big, even if they are ginormous in real life? Speccy something, you said and all artists have to know about it."

"Perspective." Ray nodded, recalling the conversation and how he'd wondered afterwards if had gone right over the child's head. Obviously, it hadn't. Charlie appeared to know exactly what the word meant.

"That's right. P'spective! Well, I haven't got any, because my seagull's a lot too big. And my boat's a lot too small." Charlie tutted solemnly. "I've been thinking that if my seagull was tired flying about and went down to my boat to have a little rest, then my boat would sink. Splash! Right down to the very bottom of the sea.

"That would be awful, wouldn't it? All the poor fishermen would have to swim home and their sandwiches would get wet, so they'd be hungry, too." His eyes and mouth formed three round O shapes. "And their watches might not work either... unless they were special ones."

Charlie brightened suddenly. "Hector-next-door – he's my friend, he's a man – he's got a special one. It's well excellent. Once, he let me wear it and put my hand in a bucket of water. For hours and hours. Guess what – the watch was okay.

"When I told Grandma, she said that was amazing and what would they think of next? It is amazing, too, isn't it, Uncle Ray? What do you think they'll think of next?"

Ray struggled to come up with an answer at such short notice. "Well," he managed eventually, saying the first thing which came into his mind, "they might come up with paints that make pictures all by themselves. Perhaps one day, I'll just choose the colours, put them on the canvas and..." he snapped his fingers.

Charlie looked unimpressed.

"I don't think that would be a very good idea. How would the paint know what you were looking at inside your head? What if... if you were sitting here and thinking it would be nice to draw that lady and her dog, down there," he pointed at the beach, "but the paint thought it would be great to... to... do a picture of a elephant and her children sleeping under a tree?

"You wouldn't like that, would you?"

Laughter bubbled in Ray's throat. He swallowed hard. "No, I wouldn't like it at all. But what I would like," he carried on quickly, "is to take a look at your drawing." Charlie passed him the pad. Ray studied it.

"It's very good," he said thoughtfully and honestly, "but you're right, your seagull *is* too big. Now, we could rub it out or... because we're artists and like to create different things... what if we decided that it wasn't a seagull at all!"

"*Not* a seagull?" Charlie questioned breathlessly. "Is it maybe a aeroplane? That would sink a boat if it landed on it, wouldn't it? That would be well p'spective. Or is it a space ship… like in *Star Wars*? Coming to save the whole world from a evil invader who lives on another planet?

"That happens. Every day, I think. I've seen loads of *Star Wars* films. My dad and me – we love them! My mum thinks they're silly. So does my friend, Chloe. My darling Daisy – I'm going to marry her, one day – doesn't mind them, but she'd rather watch things where people tell each other that they love each other. And kiss!" Blushing, the little boy shrugged. "Girls!"

Ray's mouth twitched, but he stuck with his original idea.

"Actually, Charlie, I was thinking that you might like to say that you've drawn an enormous *albatross* and that it has come to tell the fishermen that a storm's coming.

"That they should sail home now… to safety. You could call your picture THE WARNING and…" Ray stopped mid-sentence, "sorry, I'd better explain what an albatross is. It's a—"

"My grandad – that's your dad, not my dad's dad," Charlie interrupted quickly, "knows loads of stuff about albatrosses. He told me, because he knows I like interesting things, too.

"A albatross is a well big bird with wings a hundred metres, I think, long. It's a excellent friend for very old sailors. Marinades, they're called. Grandad knows a poem about them. A albatross and a sailor. He says it a lot.

"An' once," he glanced over his shoulder, then lowered his voice, "when Granny didn't know I was near her, I heard her say 'Gordon, shut up. I'm fed up listening to you talking about that'.

"That's quite rude, isn't it?" Charlie giggled, gleefully. "To tell a grown-up to shut up? But," he carried on, "I think you've just had a very tremendous idea, Uncle Ray. This'll be my p'spective albatross picture. When I finish it, I'll give it to Grandad for a present. Even if it's not his birthday or anything.

"He'll like that, won't he? And Mum and Dad will like the one I made for them and you put in that beautiful frame with real glass in it…"

* * *

At first, when Charlie had arrived home, looking not in the slightest the worse for wear after his long car journey, it had been bedlam, with everyone talking at once.

"I had a excellent holiday. Brilliant. Did you have a good time, Mum? Did you, Dad? Did you, Georgia? Did you, Beth?"

"A terrific time, darling. We stayed in the beautiful hotel, with lovely gardens and we went to the theatre and saw a musical show."

"Georgie pitted!"

"No! No! Bef pitted!"

"Back to normal!" Martin had to raise his voice to be heard over the racket.

Now, with both twins ready for bed and snuggled on her lap, Tessa watched as he removed the print – a gentle country scene – from its long-time home on the wall over the fireplace and replaced it with their son's large painting in its bronze-coloured frame.

Several feet away, his head on one side, Charlie frowned. "It's a bit not straight, Dad. The baby looks as if it might fall off!"

Martin moved one corner up. "Better?"

"A fraction more," Tessa suggested.

"Stop!" Charlie yelled, making her jump. "That is excellent! Thanks, Dad." He sidled over to Tessa and sat down on the settee beside her. "D'you really like the picture, Mum?"

"Love it," Tessa assured him, her eyes straying back to the family portrait. There was no mistaking who was who. Charlie had got everyone's hair exactly the right colour, except for the person who was wearing some sort of a cap and Telly tubby Wellington boots.

He seemed to read her mind. "I wasn't very sure how to paint the baby, but I didn't want to leave it out, cos it might be sad when it grows up, if we're all there and it's not.

"I told Auntie Katherine I was worried an' she said that all babies wear hats and boot things, so would I like to try that. I did like. It's cool, isn't it?"

"It's great, Charlie. It's the best picture you've ever done." To Tessa's surprise, her son shook his head.

"No, Mum, my albatross one is the best. The albatross that comes to stop the fishermen's sandwiches getting wet and their watches getting broken. You'll like that one when you see it. Bet you do.

"It's got p'spective, you see. I didn't know about p'spective when I painted the family. I should have made Dad very tall, and you a bit not so tall, then me – middle-sized – an' Georgia and Beth littler, an' the baby... teeny tiny.

"P'rhaps," he said thoughtfully, "I should do a new one. Prop'ly. P'rhaps I—"

"No," Tessa interrupted gently, gesturing to Martin to take the twins from her and up to bed, so she could give her little artist her full attention. "You see," she carried on when it was just the two of them, "I know it's important when you're a painter to get things looking just right, but I think you made us all the same size, because you love all of us exactly the same.

"There's more than one kind of perspective, Charlie. There's getting the things in *life* just right, too. It's difficult to explain, but it means that you have to decide what's really important to you, no matter what other people might think, or even if it breaks some rules.

"It's called following your heart..."

Charlie was silent for several seconds. Then, "You are absolutely right, Mum. You are a genius! This is my masterpiece, you know. Uncle Ray said so. I think that's because I'm called Master Charlie Harper. But when I grow up and become a *real* artist, then I'll be painting misterpieces, won't I?

"Or… I might be a man who goes out to sea in a boat and makes friends with albatrosses… or a actor… I'd like to be a actor…"

The Sound of Music

Tessa Harper had heard vague rumours about the new head teacher at the local primary school having an acting career before turning to teaching.

But because her son, Charlie, had been the main source of the story, and because it hadn't yet been properly confirmed by anyone else, she had taken the revelation with a pinch of salt.

Bright though he was, her seven-year-old sometimes got his facts muddled.

Recently, Charlie had described, in great detail, a programme he'd watched on television at a friend's house. A DIY programme about a man who had painted a well excellent roof.

"He must have had to get a enormous van to put all his paint in, because the roof was really huge!" he'd told Tessa, breathlessly. "Bigger than the Minnellium Dome, I think. An' he liked it so much, Mum, that he gave it a real name.

"It's called Christine an' it's in Africa or Spain. An' the man who drew all the gold angels and men with long beards and ladies with – I think they had their swimming costumes on – was called Michael.

"His other name was Angle. But," Charlie had paused dramatically, "when he showed people what he'd done, everyone looked up and pointed and said 'Oh!'

"He thought that was well excellent. He was very proud, you see. So now, when he signs things, at the bank or the supermarket, he writes Michael Angle Oh. An' he's *very* famous… like Bob the Builder… or the Queen… or he might be dead. I'm not sure…"

Although screaming with laughter inside, Tessa had patiently managed to sort out the correct details about Michelangelo's famous Sistine Chapel ceiling, in which country it was situated, and to confirm, solemnly and straight-faced, that yes, the artist – *not* a DIY expert – had died a very long time ago.

But, she mused, reading the letter a highly excited Charlie had just given her, this time the little boy seemed to have got his facts right. It read:

Dear Parent,

As we are all aware in this new 21st century, there are many kinds of learning processes besides the classroom environment. Children learn through play, through the media, and by exploring and demonstrating their talents.

Bearing this in mind, it is my aim to develop these talents. To show each and every little person that they have an important role to play, a special 'part', unique to themselves, but which, when shared with others, turns a straggling aimless line into a perfect united circle.

I have considered, long and hard, how to best achieve this. After much soul-searching, I have reached a decision.

Some of you may be aware that I enjoyed a career on the stage before deciding where my true vocation lay. Using that experience as a resource, I intend to produce a concert – a musical extravaganza – in which every child will be invited to participate, either on stage or behind the scenes, depending on their individual wishes.

We need your help, too, therefore I hope you will support this project by filling in the enclosed slip and returning it to me.

Yours faithfully
BYRON GRANT-HUGHES

The tear-off slip was about a meeting, next week. Tessa was mentally arranging a babysitter when Charlie's voice rang out.

"So what do you think, Mum? It's tremendous, isn't it? I told you I might want to be an actor, didn't I? An' you can make me a costume, can't you? Or *loads* of costumes, cos I might be a pirate, or a bear – like *Baloo* in *Jungle Book* – or a boy who dances."

Clothes for a boy who dances could mean anything. Shorts and a colourful T-shirt, perhaps. A pirate costume she could manage. Just! With a cleverly tied headscarf, a brass curtain ring, and an eye patch. But, Tessa winced inwardly, a bear costume?

She was hard pushed to take up a hem that didn't result in one side being two inches higher than the other! Quickly, she put that thought from her mind. One thing at a time, she decided.

Charlie's greeny-blue eyes sparkled. His words tumbled out.

"Chloe is *excellent* at dancing. She can stand on the tips of her toes. She's says it's pimps. Easy-peasy. My darling Daisy doesn't want to be a dancer. She wants to be a singer, but not a pop singer, cos she's worried that if she has to have her tummy button pierced with a ring, it might get caught in her vest and would really hurt.

"My darling Daisy is very fantastic at singing, you know? Once, when Chloe and I were at her house for tea, she sang us a beautiful song.

"It was called Edwellis and was about a flower and a family with hundreds of children, who climbed high mountains and ate strawberries for their tea. Every single day, Daisy said."

Edwellis! Tessa mentally congratulated herself on how skilled she was becoming at deciphering her son's howlers.

"The song's called *Edelweiss*, darling," she gently corrected. "From *The Sound of Music*. It's a lovely film… I can't remember if you've seen it... I'm sure that Granny's got the video..."

Charlie shook his head, firmly.

"I have *not* seen it, Mum. I would have remembered. I like mountains, you see. They're cool! Grandad and me nearly always watch the *Jungle Book* video. It's our favourite." He began to sing tunelessly and wave his arms in the air. "*Look for the bear necessities, the simple bear...*" then stopped.

"But I would *like* to see the film with Edwel... Adewel... that song in it. Can you ask Granny if I can borrow it? Or I could phone her now and ask her myself. That's a good idea, isn't it?"

Out of the corner of her eye, Tessa could see the quieter of her twin daughters, Beth's, copper head bent over her drawing book as the tot filled the page with colourful squiggles.

At the other side of the small play table, her identical sister, Georgia, had clearly become fed up with the restrictions of a few sheets of paper. Clutching a scarlet crayon in one clenched fist, her narrowed green eyes were fixed on the cream-painted wall in front of her.

"That's a *great* idea, Charlie," Tessa quickly said as the two-year-old, a determined look on her face, pushed back her chair. "And can you ask Granny if she's free for a couple of hours next Tuesday evening? To look after you three while Dad and I go to the meeting about the concert?"

* * *

On the morning after the well-attended get-together, Tessa, her oldest and closest friend, Molly, and Susie Pollock, the mother of Charlie's sweetheart, Daisy, gathered round the Harper's kitchen table.

"It's incredibly quiet here today," Molly commented. "What have you done with the dynamic duo? Rented them out to the Girls High school for their sex education lessons?

"Half an hour of *Georgia* in full flow – that would bring the birth rate tumbling down!" She grinned wickedly and looked at Tessa's burgeoning bump, visible now at four months in spite of her baggy sweater. "On second thoughts... some people *never* seem to learn..."

Gentle Susie's cheeks were faintly pink as she scolded, "Molly, you *are* dreadful!" Tessa's only retaliation was a soft chuckle, but inside her, she felt a deep sadness for her friend.

She knew all too well that Molly's light-hearted words masked her true feelings. That since Chloe's birth, seven years before, she had desperately longed for another child.

However, in spite of countless tests and being assured that there appeared to be no physical reason for her failure to conceive, it hadn't happened.

So, Tessa decided, best get off the subject, even though Molly had been the one who had raised it. She poured the coffee. "The little cherubs are with Martin's mum. She has her sister staying and she wants to show them off.

"Now... about this concert... there was so much going on last night, everyone talking at once, I think I missed a lot of the details. What's happening?"

"Actually, I'm not *that* sure, either. Only that the theme appears to be singing and dancing from the children's favourite films and pop videos." Molly snapped a ginger biscuit in two. "Chloe's got her heart set on being the ballerina in *Hans Christian Anderson*. She's watched it so often, she knows every single step."

Susie nodded. "Same with Daisy and *The Sound of Music*. Word perfect on every song. And according to her, they're going to start doing multiplications today."

Tessa and Molly exchanged a puzzled glance. Molly's mouth twisted.

"Pardon me for sounding stupid, Susie, but what's that got to do with the concert?"

Although poker-faced, Susie's bright blue eyes twinkled. "Oh, loads! They're doing multiplication to see who wants to be singers or dancers or—

"Additions!" Tessa's interruption was swift. "*Auditions*!"

"How did you work that one out so fast?" Molly spluttered.

"Living with Charlie!" Tessa replied airily. But ten minutes later she looked at Susie, horrified.

"A goat?"

"'Fraid so, Tess. Daisy's determined she'll sing *The Lonely Goatherd*. And, naturally, knowing how much *he* loves *them* and *she* loves *him*, has cast Charlie to be her most excellent pet!

"She reckons he'll be thrilled to bits, dancing around pretending he's a puppet, wearing a goat suit and big curly horns."

There was no arguing with that. Charlie would indeed be highly delighted, especially now he'd watched the video several times and that particular song over and over again. Tessa stared gloomily at the dregs in her coffee cup.

Since her son's comment that he might be a bear in the concert, she had thought long and hard about how to come up with a costume. And, eventually, had found what she hoped was the answer: an unwanted, giant teddy from a charity shop, carefully dissected and unstuffed.

But a goat… she couldn't even begin to imagine where to start with that.

Why, she wondered, couldn't Daisy have just stuck to warbling good old heart wrenching Edwellis? Her beloved Charlie could still have been at her side, but suitably and easily attired in shorts with braces, boots, and the genuine Tyrolean hat which his grandfather had brought back from Austria…

* * *

It was hectic backstage as frantic parents shrugged their excited offspring into costumes. Some of the outfits were masterpieces, Tessa couldn't help thinking.

Kneeling, she struggled to match up the Velcro strips which she'd carefully, but, she realised, unevenly tacked on to a grubby-looking, cream fireside rug.

Her mother had suddenly – and thankfully – remembered it was lurking in her attic.

"Wow," Charlie had said, eyeing it happily for the first time. "A real goat coat. Wicked!"

"Are you nervous, sweetheart?" Tessa asked him now. He shook his head, the one which would soon sport a pair of curling *papier-mâché* horns, attached to a hair band which was covered with cotton wool.

"No, Mum. It's cool!" He grinned, revealing the endearing evidence that both of his upper front teeth had simultaneously – three days ago – parted company from his pink gums.

"I've always wanted to be a goat, you know. An' Mr Grant-Hughes said he got a bad fright when he saw me practising with Daisy and the others. Guess why?"

Trying to decide which directions the horns should point, Tessa didn't immediately respond. Charlie chuckled.

"I knew you wouldn't guess. It is a bit of a hard question. Well, he thought I was a *real* one, you see. He told me he was worried that I might eat everything up, then he'd have to go and find a farmer to take me away.

"That was funny, wasn't it?"

A touch on her shoulder distracted Tessa. Byron Grant-Hughes, looking gloriously theatrical in top hat and tails, was smiling – slightly nervously, she thought – down at her.

And although his voice was bright, she immediately detected a note of concern as he asked, "All finished?" then, without waiting for a reply, quickly added, "Oh, good. I'll take Charlie to join the others."

Stooping, he murmured, "Our little ballerina, Chloe's, mother asked me to ask you if you could give her a hand, Mrs Harper. It seems to be," he added very softly, "a matter of urgency."

Chloe had been dancing, appearing in stage shows, since she was a tot. Molly had always sworn that there wasn't an ornately-ruffled tutu in the world that was unfamiliar to her, nor a single satin slipper she could not sew a precise ribbon on to.

For the life of her, Tessa couldn't imagine why her friend should so desperately need the assistance of a total novice to the dressing-up game.

A glance over her shoulder gave her the answer. Quickly, she cast her eye over her son. "You look terrific, Charlie," she said, sincerely.

"Yes, you look tremendously excellent, pet!" Oozing confidence, Daisy, the lonely goatherd, her wild curls escaping from the confines of the genuinely Tyrolean hat, her glasses comically perched on the end of her freckled nose, had suddenly appeared to round up her flock.

Don't you worry about a thing, Mrs Harper. Charlie an' me – we'll be fine," she said.

Tessa had no doubts about that. Molly, however, sitting on the floor, was looking grim. Beside her, stood an anxious-looking Chloe, her blonde hair loose and hanging halfway down her back.

"Mummy's not feeling very well. She thinks she might have a tummy upset. Auntie Tessa, could you put my hair up and help me with my tiara, please," the little girl pleaded.

This was one job she *could* do. The only way to keep her twin daughters' hair free of yoghurt and marmalade was to scoop the flaming manes into topknots. "No problem, sweetheart," Tessa said, calmly.

A few minutes later, in a fluff of crisp white net, Chloe pirouetted off. "I hope you'll be all better soon, Mum," she called over her shoulder.

"So do I," Molly groaned, "although I very much doubt if it will be a rapid recovery!"

The tone of her voice – faintly pathetic, yet tinged with a wry humour – sparked something in Tessa's mind. Head on one side, she studied the pale face and the film of sweat on Molly's upper lip.

"Tummy upset?" she questioned, finally. "Are you *sure* that's all it is?"

"Trust you to act suspicious!" Molly smiled feebly. Then, "Okay, it's a fair cop, Guv'nor! I'll come clean. I did a test a month ago. It was positive, so I did another one, last week. Today, Doctor Gilbert confirmed it. I was going to tell you when I first suspected, but… well … you know…?"

Tessa did know. Twice, after Charlie, she'd been ecstatic to discover that another child was on the way; twice her hopes had been cruelly dashed. She perfectly understood Molly's reluctance to broadcast the news. Even to her nearest and dearest. Until she was absolutely positive.

Glancing at her watch, she flung a supportive arm round her friend's shoulders. "Well done, you. We'll talk about all the ghastly gory details later. For now, it's time to find our seats…"

It was right at the end of the very successful concert, as they were about to collect the wildly-dancing goat who had almost brought the house down, the lonely herder with the voice of an angel, and the tiny ballerina who had looked as though she was floating on air, when Tessa revealed another fact she had found out that morning.

"Three of them," she whispered into Molly's ear. "Three new little people. Imagine that!"

Molly's jaw dropped. "Oh, Tess, not *twins* again! How on earth are you—"

"No, only *one*, this time. Katherine, my sister-in-law, has just found out she's pregnant. My brother, Ray, is acting as though he's the only man in the world to father a child!" Tessa gently patted Molly's stomach. "All we need now is for Susie to decide she's feeling left out!

"But even without that, you have to admit, it's getting more and more like *The Sound of Music* every day, isn't it...

Believing in Icicles - Christmas Special

It was a pretty cool Magic Grotto, with spacemen and spacegirls flying around and singing in whoopy voices. The computer graphics were mega-brilliant, too.

But he'd seen everything there was to see now. It was getting a bit boring. And Charlie Harper was starving.

What had he eaten for breakfast? Cereal or a bacon sandwich? And for his lunch? Charlie couldn't remember, because it had been ages ago. They had been waiting in this hundred mile long queue for about six or eight hours!

Mrs Pollock, had been very kind, though. She'd brought them – himself, his darling Daisy, and their best friend, Chloe – into town on a tremendous Christmas bus with a real igloo and real penguins on the roof.

She had smiled a lot, too. Once, a while ago, when she'd said, "Not long now before we see Santa. Just a few more minutes…"

That had cheered Charlie up. Because, he reckoned, if Mrs Pollock said it wouldn't be long, then it must be true. Grown-ups didn't tell lies.

And children shouldn't either. 'Specially not at Christmas.

Santa didn't like big fibbers! Everyone knew that. Even people camped on the tops of mountains and ones who lived in Australia and Canada.

So… any minute… just a few more little seconds…

Daisy dug him in the ribs. "I'm getting really fed up, pet," she grumbled. "This is pants, isn't it?"

Before Charlie had time to agree, Chloe stuck her nose in the air.

"Don't say pants, Daisy," she said, in a loud whispery voice. "It's not very nice! Just say…"

"My pants *are* very nice!" Daisy interrupted indignantly. "They're new ones – first time on – an' same as the girl pop stars wear. Anyway, it's tremendously cool to say 'It's pants' if you don't like something. I heard a girl say it on Saturday morning telly and *she* had brilliant purple hair an' a silver ring right through her nose!"

Daisy's own snub nose wrinkled thoughtfully. "Or I s'pose you could say 'It's knickers' if you wanted to. That'd be okay. Knickers is sort of the same as pants an' *everybody* wears them. Even…"

In seconds, the queue seemed to regain its cheerful pre-Christmas spirit. Grumbles were replaced by giggles. Heads swivelled.

Thankfully, Susie Pollock noticed, Daisy seemed unaware of her rapidly-growing audience. But once she did, there would be no stopping her. Then the irrepressible Charlie would join in. And Chloe would insist on having her say.

Susie felt her face grow hot.

The potential for embarrassment was endless. Parents' underwear! Royal underwear! Even Santa's smalls would likely be singled out for discussion.

Heavens, Daisy might even consider proving her point by displaying her new frillies to all and sundry…

A sudden peal of electronically-manufactured Jingle Bells was the sweetest music Susie had heard in a long time. If she'd been able to reach out and hug the owner of the jovial voice who declared, "Santa is ready for his next lot of little visitors," she'd have done so.

"Right, everyone," she instructed, preventing her daughter from elaborating further, "it's time, now. And afterwards, we'll go back to our house for tea. You must all be getting hungry…"

* * *

"My mum's a tremendous cook, but your mum makes the most excellent chips in the whole universe," Charlie told the love of his life as the three children slumped, side by side, on the sofa in the Pollock's living room. "Your Christmas tree's cool, too. I like all the pink spiky things!"

Hugging her plump knees, Daisy nodded. "They're called icicles, pet."

"*Can't* be icicles!"

"An' why *not*, Chloe?"

"Because, Daisy, icicles are *white*! Everyone knows that! I did when I was just two!"

Daisy heaved an exasperated sigh. "*Who* told you icicles are always white?"

"My mum. She explained that when snow melts on your roof and then it gets really, really cold, the water can't fall on the ground, so it freezes and leaves icicles behind."

"That's right. My grandad said that, too," Charlie contributed, "and *he* knows every single thing there is to know. Even about bats! And cheese with holes in it!"

Daisy shifted position. "They're dead wrong! You can see right through water. It's clear. Like Clingfilm. So why did your mum, Chloe, and your grandad, Charlie, say icicles were white when they really should have said that they weren't a colour at all?"

Chloe gnawed on her lower lip. "Don't know. What do you think, Charlie?"

He puffed out his cheeks. "Well, I'm thinking that icicles might be a bit pink if the sun was shining on them. Or a bit green if they were hanging off a tree. Or a bit blue—"

"Or every colour in the world if they were hangin' off a rainbow!" Daisy interrupted, pulling a comical face. "You do go on, Charlie, but it doesn't matter, cos them things on our tree *are* icicles. Even though they are pink. It said it on the packet, so it must be true!

"Or maybe it isn't," she carried on, suddenly thoughtful. "Grown-ups wrote that packet and they don't always tell the truth. It's not fair. I mean they say we must tell the truth an' then they tell us big fat lies."

Remembering how Mrs Pollock had said, "Won't be long, now!" when, really, it had been ages and ages, Charlie's lower jaw dropped. Chloe, however, looked furious.

"My mum and dad would never do that! If they say something that isn't right, then it's because they've accident'ly made a little mistake. So I think it's horrible of you to say that, Daisy. It's... it's... *pants*! And I also think..."

Withering her into silence with a fierce glare, Daisy leaned forward until her earnest face was inches away from the pretty little blonde's.

"What about Santa Claus, then?"

"What about him?" Charlie and Chloe asked in perfect unison.

Daisy didn't answer straight away. Curly head bent, she examined the fingernails she had painted with silver, glittery polish she'd found in her mam's dressing table drawer.

Then, "He isn't a person, at all!" she hoarsely revealed. "He's just a lad in a story, but grown-ups tell their children that he's real, so's they'll behave themselves an' not get under their feet while they're buying turkeys an' Brussels sprouts.

"I hate sprouts! More than I hate cauliflower! Sprouts is worse than pants! Sprouts is—"

It was Charlie's turn to interrupt. Two red spots stood out on his cheeks. "But, Daisy, he *is* a real person. We saw him today. Remember? A jolly fat man, with a long white beard, a red coat an' really cool boots. He gave us great presents.

"I got a brilliant joke book, Chloe got a set of beautiful beads she can put in her hair, an' you got some nice coloured string to make bangles with. So if that wasn't Santa, then," Charlie scratched his head, "who was it?"

Chloe had stuck her thumb in her mouth, something she only did when she was upset or nervous.

She pulled it out. "Actually, it *wasn't* the *real* Santa, Charlie," she said hesitantly. "It was his cousin or his brother, or something. My gran told me that though Santa's magic and can go down every chimney in the world in the same night, he doesn't have time to leave his workshop before Christmas Eve.

"He's too busy. Making toys and feeding the reindeers. So he gets his friends and relations to talk to children and then they go back to Lapland and give him a list of all the things we want. I think…"

Daisy sighed. "That's just another bit of the story. It's our mams and dads that buy the presents. From shops. They hide 'em up in the attic or at our aunties' houses, so we won't find them.

"Then, on Christmas Eve, they tell us we have to go to bed really early or Santa won't come. It's a fat fib. *We* have to go to bed, because they want to have a drink of sherry an' eat mince pies in peace an' kiss each other!

"An' that," she finished dramatically, "is the real truth!"

All the time she'd been talking, there had been a question in Charlie's head. He hadn't wanted to ask it, in case he didn't like the answer very much. But now he couldn't stop himself.

"How do you know all this, Daisy?"

"I heard it on the telly. An old lady – about forty and she had a orange dress – was saying about it not being right to warn little children about taking things from strangers, then say it *was* okay that a very strange man was going to come right into their bedrooms and leave them presents they were allowed to keep!

"The lady said she thought Christmas was okay, because it made people kinder to each other, but that children over five years old – like us, because we're seven, nearly eight – should be told the truth behind the leg end."

Charlie's greeny-blue eyes widened in amazement. "What's a leg end?"

Daisy held both hands, palm-upwards, out in front of her. Her shoulders shot up. "Don't know. She didn't say."

"I s'pose," Charlie suggested, "it might be something to do with a turkey. Its feet. P'rhaps the lady wasn't talking about Santa at all, Daisy. P'rhaps she wanted children our age to be told that we mustn't ever eat turkey's toes, because they're poison!"

Chloe frowned. "I didn't know turkeys had toes."

"They must have," Charlie said. "I mean if they didn't have toes, they wouldn't be able to walk. An' they do walk," he stood up, "like this."

His wobbly demonstration of the turkey trot was swiftly curtailed. Daisy was clearly impatient to get on with her story.

"I *haven't* finished yet," she scolded. "The next time I heard about Santa not being real was last night. From my cousin, John, in Gateshead. He's twelve. A canny lad. I told him on the phone about us going to the Magic Grotto today. I thought he'd be dead jealous, but guess what?"

Chloe and Charlie exchanged a worried glance. "What?" Charlie asked.

"Well," Daisy sniffed, "he laughed! John said he thought I'd know better at my age and that I should ask me mam to tell me the truth."

"And did you?" Chloe whispered.

Daisy nodded. "This morning, when she gave me my egg on toast."

"What did she say?" Charlie asked.

Daisy tutted. "That John was being daft. But when I asked her about the leg end, she pretended she hadn't heard me and went upstairs to the loo!

"I forgot to ask her any more, cos I was excited about seeing Santa and getting a present. But I'm going to talk to

Dad later. I always know if *he's* fibbing. His nose goes a funny shape."

"What? All long and pointy, same as Pinocchio's?"

"No, Charlie, kind of squashy, with a white bit on the end."

"My goodness! Is the white bit like a icicle?"

"No, it's more like…"

Further discussions on the subject were halted when Martin Harper arrived to take his son and Chloe home.

"Don't forget to ask your mum about what Daisy said," Chloe instructed briskly. "As soon as you get in the front door! Look to see if her nose changes!"

"Okay," Charlie agreed as she climbed out of the car.

His little sisters, Beth and Georgia, were still up, waiting for him to read them a story. Mum had made hot chocolate, with pink marshmallows swimming on the top. Her tummy, full of new baby, looked 'ginormous' and her face looked a lot tired.

To make her laugh, Charlie told her the best jokes out of his new book. It was only when he was in bed that he remembered.

I'll find out about Santa – and other things – tomorrow, Charlie promised himself, drifting off into sweet dreams about reindeers, rainbow-coloured icicles, and singing spacemen…

* * *

The question wasn't entirely unexpected. Tessa had been aware that it was only a matter of time before the subject was raised.

Martin had commented, recently, that he found it amazing how, in this age of in-your-face media and with his own perceptive skills, Charlie still believed.

"I was fully expecting the third degree last year," he had admitted.

Glancing out of the window, Tessa could see her husband and the twins in the garden, breaking up bread to feed the birds.

Thank heavens Charlie had waited until the girls weren't around. At not quite three, this was the first year the tiny twosome had properly latched onto the magic of Santa Claus, asking, every day, their voices quivering with excitement, "Will he come down the chimney tonight, Mummy? Do we hang up our stockings now?"

Shattering three sets of dreams would have been unthinkable. She would have had to put her principles aside and lied. Then spoken to Charlie, later. In private.

Told him the truth. Asked him to keep the secret. So his sisters, and the new baby, could share in the other magic of Christmas, the one which wasn't about little Jesus being born in a manger – one of Charlie's favourite stories.

Having refilled her coffee cup – something to hold onto – Tessa sat down at the kitchen table, opposite her son.

"About Santa," she began, "he's part of a legend about a kind man called Saint Nicholas, who loved children very much and brought them presents—"

"A legend! That's not the same as a *leg end*, is it, Mum? A legend isn't anything to do with turkey's poison toes, is it? What is a *legend*?"

Typical of Charlie to come up with a remark to lighten her painful task! "A legend is a very old and wonderful story." She smiled. "But I didn't know turkeys had poison toes, Charlie. Who told you that?"

"Oh, a old lady in a orange dress on the telly. Well, actually, she didn't tell me. She told my darling Daisy. Then Daisy told me and Chloe that Santa wasn't…" Charlie stopped.

Then, "Mum, can the baby hear what we're talking about," he carried on in a whisper. "I know it can hear music – *you* told me that – that's why I sing to it sometimes, but can it understand *real* words?"

Tessa winced. Not at the question, but because the child growing inside her had delivered an almighty kick. So strong, she imagined she could feel her teeth jangle and her eyelashes wobble. It left her momentarily unable to respond.

"I'm asking," Charlie carried on, cheerfully, clearly not bothered by her silence, "because I don't want the baby to hear any fat fibs before it's even got born, you see!"

Tessa found her voice. "It might be able to hear our voices, but I don't think it's big enough to understand what we're saying, darling. So don't worry."

"All right, I won't! You and Dad get nice presents, don't you, Mum?" Tessa nodded. Charlie grinned. "So who gives them to you? Is it Santa...?"

The moment of truth! "Well, actually it's people who believe in the same things Saint Nicholas did!" Tessa responded, frankly.

"Good people, who want to make the world a brilliant place?"

"Yes, sweetheart. Very kind people. And that's why we say that Santa Claus brought them, because according to the legend he—"

"Oh, wow! This is excellent news. The best!"

She'd done a rotten job, Tessa told herself guiltily. The perfect chance to gently put Charlie right on one of the painful truths of growing up and, judging by his rapt face, she'd blown it.

But maybe it wasn't too late. Only she'd play it a bit different this time. Put the ball in Charlie's court.

"You must have a lot of questions inside your head." The child nodded. "So why don't you ask me what you really want to know."

Charlie frowned. Shifting in his chair, his small mouth twisted this way and that. Then he glanced across at Tessa.

"There *is* something I need to know. Something tremendously important. Will you tell me, honest and true, cross your heart?"

Tessa nodded.

"Okay, then. What colour are icicles, Mum?"

She gulped. This wasn't what she'd been expecting. But...

"I don't think they're actually any *colour* at all, Charlie... they're just frozen water... although I suppose... well, if the sun shone on them, they might look pinkish or yellow... and if the sky was blue behind them, then—"

Charlie slid off his chair. He did a jubilant little dance, punching the air with his clenched fist.

"They might be a bit blue! Mum, I *knew* you'd tell me the truth." He raced towards the door. "I'm going to phone my darling Daisy, so she can ring her cousin, John, and tell him he'd better start to believe in the *real* Santa... or," mouth open, Charlie winked exaggeratedly at Tessa, "he might not get a single present... ever again..."

A Spot of Bother

"Thanks for popping in, Doctor Gilbert. I'm sorry I couldn't make it to the clinic, today, but… well, you know how it is? I did phone, though, in case you wanted to fit someone else in."

Walking along the hall, Tessa Harper's voice was raised to make it heard over the din coming from the living room, where Charlie was introducing his twin sisters to the game of Snakes and Ladders.

"Down the ladders. Whee!" Georgia was shrieking, over and over again.

Not to be outdone, her identical sister was shrilling, "An' up a snakey! Up, up a wriggly snakey!"

And Charlie… "No! It's *up* a ladder and *down* a snake. That's how you do it. And don't throw the dice so hard, Georgia. That's a hundred times it's gone under the telly! I'm getting well tired crawling about the floor…"

The racket jangled inside Tessa's head.

"My mother and my mother-in-law," she carried on, "kindly offered to stay with the patients, but I honestly didn't think my swollen ankles would carry me as far as the surgery."

She sighed as she opened the front door.

"Besides looking like an elephant, I feel completely exhausted. The only good thing is that all the children went down with it at the same time. And that none of them has been particularly ill. Just spotty. Especially Beth. In her hair and all the way south to between her toes!"

The elderly doctor smiled, sympathetically, at the harassed-looking young woman who was just weeks away from giving birth to her fourth baby.

"Another good thing, Tessa," he gently pointed out, "was that *you'd* already had chickenpox. And Martin, too."

Tessa nodded. "Yes, his mum's pretty certain about that."

Dr Gilbert patted her arm. "Good! Well, what I'd like to suggest now, is that you put those poor feet up for a while. But I suppose that's out of the question?"

"With the spotty – or should I say scabby trio – to entertain? You're not kidding!" Tessa pulled a face. Then grinned as she saw her front gate being pushed open – by a small plump figure, wearing a slightly too-tight nurse's uniform, and a cap, with a red cross on the front, perched on her wild brown curls.

"On the other hand..." she said as her son's girlfriend, Charlie's Darling Daisy, skipped towards her, swinging a small plastic case, which, Tessa knew, because it had accompanied the little girl on every visit, contained a selection of plastic medical instruments.

Straight-faced, Doctor Gilbert looked over the top of his glasses. "Ah, Nurse Pollock. How very nice to see you. Have you had a busy day, looking after all your poorly patients?"

Daisy giggled and pushed her own scarlet-framed spectacles up her snub nose.

"It's not really *Nurse* Pollock. It's me! Daisy. But I've been thinking I might be a nurse when I grow up. I'm dead good at it, aren't I, Mrs Harper, and I won't catch anything bad from people, cos I've had *everything*. Even a broken arm and once I was sick when I went to Spain for me holidays!

"Or," Daisy carried on, suddenly thoughtful, "I might work in a library, so's I can read books all day... or I could be a juggler... I can do it with three oranges! Anyway, I got work to do, now. Me mam'll be picking me up, later. In about an hour, she said."

She flashed Tessa an old-fashioned look. "How're them scabs today? Any dropped off yet? Have you counted them?"

Not waiting for an answer, bristling with importance, Daisy disappeared indoors. Doctor Gilbert chuckled.

"A juggling librarian? The mind boggles!" He glanced at his watch. "Although I'm on call 'til six, I promised my wife I'd try to nip home for a bite to eat. Don't worry if you can't get to the clinic, next week. I'll pop in again. No problem."

With that, he returned to his car and Tessa slowly made her way back indoors for a well-earned cup of tea, confident that Nurse Daisy would entertain her patients for the next sixty glorious minutes.

Bliss! Martin would be home after that. And, with a bit of luck, her unborn baby would decide on a break from practising what felt like backward flips and cartwheels...

* * *

"Am I normal?" Charlie asked as the toy thermometer was removed from his mouth. "I feel tremendously normal, you know. And I *need* to be normal, cos it's my birthday in three weeks and four days... and... some hours and minutes. So am I?"

Daisy's mouth twisted as she studied the small tube.

"Not sure, pet! I'll need to take your pulse thing first. Now, where's me watch?

"You're right. You are very tremendously normal, Charlie," she eventually declared. "'Cept for your scabs, of course. You still got quite a lot of 'em. Not as many as she's got, though. That Beth."

She flickered her eyes towards the twins, sitting at their play table on the far side of the toy-strewn living room. And frowned.

"Don't scratch, Beth! You'll make huge big holes all over your face. You'll look like one of them things me mam drains the spuds in. And pack in picking you nose, Georgia. Your head'll cave in!"

"Will not!" Scowling fiercely, the tiny redhead's finger disappeared further up her tip-tilted nostril.

"Will so," Daisy countered, skipping over and catching hold of the tot's arm, tugging gently at it.

Charlie tumbled off the settee and somersaulted across the carpet. His bluey-green eyes were alight with horrified fascination.

"Is that *true*, Daisy? Does your head *really* cave in if you pick your nose?"

"'Course it does! Me grandad said so. When we were in Whitley Bay. We made this mega sandcastle and I wanted a big tunnel through the middle of it, so I started diggin'. An' diggin' An' diggin."

Daisy sighed loudly. "Then it caved in! Me grandad said that was cos I'd taken all the inside out of it. He said that's what happens to boiled eggs when you eat all the white and the yellow stuff and to people who pick their noses all the time. One little bash and..." She shrugged.

Charlie looked pensive.

"Did you pick your nose, then, Daisy? In Whitley Bay? On the beach?"

"'Spect I must have done else me grandad wouldn't have said it, would he? But I don't do it now. Not ever. I like me head. It's got me brains in it! And me hair on it!"

Listening outside the door, Tessa grinned.

Daisy's lurid description of what could happen to a nasal explorer wasn't anything like how she would have chosen to prevent the habit. On the other hand, Georgia was too young to take the ghastly details on board.

Besides, knowing Charlie's insatiable curiosity, the conversation was likely to continue for ages. Already he'd started questioning the facts, his voice trembling with excitement.

"Daisy, does your grandad *know* a little girl whose head caved in? Or a little boy? Or a man? Or a lady? And did it all cave in or just bits of it…?"

She'd have to explain the true facts to her son later, but for now, Tessa decided, there ought to be more than enough time not only for a cuppa, but to get the evening meal prepared. In peace!

* * *

Ten minutes later, having stuck a chicken casserole in the oven and as she peeled the last potato, a shriek startled Tessa. A *very* loud shriek. From Charlie.

Followed by "Oh, no, Georgia! That's a *well* bad thing to do! Mum'll be really cross with you. She'll go mad!"

Now what? Dropping the knife into the water, without stopping to dry her hands, Tessa dashed into the living room. "What's going on in—" she stopped, mid-sentence. Her jaw dropped. "Oh, heavens," she spluttered at the sight of Beth, the more placid of her daughters, whose face was zigzagged with wobbly lines of bright green, haphazardly joining up the spectacular array of scabs.

The tot grinned and patted her emerald-coloured left cheek.

"Georgie made me pretty, Mummy. Very nice."

Her sister's curly copper ponytail swung as she firmly shook her head. Georgia waved a felt-tipped pen in the air. "No, made a *puzzle*, Bef. Dot, dot, dot. One, two, free. Clever girl!"

"She's a bit of a monster, isn't she, Mrs Harper?" Daisy remarked, cheerfully, while Charlie's frown drew his tawny eyebrows into a straight line.

"They were fighting, Mum, cos Georgia wanted to do the Tellytubbies jigsaw and Beth wanted the Tweenies one. Daisy said it was making her head ache. I was frightened it might cave in, so I found the girls their comics and told them to do a bit of colouring-in.

"And," he looked guiltily up at Tessa, "there was a dot to dot puzzle in Georgia's. I showed her how to join the lines together, then Daisy and I watched a programme on the telly.

"It was a great programme, Mum," Charlie visibly brightened, "about how policemen catch bad people by taking photos of them and showing them to everyone in the world and asking if anyone knows their names and where they live, so—"

"What I don't understand," Daisy interrupted, "is, if the police are a bit *sure* they're not very nice, why don't they just lock 'em up when they take the photos? I'd do that if I was a police person. In fact, I'm thinking I might like to be a police person… or a lion tamer!"

Charlie tutted.

"A lion tamer isn't a kind thing to be, Daisy. Lions don't like being told to do tricks. Lions want to be just ord'nary and live in the jungle with their mums and dads and the rest of their family and friends. They want to lie in the sunshine and talk to each other. An' be wild sometimes. Like having tree fights and stuff. Don't they, Mum?"

Tessa nodded vaguely. Crouching, with difficulty, she cupped Beth's heart-shaped face and tilted her chin up. There was barely a clear centimetre of pink skin.

The box which the pens had come in was lying on the floor. Tessa quickly read the label. Non-toxic – thank heavens for that. And washable. But, she realised, under the present circumstances, being washable wasn't much of a help. Charlie seemed to read her mind.

"You can't put soap and water on Beth's face, Mum, cos you might wash her scabs off and then she'll look all holey, like Daisy's mum's potato thing. What's it called, Daisy?"

"Em… a commander, I think. Yeah, that's what it is."

"My goodness," Charlie said, "is it? You get them in the army, you know."

Daisy nodded. "I 'spect they need them in the army. All them men must eat an awful lot of spuds. And yukky sprouts and smelly cauliflower. I'm *never* going to be an army person."

"Neither am I. My mum wouldn't like me to do that, would you, Mum?"

Her head spinning, Tessa looked up. "Wouldn't like what, sweetheart?"

"Me to be an army person and have to eat sprouts out of a commander."

A commander? Something else to be sorted out later, no doubt! Along with nasal hygiene and police identikit images of wanted criminals. But *much* later. Tomorrow, even.

For now, in response to Charlie's last question, Tessa simply shook her head. The little lad beamed.

"See, Daisy, I told you she wouldn't want me to do that." Putting his hands on his hips, he peered closely at his sister. "But I don't think she knows what she wants to do about Beth's face. Do you, Mum?"

Tessa puffed out her cheeks. In all honesty, she hadn't a clue. A bit of professional advice was needed. A glance at the clock assured her that Doctor Gilbert was still on call. She snatched up the telephone.

"I'm so sorry to bother you again, but…" Tessa explained the facts, ending with, "Thankfully the pens are non-toxic!"

A long silence followed. Then came a wheezing, choking noise, followed by the unmistakable ringing of helpless laughter.

"I'm sorry, Tessa," the doctor eventually managed, "but I have this picture in my head. Tell me… what colour did Georgia use?"

What difference did *that* make? Tessa raised her eyes. "Green!"

The revelation was greeted with fresh gales of mirth, exacerbated when Tessa further revealed that Charlie had declared "Good job Georgia chose a nice colour. Beth would look silly with brown lines all over her face!"

Replacing the phone, minutes later, relieved to hear that no damage had been done and, that except for trying a little baby lotion on a cotton wool bud, the felt pen would gradually fade, Tessa sank into an armchair.

Tomorrow, she promised herself, she'd keep much more of an eagle eye on the convalescents. It wasn't fair to expect Charlie to supervise the determined Georgia. Or Daisy. They were both far too young to take on that responsibility.

No, tomorrow and every other tomorrow until all her children had completely recovered and could return to school and play group, she'd give them her full attention. No matter how weary she felt.

Momentarily, Tessa allowed her heavy eyelids to droop. But only momentarily…

"Here's Dad's car coming." Charlie's voice rang out. "Wow! He's nice and early. That's tremendously cool!"

* * *

Her husband seemed anything but cool when he walked through the back door! His face was grey with fatigue and he looked at his wit's end. "Oh, dear, rough day?" Tessa asked, kissing his cheek.

Martin pushed a hand through his thick brown hair, making it stand up in spikes. "Rough is putting it mildly, Tess. Everything that could go wrong went wrong. The computers crashed. There was an almighty mix-up with a supplier. And half the office is away sick.

"There seems to be a lot of bugs going round… still, you don't want to hear all that, love. You look dead beat yourself. So… how're things in Harper's hospital?"

Tessa kept her face carefully blank.

"Well… Nurse Daisy, who can't make her mind up if she wants to be a real nurse, a librarian, a juggler, a police officer or a lion tamer – but definitely not an army person, because that involves eating veg out of a commander – has done her usual scab count. Apparently three of Charlie's have dropped off.

"And Doctor Gilbert came round. He said—"

"Hang on." Clearly puzzled, Martin stared at Tessa. "What's a commander got to do with veg?"

Removing the bubbling casserole from the oven, she stirred it, thoughtfully.

"Haven't the faintest idea. All I know is that it's something Susie uses for the spuds and it's got holes—" she stopped suddenly and chuckled. "Aha, I do know what it is. Not a commander – a *colander*. Of course!

"Anyway, as I was telling you, Martin, Doctor Gilbert called in. He says that I'm fine and the kids will be, too. In a few more days. And that's about it, really.

"Well, apart from me learning that your head caves in if you pick your nose and Beth's face being covered in bright green stripes. But not to worry, I'm pretty certain everything'll soon be back to normal…"

That evening, the children in bed, Tessa's words came back to haunt her.

"I think I'll have an early night," Martin announced. "I really do feel a bit off colour, but I'm pretty certain I'll be okay in the morning. A couple of paracetamols. That'll do the trick."

He hadn't eaten much dinner. Two or three times he'd had a fit of coughing. Relaxing on the settee, with her bulging feet up on a stool, Tessa put down the evening paper and studied her husband's face.

The grey tinge had gone. Now it was pink and blotchy. Her mouth suddenly dry, she eased herself to her feet and crossed to his armchair.

"There's a big difference in being pretty certain and absolutely positive, Martin," she murmured, moments later. "Your mum was *pretty certain* that you'd had chickenpox, but I'm *absolutely positive* you have it now," she finished, staring in disbelief at the clusters of familiar blisters covering his cheeks and forehead...

Sweet Charity

"Dad's in the bathroom, looking at himself in the mirror, again. He's bein' a lot grumpy, as well. When I said, 'Good morning, are you feeling better, today?' he didn't say 'Yes, Charlie. Thanks a lot for asking.' He just kinda growled. An' made a face like this."

Standing at the kitchen door, his pyjama top inside out and back to front, Charlie Harper's greeny-blue eyes narrowed into slits. His nose wrinkled. His lips pursed fiercely as he puffed out his cheeks. His almost three-year-old sisters giggled.

"Orrible monster!" Georgia howled, gleefully.

"Funny Charlie," her identical twin, Beth, spluttered.

"My goodness," Tessa said, holding her hands up in mock horror. "That really is scary!" Nodding, the little boy resumed his normal expression.

"Yeah. An' I don't know why he's all angry, cos really, Mum, he should be well happy. You know that gigantic scab – the one between his eyes, that Grandad said looked like a question mark? It just fell off.

"Dad didn't pick it! He sort of frowned and..." Charlie shrugged, "it fell off. So there isn't a huge big hole in his head. It fell on a tissue, too. He won't have to look for it on the floor, so he can show it to you. That's good, isn't it? Great news?"

Filling three bowls with cereal and three beakers with juice, Tessa smothered a sigh.

Great news! She could do with a bit of that, right now. Even better would be a kiss and a cuddle from the grouchy creature she could hear padding around upstairs.

As her son took his place at the breakfast table, Tessa made a mental note to have a stern word with her husband.

Having a go at her was one thing; upsetting Charlie was another. Really, it was high time Martin stopped feeling so blooming sorry for himself.

Last night, he'd been a complete pain in the neck.

"How do I feel? How do you think I feel, Tess?" Martin had responded to her question, huffily. "I should have been in Berlin this week! Remember?"

How could she forget! He'd reminded her of it a hundred times. Charlie would likely say it had been a zillion and he might have been closer to the mark!

Somehow, she'd resisted the urge to snap back that it was a pity he hadn't gone down with German measles instead of chickenpox. Then he could have still gone on his business trip and felt quite at home!

Buttoned her lip by reminding herself that it couldn't have been a bundle of laughs for Martin to catch an uncomfortable and unsightly virus from his children at the grand old age of thirty-two.

Hadn't pointed out how he had been more demanding than all three of his spotty offspring. Put together. How his endless succession of hypochondriacal grumbles had made her want to strangle him at times...

He wasn't long for this world, Martin had regularly assured Tessa during the first few days of his illness. His chest hurt. Probably the virus had affected his heart. A side-effect. He'd read about that happening.

As for the headaches! The awful weariness! The constant itching!

"I'll never be the same man, again," had become something of a catchphrase. Even the twins had adopted it into their repertoire, along with *Baa baa, black sheep* and *Twinkle twinkle, little star*.

"Scarred for life!" was another of Martin's declarations after Georgia had sprung onto his lap, accidentally knocking off a not quite dry and extremely tiny blister from the back of his hand.

All of that had been delivered with a pathos which would have merited him a nomination for an Academy Award. And she *had* been sympathetic, Tessa comforted herself, now, as she rammed thick slices of bread into the toaster.

Well, most of time…

When she hadn't been fantasising about not being an elephant-sized mother of three and a few weeks away from giving birth again; free to do a Shirley Valentine to a remote Greek island.

Wearing a whisper of a bikini, which showed off her firm, golden-tanned body. Tossing her glossy, tawny hair back from her perfectly made-up face. Sipping a chilled champagne cocktail as the sun dipped over a tranquil sea.

Planning on ordering a late and exotic room-service breakfast, for two, in her five star hotel. Not to be shared with a treacle-eyed Alexi or smooth-talking Dimitri, but with a man who looked like the Martin she had fallen madly in love with all these years ago… the one she still loved…

Charlie's voice broke into her thoughts.

"That was very excellent. You make great cereal, Mum. Oh… an' the toaster's got tons of smoke coming out of it. Shall I phone nine nine nine and ask them to send a fire engine? Or two fire engines? How many do you think we'll need?"

Not exactly tons of smoke! More a steady, blue-grey trickle. "Dratted contraption!" Tessa's hand shot out and switched off the machine at the plug. A couple of stabs at the release button did the trick.

"Isgustin!" Georgia glared at the charred slices. "Don't want that, please. Want… a choccy biscuit and more juice. And cheese and—"

"Ice cream and yoggie. And bisgetti."

Charlie tutted. "It's spaghetti, Beth. Say it. Say spa… ghet… ti."

Her flaming red head on one side, the tot glanced up at the ceiling. "Bottom!" she declared, loudly, sending her brother into fits of giggles at the precise moment the telephone began to ring.

"I'll get it, Mum." Charlie sped towards the door. "If it's a fireman, I'll tell him it's okay. He doesn't need to get his engine out. That the house isn't burning down… not yet…" Seconds later he reappeared. "Grandad Harper wants to know if I'd like to go out with him, this morning. To buy some boots. And he wants me to wear mine, too. My wellies…"

* * *

Following the marshal's instructions, a puzzled Jim Harper negotiated the spongy grass. His grandson had been unusually quiet on the latter part of the journey.

Perhaps, he considered, the little lad was still suffering from the after effects of chickenpox.

"You all right, mate?" Jim asked as he pulled up, halfway along a row of neatly parked cars.

Charlie slowly nodded and peered out of the window.

"I'm fine, Grandad. Thank you for asking. But I'm a bit mixed-up, cos you said we were going to get you some new boots and now we're in a big field. I'm wondering where the shoe shop is!"

Jim grimaced. He obviously hadn't made his intentions clear on the phone. He shook his grey head.

"No, Charlie, We haven't come to buy boots… we've come to a Car Boot Fair. And that means it isn't about buying boots for people's feet, it's all about buying stuff from the boots of people's cars!

"Things they don't want any more," Jim explained. "Bits and pieces they've been keeping in their attics… or maybe their garages… and now they're fed up looking at them!"

Charlie's head immediately swivelled. His expression suggested total disbelief. He was silent for several moments.

Then, "Say 'Honest', please. So I know you're not trying to do a trick to me. My darling Daisy Pollock… I'm going to marry her when I'm twenty-four… she says that's the right age to do it, cos then we'll have loads of money in the bank and a nice house to live in and she's going to buy little glass things to put in her eyes, so she doesn't have to wear her real glasses under the white thing over her face…" Charlie paused. He frowned.

"What was it I was telling you, before I got mixed up, Grandad?"

"About you wanting me to say 'Honest'," a bemused Jim obliged.

"Oh, yeah! That's right. Well, my darling Daisy says it's not nice to say to people 'You're telling me a lie.' In case they're not, I s'pose, cos then they might get a bit sad.

"Daisy says we should just ask them to say 'Honest' instead. That's quite kind, isn't it?"

Struggling furiously to keep his face straight, Jim could only nod his agreement.

"So will you say it, please, Grandad?"

"Honest, Charlie."

"Thanks very much." Charlie unbuckled his seat belt and opened the car door. "I've been thinking," he said, as the pair headed for the adjoining field, festooned with balloons and banners announcing MASSIVE CHARITY BOOT FAIR, "why should we want to buy things that other people don't want?"

A reasonable enough question. "Ah, well, Charlie, you know what they say… about one man's meat being another man's poison?" As soon as the words had left his lips, Jim realised he'd made a mistake.

His little companion was just days away from his eighth birthday; it was highly unlikely that the lad would have the slightest clue what the saying meant.

His suspicions immediately proved to be correct. Charlie stopped dead in his tracks, two crimson spots on his cheeks, his eyes huge in his face as he stared, horrified, at the nearest banner.

"Charity," he read the word aloud. "I know what that means. It means you give some of your pocket money to people who aren't as lucky as you are. Sometimes they're ill and sometimes they're not. Just sad and cold and hungry. You give them money to make them feel better and a bit happy.

"Or, you send clothes and toys and stuff to nice families who live on the top of volcanoes and in trees in the middle of deep rivers.

"But," Charlie shook his head, "I didn't think we sent 'em poison meat! Isn't that a cruel thing to do to someone you don't know very well? Doesn't it make them feel sick? An' is it only the men who eat the poison meat and give the not-poison stuff to the ladies and their little children?"

By the time Jim had sorted that one out, and the logic behind today's event, they had already started browsing. Charlie patted the bulging pocket of his jacket. The coins jangled.

"I'm well rich! It was excellent of you giving me all this money, Grandad, so I can give it back to the charity people and still get loads of stuff. An' when I go home, I'm gonna tell Mum that we could clean out our garage and our attic and sell things for charity.

"But not soon." He tsked. "Mum might want to sell Dad, you see. And you wouldn't like that, would you? Cos he's your little boy and you wouldn't want not to know who had bought him or where he lived or anything.

"I wouldn't like it, either. I love him a lot. It's just that he's – well, ever so grumpy, now!" Charlie stopped and looked around him. Then lowered his voice. "I heard Mum tell Granny Allen that she felt like giving Dad a kick in the pants!

"But I don't think she really meant it. Mum doesn't like people kicking each other. What do you think, Grandad?"

The word 'frustrated' sprang into Jim's mind as a way of explaining his son's surly behaviour. But, reluctant to try to explain what that meant, he chose his words carefully, this time.

"I think that your dad's grumpy because he's been ill and he knows that he's made a lot more work for your poor Mum. I think he feels a bit – do you know what guilty means, Charlie?"

"I do!" Charlie sighed. "Once, when I was just six, I broke my *Star Wars* mug. I didn't want to tell Mum about it, cos she'd bought it for me as a very tremendous surprise. It wasn't even my birthday or Christmas or anything. So I hid it and she looked everywhere for it.

"I felt well bad. My tummy went all funny. So I wrote her a letter and said I was tremendously sorry. And guess what Mum said?"

He was so endearingly honest. So uncomplicated. One of the saddest days in his life would be the one when Charlie began to display adult tendencies. He would soon be eight. Children seemed to grow up so fast, now. Jim felt a lump spring into his throat.

"What did your mum say?"

"She said it was okay and that everyone – even the Queen – had accidents! And that my only little mistake was not telling her." Charlie grinned, suddenly. "That's what Dad's doing! He's feeling all guilty that he hasn't told Mum he's feelin' sad. I should have thought of that.

"But it's okay. I know what to do. I'll help him write a very nice letter, tonight, when I give him his special present."

Bless his heart! "I didn't know you had bought him a special present, Charlie," Jim said, softly.

"Oh, I haven't. Not yet. So I'm gonna do it now. Out of people's boots. I'm going to buy a charity present for everyone in the family. To make them – and the poor people – happy. Come on, Grandad…"

* * *

"I bought this ginormous bag of magnet letters for only 40 pence," a delighted Charlie told an exhausted Tessa, that evening. "They're for Georgia and Beth. To stick on the fridge and the freezer and learn how to spell and read things. Good idea, eh? We can teach them little words, 'til they're a bit bigger. Little words like cat… and dog… Mum… Dad…"

Tessa dismissed from her mind the abbreviated, three-letter substitute for 'bottom' which Georgia had come out with earlier, and forced herself to concentrate on her son's other bargains: an almost mint condition, brand-named baby toy for his new sibling and a very attractive *art deco* style vase for herself. But nothing, as far as she could see, for Martin.

He must have really upset Charlie, this morning, she thought, nibbling on her lower lip. How ought she to handle the situation? By having a little word with Charlie? Another gentle go at Martin? Or would it be better just to leave things alone for the moment? Let the dust settle…

"Where's Dad, Mum?" Charlie's voice suddenly rang out. "He hasn't got his present yet. An' it's well brilliant! It'll make him happy again. An' if it doesn't," Charlie shrugged, "well it won't matter. Cos he'll look like he is when he's wearing it.

"Now… where did I put it? Oh, I know, it's in the kitchen. I dropped it when I was rushin' in to give you and the girls your charity stuff. But, don't worry, Mum, it won't have got broken."

Bewildered, Tessa shook her head as her son sped off. Then she heard Martin's voice floating through the open door. "Hi, son, did you and Grandad have a good time?" Followed, moments later, by a sound she hadn't heard in ages. Helpless laughter. Martin's laughter.

And Charlie's response, "That looks really cool, Dad. Come on, let's go and show Mum and the girls…"

The jeans, the trainers and the jumper were familiar, but that was all that was recognisable about her husband. Tessa stared, open-mouthed, as her giggling daughters dashed towards the tall figure, standing in the doorway.

"Daddy's got a nice new face!" Beth hopped from one foot to the other.

"An' very pretty hair. Yellow. Like a 'nana!" Georgia agreed.

"It's cool, isn't it, Mum? And it's made out of real rubber, so Dad could wear that smiling mask, even if he goes out in the pouring rain!

"He can wear it when he goes to work… and when he goes to Germany… he could wear it to the shops… and no one'll know he's got chickenpox! An' it only cost seventy-five pence. For charity.

"That's great news, isn't it?" Charlie finished.

It was, Tessa agreed, watching as her comically masked husband scooped up each of the twins and danced round the room. The best news.

"What did you buy for yourself at the Boot Fair, Charlie?" she asked, later that evening.

"Nothing, Mum. I was going to, then I remembered that it's my birthday the day after the day after tomorrow and I'd get lots of presents.

"So I gave the money I had left to a lady who said it would help build new houses for people who live in very windy places and ones in Africa who can't see very well…"

Echoes of the Past

"Wake up, Daddy. It's hapty bifty, dear Charlie, hapty bifty to you. Open your eyes. Open 'em!"

What choice did he have, with crab-like fingers pinching his lids towards his brows? Martin hauled himself into an upright position.

The illuminated display on the alarm clock showed 06.05. There was no sign of his wife. Cross-legged, on Tessa's side of the bed, sat a small red-haired girl.

Not quite three-years-old Georgia grinned. Or was it her sister, Beth, Martin wondered, blinking.

"Good boy! B'illiant!" A sloppy kiss landed on his rough cheek. "Come on, Daddy. Come an' see Charlie – an' sing."

Sing? At this hour? Martin slid back under the duvet. Whichever twin it was began using him as a trampoline. At that moment, he felt he knew who he was dealing with. But just to make absolutely certain...

"Who are you?" He peered, comically, over the top of the quilt.

"Bef Harper."

Little fibber! "I think you're Georgia Harper."

"Not Georgie. Bef." The tot scrambled off the bed and placed her hands, bossily, on her hips. "Mummy said tell Daddy to 'urry up."

She wasn't going to weaken. Georgia never did.

"Okay, Beth," Martin said, "I'm coming. Where is Mummy? Making sandwiches for the party?"

"No, she's in Charlie's bedroom. Singin'. With Bef."

"But you said you were Beth."

Her green gaze drilled into him. "I am Bef. On Tuesday."

"Georgia, it's Saturday, today."

"I'm Bef on Sat'rdays, too. An' Mummy's got a sore tummy…"

* * *

She should have been firm, Tessa scolded herself. When Martin had suggested an Indian takeaway, late last night.

Then again, she had been relieved he'd finally got his appetite back after his rotten bout of chickenpox. And after spending hours ramming sausages onto sticks, concocting coconut hedgehogs and fiddly little cakes with each guest's name piped in coloured icing, her own tummy had been rumbling…

"Tess… you okay, sweetheart? I mean it's not… for another couple of weeks… ?" Hot on the heels of Georgia, a worried-looking Martin hurried into Charlie's bedroom.

"Don't panic. I know the difference between indigestion and labour." Tessa grinned, wryly. "I've been there often enough! With me, it always starts with backache. This is all up front! Serves me right for being a little piggy, last night."

"Little piggy," Georgia hooted, while Beth made realistic snorting noises. Charlie, surrounded by crumpled wrapping paper, chuckled.

"Hi, Dad. I'm eight, now."

"Sing hapty bifty, dear Charlie," Beth instructed.

As Tessa made her escape, Martin obliged before admiring his son's presents – the ones which had arrived, by post, throughout the week, from long distance family members.

"Uncle Ray and Auntie Katherine sent me a tremendous book showing me how to draw foxes and polar bears and whiskers and proper fur. An' noses and stuff.

"Auntie Kate sent me something well brilliant, too. Look."

Martin accepted the narrow, oblong box.

"That is a beautiful pen, Charlie. If you take very good care of it, you'll still be using it when you're eighteen."

Charlie puffed out his cheeks. "Wow! Then I will take very good care of it. It's called a fountain. You put real ink in it. I was going to get some purple, cos Uncle Ray always writes purple and it's cool, but I've changed my mind.

"That's *his* special colour. If I got purple, too, then no one would know if I was Charlie or Uncle Ray. They'd get all mixed up. So I'm going to get green. Or orange.

"With this!" Charlie held up a ten pound note. "Your cousin, Frank, sent me this, Dad. I'm going to write to him and say thanks very much. With my new pen and… can you get stripy ink… orange and green?"

About to say he wasn't sure, Martin's attention was distracted. Concentrating on Charlie, he hadn't noticed the twins leaving the room and returning again.

But they had to have done, because now they were sitting, side by side, in front of him, perched like two proverbial peas in the pod on their potties.

Martin studied the identical little faces. "Charlie, *do you* always know which one is Georgia and which one is Beth?"

"Easy-peasy. That's Georgia on that side," the birthday boy pointed, "and that's Beth."

"Are you really sure?"

"Yeah, I'm sure. Cos it's not Tuesday, is it?"

Martin suspected what was coming, but he still had to ask. "What happens on Tuesday?"

"Oh," Charlie said, airily, "Georgia's Beth on Tuesdays."

"And Beth's Georgia?"

"No, Dad, Beth's always Beth. Although, about a week… or a month ago… Beth told me she was Georgia and that was on a Wednesday. Or it might have been a Friday…"

* * *

Getting herself moving had done the trick. Not a hint of a twinge. She felt as fit as a flea, albeit a rhinoceros-size one. Tessa hummed contentedly to herself as she covered trays of freshly-made peanut butter, and cheese and tomato sandwiches with clear film.

Overhead, she could hear occasional fresh bursts of 'Hapty bifty, dear Charlie'. The longer Martin could keep the children upstairs, the better.

She still had a fair bit to do to make sure Charlie's party went without a hitch. That it would be one he would remember for the rest of his life…

"I 'spect it'll be my very last party, Mum," he'd solemnly told her when they had first started making plans. "Cos next year, I'll be a bit too old for games and things. Next year, we'll have to do more grown-up stuff… like my friend, Li. He's goin' to be nine soon.

"When he is, his Dad's going to take Li and me and some other big boys to the cinema, then we're going to come back to Li's dad's restaurant and have brill Chinese food.

"Not in little boxes. On real plates! With other grown-ups! At night! That'll be cool, won't it?"

Although, at the time, she had agreed that yes, it would be extremely cool, Tessa had also felt a sense of regret. Remembering, she experienced the same sensation now.

It was all happening so fast.

At this rate, Charlie would soon be demanding to have his eyebrow pierced; insist on wearing weird clothes; his clear, uncomplicated dialogue replaced by surly grunts…

A sharp rap on the back door was a welcome intrusion into her uncomfortable thoughts. With a warm smile, Tessa greeted her next-door neighbour. Her life-saver, she frequently referred to him. On call in any emergency; a well-brilliant friend and the best gardener in the universe, according to Charlie.

"'Morning, Hector. Come in. Sit down. I'm just about to put some coffee on."

"Thanks, love. I wouldn't normally bother you this early, but," the elderly bachelor placed three packages on the table, "I've been hearing little voices for quite a while now, so I reckoned you were all up and around.

"And I was wondering – is there anything you need doing? Since I'm at a bit of a loose end…"

There wasn't. Well, only things she could see to personally. Tessa was about to tell Hector that when something in his expression stopped her. He didn't look his usual bright and breezy self. A bit down in the dumps.

"Actually, there is something," she said quickly, glancing at the clock on the wall. "In an hour or so, the men will be coming to put up the bouncy castle we've hired for the party.

"Martin's taking Charlie into town to spend his voucher. He insisted that was what he wanted from us, this year, so he could choose his present himself. I've been racking my brains wondering how to keep the girls amused while the castle's being inflated.

"Once they see what's going on, they're going to be impossible! So perhaps—"

"No problem, love. I'll take them next door. We'll do a bit of digging. They love that." Hector's bright smile momentarily faded. "Eh, you won't be putting them in their party dresses, will you, Tessa? Never seen anyone like your Beth for getting in a mess."

"Tell me about it!" Tessa sighed as the tot in question skipped into the kitchen, her nose and chin coated with toothpaste.

"Brushed my teef! 'Lo, Hector."

"Sorry, Tess. I wasn't paying attention!" Martin looked sheepish as he tried to disentangle Georgia's tightly clinging arms, which were threatening to cut off his circulation, from round his neck. "Morning, Hector."

"Hector!" Charlie whooped. "You're my very first visitor now I'm eight. That means you're extra special. You can have the first go on the bouncy castle."

Tessa watched fondly as a flush of pleasure spread across the old man's face. Typical of Charlie to know how to bring a true sparkle back to someone's day! Make them feel important. And wanted.

"Happy birthday, mate," Hector said, giving Charlie the largest of the parcels. He reached out again and picked up the smaller two.

"And these are for you," he told the twins. "They're called unbirthday presents."

With only one piece of sticky tape removed, Charlie stopped. He wrinkled his nose. "A unbirthday present? Is that true? Or are you havin' a joke with us?"

"Oh, it's true all right," Hector replied. "You get birthday presents on your birthday and unbirthday presents when it's not. Not always, but sometimes. That's what makes them special."

"Well I never," Charlie responded thoughtfully. "An' I 'spect you might sometimes get unChristmas presents, too and un... un... all sorts of presents. That's well good, isn't it, Mum?"

Tessa nodded. "Actually, I think we've got an unbirthday present for Hector, haven't we, sweetheart? In the top drawer of the sideboard?"

Five minutes later, as Charlie admired his "tremendously excellent" gardening set for the umpteenth time, and the twins demanded to 'go diggin' with their new little trowels, Hector Smythe's pale blue eyes misted over as he looked at his own unexpected gift – a large, framed photograph of Charlie, Georgia and Beth.

"It's great, isn't it? We had it taken at my school," Charlie explained. "Mum brought the girls round and the man took us all together. We had to get one for you, Hector. Cos we're sort of your family and you love us and we love you? Don't we, Mum?"

This time, Tessa didn't reply. Instead, she stared in fascinated horror at the large puddle forming on the floor at her feet and clasped her hands at the small of her back.

"Ouch!" she whimpered.

"Mummy's done a big wee-wee!" an excited Georgia... or was it Beth... squealed.

* * *

The party, overseen by both hastily-summoned sets of grandparents, was in full swing. The garishly-coloured bouncy castle was proving to be the main attraction. Mary Allen wobbled her way across the grass and collapsed into the vacant chair beside her daughter's mother-in-law, Sheila Harper.

"I've always wanted have a go on one of those things, but much as I hate to admit it, I am too old to appreciate the delights of not having my feet firmly on the ground. Still, Hector seems to be enjoying..." Mary stopped.

Sheila's head was tilted towards the low hedge, which protected the vegetable garden from the lawn – frequently used as a football or cricket pitch.

"I think Charlie's getting a lesson in the facts of life from his bride-to-be," she whispered. "Listen..."

"No, pet, your mum didn't wee the floor," Charlie's darling, Daisy Pollock's voice was clear and confident. "She knows better. The baby just got fed up swimmin' around all the time, so it made a hole in the side of its pool, so it could shout 'Let me out'."

"But I didn't hear it shout anything, Daisy."

"It might have spoke it in another language. French. Or Indian."

"Oh, right. My mum did have a curry, last night! So did my dad."

"There you go, then, Charlie. It said 'Let me out' in Indian an' you didn't understand."

Mary stifled a giggle as her grandson earnestly carried on.

"Do all babies have swimming pools, Daisy? Inside their mum's tummies? Did I have one?"

"Course you did. Everyone in the world has one. But they're not real pools. Not big blue things with divin' boards and them chutes you slide down. They're more like balloons. An' when the baby doesn't want it any more… I think it eats it. I think it tastes like… ice cream. Or chips!"

A long silence followed, then, "But why, Daisy? *Why* does it have a swimming pool?"

"Well, it's to give the baby somethin' to do, while it's waiting to get born. It doesn't have any books… or computer games… or anything else to play with. Oh, yeah, an' it's to stop the baby's legs and arms getting broken. You know, if its mam bumps into something? Or falls over?"

"I see," Charlie said, but Mary could tell by his tone that he hadn't a clue. Another little detail to be sorted out at a later date, she supposed. Tessa was so good at things like that. Tessa could answer even the most embarrassing questions without flinching.

Charlie's voice rang out again. "Before I have another go on the bouncy castle an' blow out my candles, d'you know how babies actually get inside their mum's tummies?"

This time, Daisy didn't sound quite as confident.

"That is a mega tremendous mystery! I think it's got something to do with kissin'. An' going to Blackpool. Or Scarborough. Only your *mam* can tell you what *really* happens. Mine hasn't. Not yet."

"Mine will, Daisy. My mum always tells me the truth. I'll ask her, then I'll tell you all about it…"

Sheila had her fist pressed against her mouth. Mary was struggling to suppress her own laughter, when she felt a hand on her shoulder.

"Martin's just rung. It's a boy!" her husband, Gordon said. "Mum and baby both well. And believe it or not, grannies, Tessa's bringing him home. This evening."

* * *

"He was in a bit of a hurry," one of the midwives had teased. "Something planned? A hot date?"

"His big brother's birthday party," an elated Tessa had replied, stroking the fuzz of chestnut-coloured down on the baby's head, gazing at the very familiar little features.

"Does Sam really look just like me, Mum?" Charlie asked her now, sitting on the bed, cradling his new sibling. The way, she clearly recalled, he had tenderly cuddled his little sisters, who had gone to spend the night with their paternal grandparents.

"Exactly the same, sweetheart. Dad will get the photo albums out, tomorrow, and you'll be able to see for yourself. It'll be just like looking at your twin brother."

Charlie's jaw dropped. His greeny-blue eyes widened.

"You don't think, do you, Mum, that maybe Sam *is* my twin brother. That he forgot to get born when I did. P'rhaps he went to sleep, or something. Then, today, he wakened up and remembered it was our birthday, so he made a hole in his swimmin' pool and shouted out in Indian that he was fed up waiting."

Something had obviously been going on while she was away! Eyebrow raised, Tessa looked towards the door, where her mother was standing.

"Tell you about it later," Mary mouthed. "When you're feeling stronger!" Nodding, Tessa turned her attention back to Charlie.

"Darling, I'm so sorry I wasn't here for your party. And I'm really sad you didn't get time to spend your voucher. I hope you're not too disappointed.

"Dad said he'd take you into town, next Saturday," she carried on. "We also decided that you should have an extra treat. We don't know what, yet, but it will be something very special.

"What would help us would be if you could tell us what you'd like to do…"

Charlie tutted. "I am not disappointed. I'm not even a tiny bit sad, although I did miss you and Dad.

"But I've had a tremendous day. Bein' eight. I got loads of presents, the food was brilliant, and my darling Daisy told me tons of important stuff I didn't know about.

"The very best thing, Mum, was me getting a twin brother." Charlie expertly swapped the baby from his right to his left arm, as though he had been doing it all his life. "That is so cool. If Sam wants to be me, sometimes, he can. On… Thursdays…

"An' p'rhaps, tomorrow morning, you might like to have a go on the bouncy castle. The kind men told me they won't be coming to take it away 'til the afternoon.

"We could have great fun," Charlie assured her. "Bouncin' around. Just you and me, Mum. We could talk all about kissin' an' Blackpool and Scarborough…"

A Little Glimpse of Heaven

"All of you have a tremendous day. I'll be thinking about you," Tessa Harper had said at the front door, kissing her husband and son goodbye and waving to her neighbour, Hector, who was waiting patiently on the pavement, dressed in his best suit; complete with collar and tie.

"We will," the trio had assured her.

Now, an hour or so later, hunched forward in his seat and hugging his jeans-clad knees, Charlie Harper grinned at Martin, his similarly-attired father.

"It's great bein' eight and having another birthday, even though I wasn't too sad that you and Mum missed bits of my first one, cos she had to go to hospital, to get Georgia and Beth and me a new brother. Sam is the best present in the whole universe!"

Charlie's greeny-blue eyes sparkled as he rattled on.

"An' I'm really glad you made your mind up not to bring the car, Dad. In case you couldn't find a place to park it in London. Trains are tons better!

"I've liked 'em since I was about… three… or four. Once, ages ago, when I was with Mum and we had gone to buy her a new orange dress, and she needed me to say her bottom didn't look too big in it, I met a enormous, beautiful lady on a train."

Charlie pushed a hand through his thick, chestnut-coloured hair.

"She was brilliant, that lady! She had tons of jangly beads an' a tremendous hat, with a mega-long feather in it. It was green. The hat – not the feather – green like cabbages and frogs. She let me try it on. It was cool!"

Barely pausing for breath, Charlie turned his attention to Hector Smythe, seated beside his father.

"Even better than trains, is that you're coming with us, Hector. My darling Daisy thinks so, too. And so does Chloe and my other best friend, Li.

"He's Chinese, you know." Charlie glanced across the passage at the wiry boy with the shock of glossy black hair and liquid-dark almond eyes, who was deep in conversation with petite blonde Chloe.

"That's funny, isn't it? Cos Li was born here. In Eddingfield. 'Zactly the same as me. And I'm not Chinese – I'm English. An' a bit Scottish, too – my great grandma Allen was Scottish, before she died and wasn't anything any more. Well... I 'spect she's an angel, now."

Charlie shifted position.

"Anyway, Hector, we can talk about all that stuff another day. I just wanted to tell you that we think you're mega-cool and thanks for comin' to help Dad look after us all."

A smile lit up the elderly bachelor's face. Never in a million years had he ever imagined himself being described as cool. Mega or otherwise. Now it was a regular occurrence.

Not only 'cool'! 'Brilliant', too. And 'tremendously' 'excellent'.

Without doubt, Hector reminded himself for the umpteenth time, the best day of his life had been seven years ago, when Tessa and Martin Harper, with their baby son, Charlie, had moved in next door.

From that moment, his solitary, frequently lonely in spite of his varied interests, existence had changed. And had kept on getting better and better.

Now there were nearly three-year-old twin girls, Georgia and Beth, and tiny Sam... just a couple of weeks old... the living image of his big brother.

"Thanks," Hector said. "I think you're all pretty cool, too!" Cute and chubby Daisy, who was seated beside her boyfriend, Charlie, pulled a comical face.

"It's decent of you to say so, Hector, but I'm not really cool at all. In fact I'm well hot. Meltin'!" She peered out of the window. "Are we nearly at that eye thing?"

Martin offered a conservative estimate. "About fifteen more minutes."

In less than half that time, the train pulled into bustling London Victoria. "Stay together," Martin firmly instructed. "Charlie and Daisy with Hector; Li and Chloe with me."

Charlie's eyes widened at the sight of the escalator leading up to the shopping mall. He carefully studied the bars, the restaurants and smaller shops on the lower level.

"It's like another town," he eventually said, his voice filled with awe. "I wonder if people come here to go on their holidays, then change their minds an' stay at the station instead, for two weeks, cos it's very interesting."

Hector chuckled. "I doubt it, Charlie." Behind her glasses, Daisy's round hazel eyes showed confusion. She spoke slowly. Hesitantly.

"Me nan... not the one who lives in Gateshead, the one who lives in Bradford... well, I once heard her tell me mam that stations are the same as real life.

"Me nan said it was all about... people comin' and goin'... sayin' 'hello' and 'goodbye'... laughin' and cryin'... takin' all their luggage from one place to another... an' sometimes never comin' back again..."

Thoughtfully, Daisy tugged on the tight curly ringlet, which had escaped the confines of an orange hairband, pulling it straight before releasing it to recoil itself.

"But I don't really know what she was talkin' about," she carried on, briskly, "so, come on, Charlie, pet, come on, Hector, let's go and see the Queen havin' her dinner... bet she never eats that cheese that smells of me dad's socks when he's been playin' football..."

* * *

Collecting the pre-booked, by telephone, tickets was as easy as Martin had been assured by friends who had already taken a flight on the London Eye.

Just one swipe of his credit card and he was able to rejoin Hector, who had taken the children to the gift shop in order to buy an illustrated guide of the modern white structure.

"In case their questions are a bit too technical for my old brain," the retired engineer had said, with a twinkle in his blue eyes.

"Guess what, Dad," Charlie waved the glossy brochure in the air, "you can buy this in every language in the whole world. This one's in English, cos that's what we talk. Daisy wanted us to get one in French, too, so she could learn to speak it on the way home on the train, but it cost a lot of money, so we didn't.

"Li saw one in real Chinese. But he couldn't read it. He can talk it, though! That's well clever, isn't it?"

Shy Li's creamy cheeks pinked faintly at the compliment. Then, "Do you know that the wheel never stops moving?" he queried, solemnly, as they took their place in the queue.

"Doesn't it? How do you get on, then? Do you have to jump?" Through narrowed sapphire eyes, Chloe scanned the crowds. "What about that lady over there – the one in the wheelchair? *She* won't be able to jump, so what's she going to do?"

"I reckon," Daisy said, matter-of-factly, "that there'll be loads of big strong men waitin' and they'll just pick up the wheelchair with the lady in it and bung the lot in when the door opens. Then, whoosh, off she'll go and have a great time, spinnin' around."

"Or," Charlie suggested, "perhaps the lady's been practising jumping. At home. Just a bit. Even if she does have sore legs. Because she really wanted to see interesting stuff, like roofs and towers and Mars!"

Li giggled. "It doesn't stop, but it doesn't go fast, either. It kind of crawls along. Like a tired snail. At just one mile an hour. So, there's lots of time for everyone to get on. And off. Even people with walking sticks and wheelchairs.

"My dad told me. He saw a programme about it on the telly."

"Your dad's well brilliant," Charlie said, nodding. "So's mine."

"And mine is," Daisy declared, "even though me mam calls him a 'daft lad' sometimes. Oh, we're movin'."

"My daddy's lovely, too," Chloe said as they shuffled along, "and he promised me he would still love me loads when our new baby gets born. I was a bit worried that he might not, 'cause there's only been just me for ages and ages…"

Charlie patted her arm. "Don't worry about a single thing, Chloe. New babies are brilliant. And mums' and dads' hearts just grow bigger all the time, so they can love all their children. Exactly the same!

"Actually, everyone's heart grows bigger, every single day. That's so they can love their best friends, too." Turning suddenly, Charlie grinned up at the man, who had heard every word of the children's conversation.

As he boarded the capsule for what he considered to be the trip of a lifetime, something he would never have undertaken on his own, Hector Smythe quickly swallowed the lump which had sprung into his throat.

"Incredible bit of technology," he told Martin, minutes later, looking round the capsule. "Unique design," he added, approvingly, eyeing the curved structure, which allowed uninterrupted views of the Thames riverbank.

Shrugging out of his jacket, Martin nodded.

"Amazing! I thought we'd all be crammed in. That we'd have to find our spot and stick with it. Never for a minute did I imagine… well… this much space!

"The kids'll be able to take a look at whatever they fancy. Charlie's got the guide book, hasn't he? He's a good little reader for his age.

"In fact they all are... and if there's anything they can't work out for themselves, then," Martin glanced over his shoulder at the lively-looking young woman, whose back was to the door – 'I'm Emma, from Australia, and I'm your guide for this flight' she had introduced herself – "they only have to consult the expert..."

* * *

It didn't take long before the first questions were asked.

"Emma," Daisy queried, shrilly, "what are kangaroos like? Do they eat you? Or are they quite friendly?" Then, without waiting for an answer, added, "Is it true what me dad said... that these blokes who work over there," she pointed at the Houses of Parliament, "are paid good money for doin' nothin'?

"An' why is it so bloomin' hot in here? Worse than it was on the train! If I'd known, I'd have worn me bikini... it's a nice one... purple with yellow spots..."

Emma smiled, apologetically. "I'm very sorry, Madam," she told Daisy, who giggled. "We are having occasional problems with the air conditioning," she addressed the others, "so if anyone is feeling uncomfortable, then we suggest they take off their—"

"Not their clothes!" Li spluttered, looking horrified. "That wouldn't be at all polite!"

"I don't see why not." Daisy shrugged. "I mean, it's not as if anybody's got different bits from anybody else, is it? Boys have boy's bits and girls have girl's bits. Boy's bits are called—"

"There it is!" She was cut short, mercifully, Martin thought, by an excited Charlie. "Look... over there... the Queen's very own house. Buckingham Palace. An' I think...

yeah… I can see her… she's not having her lunch, though. I 'spect she can't make her mind up whether to cook sausages or pizza, so she's walking her dogs in her garden… to have a little think."

Chloe hopped from one foot to the other. "You're right, Charlie. And I can see her husband, too. He's cutting the grass. With a lawnmower made of real gold."

As Hector murmured about how imagination was a wonderful thing, a ripple of laughter filled the capsule. Daisy treated her fellow passengers to an indignant glare.

"There's nothing very funny about that! Grass has to be cut, you know, even if you're a royal prince an' a duke of somethin' an' you're married to someone quite important!"

More chuckles. Daisy's scowl intensified. Martin jumped in quickly. "Look," he pointed, frantically. "There's Trafalgar Square, where we went, last year, to feed the pigeons. Remember, Charlie?"

"I most certainly do remember, Dad. A pigeon sat on my head. It was great! It tickled."

"Yukky! I'd hate a bird to land on my hair. It might…" Chloe wrinkled her nose, "well… you know… do something horrible…"

Daisy laughed. "Me nan says it's lucky if a bird plops on your 'ead, but me grandad says it's a good job cows don't fly." She looked up at Martin, thoughtfully. "What does that mean, Mr Harper?"

It meant, Martin decided, that it was definitely going to be yet another of 'these' days! To his relief, an explanation proved unnecessary as the guide's voice rang out.

"If you look to the east, the Millennium Dome is just coming into view. And, next to it, are Canary Wharf and the Canada Tower, one of the tallest in…"

As all four children charged across for a better view, Hector sat down heavily on the oval seat in the centre of the capsule. Digging in his pocket, he pulled out a handkerchief and wiped his forehead.

"You okay?" Dropping down beside him, Martin looked at the pale, perspiring face with concern. After few moments, the elderly man nodded.

"Just felt a bit woozy. Young Daisy was right. It is bloomin' hot in here. Almost takes the breath away from you. Give me a minute, Martin. I'll be fine." He smiled, wanly, and dabbed at his face again. "I wouldn't have missed this for the world, you know. Not for anything. Something to remember for the rest of my days… thanks for inviting me…"

* * *

It didn't take Martin long to realise that his hope of a quiet journey home, that all four children would be worn out by the events of the day, wasn't about to happen.

Their chatter had been non-stop. Even Li's voice was raised by several decibels.

"The Millennium Eye was brilliant," he eagerly declared, "but I also liked the Tate Modern art gallery. It was very interesting. Lots and lots of colour."

"And lots and lots of upside-down pictures! Why did they stick 'em up that way, Mr Harper?"

Charlie answered for his father. Answered very seriously. "Well, Daisy, actually they weren't upside down, at all. I know about modern art. My Uncle Ray, he's a brilliant painter, told me all about it, when he was teachin' me how to draw properly.

"He said that some artists see what they're painting different from other artists. And they paint what they see… inside their heads."

Daisy remained singularly unimpressed. "Well, I'm thinkin' that they must be cross-eyed inside their heads. Or just plain daft, maybe!"

Martin secretly agreed with the little girl's comments. Many of the paintings had reminded him of the garish daubs which his small twin daughters produced on a ten-a-penny, daily basis.

And he hadn't been able to make head nor tail of many of the other exhibits, either: twisted metal structures; chunks of marble; silver wire... miles of the stuff.

As for Hector – he had looked positively bemused for most of the visit, frequently murmuring 'Give me a Monet or a Turner..."

But Martin wasn't allowed time to dwell on the matter. Chloe, smudgy mauve shadows under her eyes, but still firing on all cylinders, sat bolt upright.

"I liked lunch! Never, in my whole life, have I eaten slippery orange fish that hasn't been cooked! I'm going to ask my Mum to let me have some. Every single day."

Martin winced. Chloe had been the only one who had wanted to taste his all-time-favourite treat. And had certified it 'Well brilliant!' And 'Could I please have another tiny bit?'

Her forthright mother, Tessa's best friend, Molly, would hardly be amused to receive a request for expensive portions of smoked salmon on a regular basis.

Ah, well, he decided, philosophically, he'd cross that bridge when he came to it. If push came to shove, he's simply point out to Molly that encouraging children to experiment with new tastes was part of their education.

"And what did you like best?" Satisfied he had an excuse in the bag, Martin turned his attention to his old friend, who, to his surprise, had managed to stay awake.

A brilliant smile flashed across Hector's lined, weary face.

"I can't remember enjoying a day quite as much as I've enjoyed this one. As for what I liked best... well, it was all good, but the Millennium Eye trip will stay in my mind for ever.

"Incredible! It really was like getting a little glimpse of heaven..."

Saying Goodbye

"It's cool when nice days come on Saturdays and we don't have to go to school and can do other interesting things instead." Eight-year-old Charlie Harper studied the watch he'd bought with some of his recent birthday money, then looked up at Tessa.

"It is quarter past nine," he carried on. "Just... five... ten... fifteen more minutes, then I'll be going next door to Hector's an' we'll start making him a tremendous new rockery. It's gonna be a Alpine one, Hector says, with flowers that come from countries with mega mountains and tons of snow.

"That'll be great, won't it, Mum?"

Tessa fondly ruffled her older son's thick chestnut hair. Most things in Charlie's life were 'great', 'tremendous' or 'fabulous'; 'cool' and 'brilliant'. Besides that, the close bond between her little boy and their elderly bachelor neighbour never failed to fascinate her.

Generation gap? Not even a suggestion of one. Best mates? Absolutely!

Her thoughts were disturbed as her twin daughters stormed into the kitchen. Oh-oh, trouble, Tessa immediately thought. Not quite three-year-old Georgia's green eyes flashed fire.

"Don't like Bef," she shrieked. "She's 'orrible!"

"Not 'orrible, Georgie. Very good girl!" her carbon copy sister stated firmly.

"No! Pants!"

"You're pants!"

Tessa decided she would scream if she heard that word, the one all the children now used to describe anything – or anyone – they didn't like, just once more. Charlie tilted his head.

"Mum, I can hear Sam crying. I 'spect he's hungry. New babies are always hungry, aren't they? They make tons of noise, too. Same as Georgia and Beth!" He checked his watch again. "Actually, I think I'll go and see Hector, now. He'll be happy that I'm nice and early, cos we'll have time for a nice cup of tea and a good chat before we start our hard work."

Charlie charged out of the back door, narrowly avoiding a collision with Martin, who was returning from picking up fresh bread and family weekend favourites from the bakery.

"See you later, Dad," Charlie whooped. "Have a great morning. I'm going to. With Hector." About to wriggle through the gap in the tall hedge, he called over his shoulder. "Mum's in the kitchen. So are Beth and Georgia. They're fightin'. And Sam's upstairs, screaming. It's pants, really!"

"Sounds like very large pants!" Martin raised his eyes, comically.

It didn't take long, however, to restore peace in the Harper household. Mollified by identical gingerbread men, the previously-warring twins, flaming red heads close together, were in the living room, happily working together on their favourite jigsaw puzzle.

Baby Sam had needed only a top-up, a dry bottom and a cuddle, before snuggling down again for another snooze.

"I still feel enormous. I shouldn't really..." Tessa was licking her lips and picking up a chocolate-filled croissant when Charlie reappeared in the doorway. Looking puzzled.

"I think Hector must have forgot we were goin' to make a Alpine rockery today," he said, slowly, "cos he's not there. I knocked on the back door and I rang the bell on the front one and he didn't come.

"An' he also forgot to open his curtains and take his milk indoors, before he went out…"

* * *

Because he had a key, Martin had been able to let himself into Hector's house. And had immediately telephoned the old man's doctor. Then Tessa. To give her the sad news. But it was almost an hour before the formalities were settled and he was able to return to his now-silent home.

Tessa was exactly where he had left her: sitting at the table; the croissant untouched; a layer of skin settled on her still-full coffee cup; face pale; grey eyes, heavy with sorrow, staring into space.

"Sweetheart?" Martin put his arm round her shoulders. She looked up.

"Mum and Dad came. I rang them. They've taken the twins and Sam. Just for a while. Until Hector was… until they took him…" Tessa's voice broke and she bit down hard on her lip.

"But Charlie's here," she carried on, after a moment or two. "He point blank refused to go. I've never seen him that… well, defiant!"

"You've told him?"

Tessa nodded. "He was looking out of the window and saw Doctor Gilbert's car. He wanted to come straight round and cheer Hector up. Even asked if I thought he might have caught chickenpox.

"I had to tell him… Martin, but it was the hardest thing I've ever had to do. In my whole life. And I think I must have handled it badly. Charlie looked at me as thought it was all my fault! He's very very angry," she finished, a single tear rolling, unchecked, down her cheek.

Anger might not be such a bad reaction. Anger could be worked through. Discussed and dealt with. Martin decided it was preferable to a desperately sad Charlie, although that, he knew, would come later.

"Where is he?" he asked.

Tessa sighed. "In his bedroom. I went up, but he told me to 'Go away and not come back again'."

With a heavy heart, Martin climbed the stairs. There was no response to his light rap on the child's bedroom door. He tried again. Still nothing. Taking a deep breath, he opened the door. Charlie lay on his bed, dry-eyed, arms linked behind his head, staring at the ceiling.

"Can we have a little talk, son?" Martin settled himself on the *Star Wars* duvet. "About Hector? It's very sad, I know that, but I wanted to tell you that he looked as if he had just fallen asleep and he was smiling, like he'd been thinking very happy thoughts.

"I thought that if you knew that, it would—"

Suddenly, Charlie, two crimson spots on his cheeks, sat bolt upright. His bluey-green eyes narrowed. "No, we cannot have a little talk about... anything," he interrupted furiously. "I don't feel like talkin' and I don't believe you and Mum are telling me the truth. Hec... people don't just go to bed and die!

"People have to get ill or get hit by a bus or fall off a mountain to get dead. And they don't smile, either, Dad. Unless they are very silly and Hector is the most brilliant, clever, tremendous person in the universe. Now, please go away."

Charlie flopped down again and returned his gaze to a point above his head.

Should he? Go away? Martin mulled the question round in his mind. And decided it wasn't the best course of action for the confused little chap who was facing his first loss of someone he had dearly loved.

Wordlessly, he rose, crossed to the window and looked out over Hector Smythe's sunlit garden. Ablaze with colour and life, the lawn was a square of lush, brilliant green.

In the far corner, lay the newly-delivered heap of rich top soil; a selection of rocks and large stones; and, in the greenhouse would be boxes of plants carefully chosen plants for a perfect Alpine rockery.

One which, now, would never be assembled. Hector's house would be sold. New people would move in...

For the first time, hot tears sprang into Martin's eyes. The initial shock had gone. Now he felt only a deep sadness.

"Charlie," he said very softly, not attempting to stem the flow of his grief, "it's all right to be angry. Everyone gets a bit angry when they lose someone special. But," he turned, "it's also okay to be sad. And to cry, if you feel like it."

Charlie's head swivelled. "I do not want to cry. I do not want to do anything. 'Cept to stay here. All by myself!"

* * *

Sam was unusually restless. As she put him back in his cot for the fourth time in as many hours, Tessa wondered, if at just six weeks old, the baby had been affected by her own sorrow. And the fact that his big brother hadn't given him his usual bedtime cuddle, while he told the tot, in great detail, the events of his day.

Charlie had eventually come out of his room. But it was a different Charlie. This one was silent and unsmiling. And had refused anything to eat. An extremely rare occurrence, which prompted Georgia to remark, "Charlie must have a poorly tummy." And, equally rare, her comment to go unchallenged.

About to get back into bed, in the hope of a few hours' uninterrupted sleep, Tessa was suddenly distracted. By an unfamiliar sound, but one she instinctively recognised.

It was the sound she had longed for. Prayed to hear. Aware that when it happened, it would signal the start of the healing process.

Barefooted, she dashed from the room, sped along the hall and opened Charlie's door. His bedside lamp was on, softly illuminating a crumpled face awash with tears.

"Sweetheart!" Tessa pulled the sobbing child into her arms, stroking his damp hair away from his hot forehead. "It's all right," she soothed, gently rocking him, just as she'd done with little Sam, moments before.

"It is not all right. It's terrible! Worse than pants!" Hiccupping and shuddering, Charlie wept on. Then, agonisingly slowly, the storm abated and Tessa's arms were suddenly empty again as Charlie removed himself from her embrace and settled back against his pillows.

He wiped his nose on the sleeve of his pyjama jacket.

"Mum, I really need to have a chat. Will that be okay? In the middle of the night?"

"Of course it's okay, darling. We'll talk about anything you want to talk about."

"Right! Well, I need to talk about God and why He made Hector die, when there are loads of mega-bad people in the world who nobody would," Charlie gulped, "miss a lot and who weren't gonna make a Alpine rockery that you would be able to see out of the window and be well happy.

"An' also," he carried on, "why did Hector die when he wasn't even ill?"

Oh, heavens! How God worked was out of her league. Charlie would have to talk to his friend, the vicar, about that one. But, Tessa accepted with mild relief, she could offer a suggestion on the second question.

"Actually, Charlie, I don't think that Hector's been feeling very well for quite a long time. He's been having a bit of trouble with his heart, you see. That happens to some people when they get older.

"Doctor Gilbert gave him pills and they did help a bit, but…" Tessa struggled for the right words, a simple explanation, finally coming up with "Hector's heart had been working very hard all these years and… it suddenly stopped. It just, well, kind of ran out of power."

"Like the battery in my torch sometimes does," Charlie murmured.

"Yes. A bit like that. And there is one thing we should feel happy about, though," she continued, quickly, as his lower lip trembled, "and that is that Hector died very peacefully. It didn't hurt him. He just went to sleep and didn't waken up again. I expect," she added, "he was having a lovely dream, too."

Charlie nodded, thoughtfully. "That would be better than getting run over by a bus or something. But I think you might be wrong, Mum, about what happened to Hector not hurting.

"I think my heart's got broken, too, and it hurts a lot! Just here…" as his voice tailed away, the little boy's tears flowed again.

It was an hour later before his eyelids drooped. As Tessa wearily returned to see to a wailing baby, Charlie's parting statement, delivered in a drowsy voice, rang round in her mind.

"Hector took me to the cemetery once an' he showed me where his mum and dad live. Under a nice tree and they had a big piece of silver stone with their names on it, so everyone could say hello when they passed by.

"Hector said that's where he was going to live when he wasn't next door, any more. An' Mum, I want to go and see Hector move into his new house and take him a nice bunch of flowers… with you and Dad… cos he hasn't got brothers or sisters or anything. We're his family, Hector said…"

* * *

Charlie's revelations about the funeral arrangements had proven to be accurate. Hector's last wishes, perfectly detailed and to be administered through his solicitors, Barnes and

Brooke, were for a service at the local church, followed by him being reunited with his parents.

There would also be a buffet lunch, afterwards, at the Bowling Club.

When she'd been given the facts, via the phone, by Mr Barnes himself, Tessa had firmly stated to Martin, "I don't want Charlie to go! He's only a little boy. It'll be too much for him."

"I disagree, Tess. If it had been a cremation – well – I'd have needed to give that a lot more thought. But a burial... I think Charlie will take a lot of comfort in that. In seeing his friend being laid to rest in an enormous, beautiful garden!

"For all we know, there might even be an Alpine rockery or two!"

His half hearted attempt at humour had missed its mark.

"It will only upset him," she'd insisted. "Just when he's beginning to smile again."

But Martin had had an answer for that, too. An answer which had made perfect sense.

"He's only smiling on the surface, sweetheart. Deep down, he's still struggling to make sense of it. This way – and it's what he wants, remember – he'll be able to say a proper goodbye..."

Days later, leaving the flower-filled church, in which Charlie had occasionally wept and clung to her arm as though terrified that she might suddenly leave him, too, but had also sung All things bright and beautiful lustily, then had said, loud enough for everyone to hear, "That was Hector's and my very favourite hymn and he must have wanted us all to sing it, so I would know he was thinking about me," Tessa was glad she'd withdrawn her protests.

Even more so when, under bright blue skies, in the tranquil cemetery, to the sound of birdsong and surrounded by everything which Hector Smythe had held dear, when three eight-year-olds, Charlie... his beloved girlfriend, Daisy, newish to the area... and Chloe, who had known Hector for a great deal of her life... linked hands as the coffin was lowered.

"You were a great lad, Hector, pet," matter-of-fact Daisy said. "Have a good time with your mum and dad. Remember to tell 'em about us. Oh, yeah, an' tell 'em about the London Eye an' how we all had a brilliant time."

"I wish you weren't dead, Hector. I really, really wish..." Chloe said huskily, clutching a posy of wild flowers, neatly tied with a pink ribbon.

"I'll love you every single day of my life, Hector," Charlie contributed. "So will Mum and Dad. And Georgia and Beth. And Sam... because I'll teach him everything you taught me... about how to make your carrots grow the right way up.

"Oh, yeah, an' I'll bring you some of mine when they're ready to pick. When I come and visit you. And some onions, too. And any other interesting stuff.

"I'll come loads of times." Charlie glanced, sideways at the two girls who nodded. "We'll all come loads of times and tell you our news... like we *always* do..."

"You're a very clever husband," Tessa told Martin, as the mourners – a respectable turnout of bowlers and anglers, former business colleagues and fellow members of the charity committees which Hector had sat on – assembled for lunch.

"It did do Charlie a lot of good and—" She stopped as a stocky, grey-haired man touched her arm.

"Mrs Harper?" He turned to Martin. "Mr Harper?"

"Yes," the duo answered in unison.

"I'm Colin Barnes. Mr Smythe's – Hector's solicitor." An embossed card was thrust into Martin's hand. "I know this is a sad day, for all of us, but I really need to talk to both of you. Perhaps you would be good enough to ring my office for an appointment. At your earliest convenience, please…"

From Hector, With Love

My very dear Tessa and Martin, When you moved in next door, I could not have imagined, for a moment, how my life was about to change. I remember the freezing cold day when you arrived as though it was just yesterday. Tessa, you appeared barely more than a child yourself, yet you were cradling your own infant, so tenderly. And Martin, you looked at the end of your tether. I will never forget the way you gripped my hand when I offered to get your central heating boiler going! Or how we all sat in my living room later, eating fish and chips, chatting away, as though we had known each other for years.

But, on reflection, the best part of that day was when Charlie was placed in my arms. Lacking relatives, I'd never held a baby. In all honesty, the very thought terrified me! But it was so easy. Charlie looked up at me. He chuckled. I sensed, there and then, that I had a new mate! And I was right.

Since then, things have just got better and better. I feel I belong to a family again. That I am an honorary 'Grandad' to Charlie, Beth and Georgia. And the expected baby, who, sadly, I suspect I will never get to really know...

My dear friends, please do not feel awkward about what I have done. The children have given me so much joy. You have all given me so much joy.

Accept this legacy with my deepest affection and gratitude. In the hope that it will enrich your lives, in the way you have enriched mine.

Your friend
Hector

Mary Allen's eyes were moist as she returned the hand-written letter to her daughter, Tessa, who was staring, blankly, into space.

"You had no idea Hector was going to do this?" Mary asked, hoarsely. "I mean... he never said... anything? Not even a *little* hint?"

A still-shaken Tessa shook her head. The visit to their late next-door neighbour's solicitor, two days ago, still seemed like a dream.

"When Mr Barnes asked Martin and me to get in touch with him after Hector's funeral, we thought... actually, Mum, I don't know what we thought!" She smiled shakily. "Except that perhaps Hector had left his precious gardening tools to Charlie, knowing how much they would mean to him and that he'd take good care—"

"Instead of that, he's left him the whole garden. And the house to go with it!" Mary interrupted.

"Not just to Charlie, to the girls and Sam," Tessa pointed out. "And with provisions that should we have more children, the trust funds would be extended to include them.

"There's a fair amount of money, too. And stocks and shares. I knew Hector liked to dabble in the stock market, his 'little hobby', he called it, but," she puffed out her cheeks, "I never realised how *good* he was at it!

"Several charities have benefited from his skill and when each of my children reaches their twenty-fifth birthdays, they're going to be quite comfortably-off young adults..."

Tessa's voice tailed away. Both women sat in silence for several minutes. Finally, Mary stood up.

"I need a cuppa." At the sink, filling the kettle, she turned. "Have you and Martin any idea what you're going to do with your own legacy? Ten thousand pounds is quite a lot of money, you know."

Quite a lot of money? It was a small fortune. But everything had happened so quickly. They hadn't had time to discuss the matter. Nor, Tessa told herself, were they over keen to do so. Not at the moment. It would only underline their loss, reopen the void in their lives that Hector Smythe's sudden death had left.

"Not yet," she told Mary. "And we haven't said anything to Charlie, either, but we're going to. At the weekend. He's old enough to partly understand what Hector has done for him."

"And how much he loved him... loved you all," Mary murmured.

* * *

On Saturday afternoon, Georgia and Beth were at the birthday party of one of their friends from playgroup. "Twelve three-year-olds... you should have heard it, Tess. It sounded – and looked – like a houseful of rampaging baby gorillas!" a harassed-looking Martin had spluttered on returning home after dropping his twin daughters off.

Baby Sam, having enjoyed a gentle kicking and cooing session in his little bouncy chair, had nodded off. Charlie was on the telephone. Moments later, he bounded into the living room.

"I'm a very cool person, today," he proudly announced, collapsing onto the settee. "Tons of people are phoning me. First it was Li. *He* wanted to know if *I* wanted to play football. I said I was sorry, it would be tremendous, but I couldn't. Though I might be able to tomorrow.

"Next it was Chloe. *She* wanted me to come round and watch her new video. I said that would be great, but I was really, *really* busy. I told her I might be able to come round tomorrow. Or another day, if I'm going to play football...

"That one," Charlie nodded at the door, "was my darling Daisy Pollock."

Tessa smiled. "And what did Daisy want you to do?"

"Not anything, really." The eight-year-old shrugged. "She said she just wanted to say hello to me. That was kind of her, wasn't it? Then I said that I only had time to say 'hello' cos you and Dad and I were going to have a mega important talk.

"But," he shifted position, "I did say goodbye to her as well. A *proper* one. You must *always* say a proper goodbye to your friends, mustn't you? Or they might think you don't care and stop bein' your friend. I wish I'd been able to say a proper goodbye to Hector…"

A lump lodged itself in Tessa's throat. She stared down at her feet. Not one of them had been able to say a proper goodbye to Hector. It simply hadn't been possible.

And she wanted her still-grieving son to understand that. To accept and come to terms with yet another fact of life.

It couldn't, Tessa comforted herself, be any more awkward than the recent session when she had explained, after a grilling from Charlie and as frankly as she could, without getting too emotional, how babies got into their Mum's tummies in the first place.

And Charlie's reaction. Staring at her, horrified, protesting: "You're havin' a joke with me, aren't you, Mum? People wouldn't do anything like that! It would be a bit rude! 'Specially if they did it in Blackpool, like Daisy's mum said. Or at the supermarket. Or on a bus!"

Things had got progressively and embarrassingly worse after she had assured her son that, for two people who had married because they loved each other very much, it was a beautiful way to become even closer. And, also, it was the only way to make a baby, in the privacy of their own bedroom.

IVF and all the other skills of modern medicine could wait, she had decided.

After a series of facial gymnastics – mouth twistings, nose wrinklings, eyebrow wigglings – Charlie had then asked: "So… how did the first two people in the universe… Adam and Eve… how did they know they had to do that? Did God give them an instruction book? With pictures about what buttons to press? Like you get with a new computer and a washing machine?"

Immediately followed by a thoughtful: "The Queen's got four children, hasn't she, so she and her husband must have... well... you know... four times... or did the Queen get someone else to do it for her, cos she was too busy doin' some reigning?"

And "When I tell my Darling Daisy about this stuff, I don't think she'll be well happy, you know. I 'spect she'll say we'll just kiss a bit and never, *ever*, go to Blackpool."

Somehow, she had coped. With Martin's help. And, together, they would handle *this* situation. By giving Charlie the facts and answering his questions. Honestly.

Raising her head, Tessa met her husband's eyes. He nodded and began to explain to his son about the precious gift he and his sisters and brother had been left. By their very special friend.

Charlie listened, calmly, until his father had finished. Then his lower lip trembled.

"What's wrong, sweetheart?" Tessa reached for his hand. Charlie's fingers gripped her wrist.

"Well, Mum, I don't want to go and live next door with Beth and Georgia and Sam! I love them loads, but I'm not very good at cooking. I can only make cereal and sandwiches. An' I really hate Sam's yukky nappies. An' the way Georgia and Beth are always fighting.

"An' I'd miss you and Dad. A lot. Though I 'spect you would let us come to tea, sometimes... to have chips an' stuff..."

Minutes later, after rapid explanations from both his parents, about how Hector's house was being sold and that the money from it would be put into the bank for him and his siblings until they were grown-up, he was smiling again.

"Oh, that is mega brilliant news! Wicked! How tremendously kind of Hector. He knows I'm going to marry my darling Daisy Pollock when I'm twenty-four." Charlie sprang to his feet and dashed towards the door. "Is it okay if I ring Daisy, now, Dad? To tell her that we'll wait just one more year? 'Til we're twenty-five?

"Then we can buy a excellent house. An' a helicopter. An' a horse. An' to ask her if she wants to come with me, tomorrow, to visit Hector and say 'Thank you very much'? She *will* want to. I know that. Daisy always thought Hector was a decent lad. Now she'll know she was right!"

Martin nodded. Charlie sped off.

"He's got his priorities right," Tessa said. "He *could* have played football with Li. He *could* have watched Chloe's new video. Instead, he's going to visit his special mate. Martin, perhaps we *all* should go to the cemetery and pay our respects to Hector.

"Like him, I never realised, on the day we moved in here, just how much he would change our lives…"

* * *

A removal van was parked outside. Ankle-deep in a clutter of colourful books, stuffed animals, and undressed dolls with peculiar haircuts – Georgia's latest skill – Tessa watched the comings and goings from behind the twins' bedroom curtains.

Hector's well decorated and perfectly maintained home had sold quickly. She had gleaned from her contact with his solicitor, Colin Barnes, that a young family would be moving in. Three children, although he wasn't certain what age groups they fell into.

"I can only pray that they're not too noisy," he'd said, solemnly, causing Tessa to chuckle. In conversations, she had learned that Mr and Mrs Barnes had never 'been blessed', as he had put it.

"Oh, they will be," she'd assured him, brightly, thinking of the bedlam that occurred, daily, within her and Martin's four walls. "If they're fit and healthy, they'll be *very* noisy indeed. Whether they're brand new or sixteen!

"But that won't be a problem. After a while, you don't even hear the racket."

His smooth, kindly face had registered total disbelief.

Leaving his office, that day, Tessa had congratulated herself that she hadn't suggested that if perhaps Mr and Mrs Barnes had indulged in a sojourn in Blackpool, then abundant blessings might have been bestowed on them!

But, at the moment, there was no sign of any little people, next door, either. Only a few glimpses of a couple, who appeared to be around the same age as herself and Martin, directing the removal men.

The fair-headed man was extremely tall – had to be six feet five. At least. The woman, small and enviably slim, with a waterfall of glossy black hair, tumbling across her shoulders and down her narrow back.

They'd looked, Tessa decided, very nice. Perhaps she ought to offer a cup of coffee. Or would it be better to hang on until all the furniture was indoors?

Hearing her own doorbell ring, she quickly dropped the corner of the curtain. It could be one of her new neighbours, needing some advice. Or an ice-breaking few spoonfuls of sugar...

"It's okay, Mum. Beth and Georgia are watching a video. Sam's still sleeping. I'm answering the door," Charlie called up the stairs. "I 'spect it's my darling Daisy. She said she'd likely come round. To make sure that nobody horrible was moving into Hector's house.

"Daisy's not very happy about horrible people, you see. She doesn't like people who look like witches or ones with rings through their noses... Oh, hi, Daisy. These are tremendous trousers. Brilliant zips! Tons of pockets."

"They're called cargo pants," Tessa, reaching the bottom stair, heard her son's plump sweetheart tell him. "And this is my new top. It's cool, isn't it?"

Head on one side, Charlie studied the hardly-there crimson T-shirt. "I think, Daisy, that you might have been better getting a bigger one. Yours is a bit too short. I can see your... well... some of your tummy!"

Tessa stifled a giggle as Daisy's hazel eyes, enormous behind her glasses, met her own in a glance of pure exasperation. The little girl's wild curls bounced as she shook her head. She sighed loudly.

"Men! Honestly, Mrs Harper! Charlie, pet, you're not mega good at fashion, are you. This is *meant* to be short. It's called a *crop top*. All the pop stars wear them. Well... the girl ones do.

"I'm cool, me, when I'm wearing this. Now, what about them folks next door. Do you think they're decent? What are the children like?"

When Charlie admitted that he didn't know, that he hadn't seen any children yet, Daisy caught hold of his hand.

"Tell you what, pet, we'll go outside, sit on the wall, and wait for them. Then we'll know..."

* * *

This time, it was Martin's turn to witness the new arrivals. From behind the curtain in his and Tessa's bedroom.

Charlie, having earlier scrambled through the gap in the dividing hedge and returning to his own territory with a shy-looking tall blond boy, a petite raven-haired girl and a small, curly-headed, jeans-clad figure of indeterminate gender, appeared to be in charge of the proceedings.

Slowly, carefully, Martin opened the window in order to hear, as well as see, what was going on. So he could tell Tessa about it, later.

She'd be bound to ask.

"I'm Charlie Harper," his son was saying, "and this is Daisy. Daisy Pollock. We're both eight. I live here. Daisy lives quite near, but she used to live in Gateshead. That's a very long way away.

"I've got twin sisters," he carried on, "called Beth and Georgia – they're three – and a baby brother called Sam."

"I'm Tristan," the tall lad said, "Tristan Warren-Smith. I'm nine. This is my sister—"

Martin grinned as the little girl, dark eyes flashing, long lashes fluttering, sidled up to Charlie. "*My* name is Sacha Gabriella Warren-Smith," she firmly interrupted her brother. "And I'm seven, but Mummy says I'm really a *lot* older, because I'm quite sensible and Tristan can be very silly.

"This," she waved a dismissive hand towards the sturdy little person, thumb in mouth, standing behind her, "is Piers! He's four and," she glared at her small brother, "he's a menace. Quite horrible at times."

Throughout the exchanges, Martin had been watching Daisy's face. Clearly, she had been unimpressed by Sacha's over-familiarity with her sweetheart, Charlie, but had held herself in check. Now her cheeks were crimson as she crouched by Piers. Then looked up at her adversary.

"Strikes me, Sacha," Daisy said, "that your brothers are canny lads. Both of 'em. But I'm thinking that *you* might be horrible. A pain in the neck. Or the bum, as me dad says when me mam isn't listening!"

"You're right, Daisy," Tristan's smile split his solemn face.

"Bum! Bum!" Piers shrieked, collapsing in glee against Daisy. "Pants! Pants!" he roared.

* * *

"Caroline and Jeffrey seem very pleasant, don't they?" Tessa said, in bed, that night. "And the children are lovely... little Sacha's so sweet... I'm sure they'll all get on fine with our lot."

Martin pulled his weary wife into his arms. She'd been marvellous, supplying an impromptu meal for their new neighbours. And Daisy, who had invited herself to supper. To keep her eye on things, Martin had supposed.

So Tessa didn't need to hear, right now, that there were already rumbling of unrest, caused by Sacha announcing that Charlie would be her new boyfriend; and Daisy's furious reaction as purple faced, hands on hips, she had hissed, "Oh, no, he won't..!"

No Rain in Spain - Summer Special

Charlie Harper was clearly ecstatic about his new holiday haircut; Tessa, his mother, was *not* quite as enthusiastic about the gelled, chestnut-coloured spikes.

But not wanting to take even the slightest edge off his excitement over his impending trip with his maternal grandparents, she waited until he had scampered off to reveal his 'cool' look to his little twin sisters, Georgia and Beth, before asking the question which was uppermost in her mind.

Elbows on the table, her chin resting in her cupped hands, she looked into her husband's eyes. "Why, Martin?"

He fluttered his dark lashes, dramatically. "Oh, questions, questions! Why do little birdies not fall out of the sky when they're tired? Georgia wants to know that! Why do noses run and where does all the gunk live while it's waiting to come out? Charlie asked me that last week. And Beth wonders—"

"Martin! You *know* what I mean. You were only supposed to be taking him for a trim and now he looks like – well – like all the girls' dolls after Georgia found the scissors I thought I'd so carefully hidden."

"He *doesn't…*" Tessa paused, momentarily, "look like *my* Charlie!"

"No, but he *sounds* like your Charlie. At least he did in the barber's." Martin chuckled.

"The poor bloke having a razor cut in the next chair, nearly lost an ear when *your* son announced that 'I need to have my hair cut humungously short, today, please, cos it'll be easy-peasy to dry. I don't want to land in Spain, tomorrow, all dripping! I don't have a umbrella to take on the aeroplane with me to catch the water, but my granny has, so she'll be okay. Grandad'll be all right, too. He doesn't have a lot of hair to worry about!'"

Tessa's jaw dropped. "Why on earth would he say something like that?"

"Because *your* Dad's been singing a well-known song to him. You know the one? About the rain, in Spain, falling mainly on the plains… ? *Your* Charlie translated it to mean *in* the planes!

"We got it sorted out. Eventually!"

Imagining the conversation, Tessa grinned. "Not before the scalping process, though," she murmured.

"By then it was too late. A lad Charlie knows from school had come in. A 'really cool guy' apparently, with a trendy, spiky haircut! I didn't have the heart to say 'No.'"

Martin shrugged. "Look on the bright side, sweetheart. You only have to look at it for the next twenty-four hours. Hair grows faster in hot weather. When he returns from Benidorm, in two weeks' time, he'll be *your* Charlie again. Full of tales about his 'tremendously excellent' adventures, no doubt…"

* * *

"This is the most tremendously excellent second of my whole life, Granny! Thanks a lot for bringin' me on holiday with you." Inside the crowded airport terminal, his greeny-blue eyes sparkling, Charlie puffed out his cheeks.

"There must be millions of people here, goin' to places like… like… Egypt. There's a thing called a stinks there, you know. An' a dead king and his mummy lives in it!"

Mary Allen stifled a giggle, grateful all over again that Tessa and Martin had agreed to her and Gordon's offer of taking Charlie on his first foreign holiday.

"We'll take very good care of him," she'd assured her daughter. "And it'll do your dad a world of good. He's still only seven himself, inside! Having someone he can build sandcastles, go on long walks, and be *daft* with is his idea of paradise…"

"It's called the Sphinx, Charlie," Mary gently corrected, now.

He appeared not to have heard. Jiggling from one trainer-clad foot to the other and back again, he waved. With both arms.

"Here's Grandad. He's given our cases to the nice lady who's going to carry them to the aeroplane for us. That's kind of her, isn't it? She must be well strong! Is she the same lady who's going to bring us our lunch when we're zoomin' through the sky?

"Hi, Grandad, I can't wait to have my lunch," Charlie babbled on.

"My girlfriend, my darling Daisy Pollock – she went to Spain, once, on a plane – and she had chicken things and pasta stuff and pink pudding with hard bits in it and cheese!

"D'you think we'll have that? Same as Daisy? Or a burger, or somethin'?"

Gordon knew better than to voice his opinions on mid-air catering in front of Charlie. Mary would have his guts for garters if he said *anything* to dampen the lad's high spirits.

Instead, he concentrated on his grandson's new look. "Does Daisy like your haircut, Charlie?"

"Yeah, she really does. She says I look like a pop star and she thinks the gel," he proudly patted the sharp spikes with the palm of his hand, "smells like oranges. Daisy loves oranges. They grow oranges in Spain. On trees. My dad told me.

"I can't wait to see a tree with *real* oranges growing on it… I can't wait to swim in a *proper* blue pool – I've got my 50 metre swimming badge, you know, and I can *nearly* dive without my tummy making a plopping noise on the top of the water... and I can't wait to say 'Bonnie days' to the nice people who live in Benidorm.

"Daisy said that means 'Hello. I hope you are well.' Does it, Grandad?"

"Mmm, yes, something like that, Charlie."

* * *

"Can we send a postcard to Mum and Dad and Georgia and Beth and Sam today, to tell them I've got twenty-seven freckles on my nose?" a golden-coloured Charlie asked, finishing his breakfast in the hotel dining room, a week later. "An' to say that I have *not* got sunburned, even though it's well hot, 'cause clever Granny *always* puts that good stuff on me?

"An' to say that I can dive prop'ly now... an' swim one hundred metres, easy peasy... an' about that excellent castle we went to, where the brave men riding beautiful horses pretended they were fightin' an' killin' each other, but they were OK really, cos they all came out at the end and bowed, and we all clapped and cheered?

"An' also that we had a *whole* hot chicken *each*, off a spinnin' turny thing with a fire underneath it? An' that I was up *so* late that it was nearly tomorrow... an' I wasn't even a little bit tired?"

Charlie licked his lips, thoughtfully.

"P'raps we could send *two* cards, then I'd have enough room to tell 'em all about the tons of well amazin' food we get here in Spain..."

Where did he put it all? Mary couldn't help wondering for the umpteenth time.

This morning, Charlie had demolished a mammoth portion of fresh fruit salad – including lots of carefully-selected orange segments. "So I can think of my darling Daisy, while I'm eatin'," he'd explained, with a dreamy smile.

After that had come an enormous bowl of cereal and yoghurt. Followed by a boiled egg and two crisp rolls – one with butter; the other thickly spread with strawberry jam. Finally, a sugar-coated bun!

Just as the expression 'Hollow legs' sprang into Mary's mind, it suddenly struck her that Gordon was eating a lot more than he usually did on holiday, without displaying any visual evidence.

And that in just a few hours both the men in her life would be 'well hungry' again! Sniffing the warm air for the merest suggestion of lunchtime paella – something which Charlie had declared to be the 'most excellent rice stuff in the universe'.

If she ate even half of what they managed to put away, she'd be as big as a house, Mary decided, finishing her coffee. But then again, she forced herself to admit, she didn't exercise like Charlie – and Gordon – did.

While she had sprawled on a sun lounger, shaded by a huge umbrella, engrossed in her blockbuster novel or taking the occasional cooling, leisurely dip in the pool, the pair had gone on long adventure treks.

Up into the hills, looking for wildlife. Exploring the quieter bays along the coastline, searching for interesting shells and pebbles. Even roller-blading, Mary nearly having a fit when Gordon admitted that he had had a go, too.

"You could have broken your neck, you silly old man," she had scolded, out of Charlie's earshot. Her rebuke was met with a twinkling grin from her fit-looking, sun-tanned husband.

"Easy-peasy, lemon-squeezy! Tremendously excellent! I'd like a pair of blades for my birthday, please, my darling. And a safety helmet, knee pads, elbow shields…"

At least she'd get some exercise today, Mary consoled herself. A more gentle, safer, kind. Better suited to her advancing years! She checked the time on her watch.

"The coach leaves in half an hour," she said, "so have you boys got everything you need or do you have to go back upstairs to the room?"

Charlie tutted. "You're making a mistake, Granny. Grandad's not a boy – he's a man. A *real* one. I know what the difference is between a man and a lady. D'you want me to tell you? Yeah, I bet you do, so I will."

Oh, heavens. The two middle-aged couples at the next table – who had made friends with Charlie on their first meeting – were unashamedly eavesdropping, all four wearing wide grins. Mary held her breath as Charlie began his explanation.

"Well... men have to do this thing to themselves in the bathroom, every morning. And ladies don't, cos they don't have the same bits of stuff as men have. You see, men—"

"Sweetheart," Mary interrupted quickly, feeling her face grow hot and making a big deal of looking at her watch again, "if you want to buy some postcards from the hotel shop, you'd better go now. And don't you want to put your hair gel on?"

To her dismay, Charlie shook his head. "It's OK, Granny, thank you for askin', but the hot sun makes my gel go all sticky, an' I'm gonna buy my cards on the top of that mountain place.

"Mum and Dad'll like that. I might buy my darling Daisy one, too. She likes mountains. She likes ones with snow on them, but I don't think she's ever seen one with a whole country at the very top!

"Neither have I. An' I can't wait to go to... what's it called, Grandad?"

"Guadalest, Charlie. And it's not a country, it's more like a village."

"Oh, right. That's still cool! I still can't wait. About men and ladies... men have to go into the bathroom *every* single morning... before they go to work, or play golf, and then they shave the bits off their chins.

"'Cept for men who like beards! But ladies never *ever* have to do that. They're always nice and smooth, you see. That's interesting, isn't it?" Charlie finished his lengthy explanation and sprang to his feet.

"Now, let's go and get on the coach. It'll be great. Well exciting. I can't wait…"

* * *

The following morning, over another gigantic breakfast, Charlie treated his fellow-diners to a step-by-step account of his day trip.

"Guadalest was amazin'. About a million years ago, some men with big axes cut ginormous holes in the mountain and all their friends an' their families an' their cats and dogs walked through, and said, 'This is very beautiful. We'd like to live here.'

"Not the cats and the dogs. They didn't talk. I 'spect they jus' miaowed and barked, instead. To show they were well happy, too.

"So the men made steps, then built houses. *And* shops. They thought it would be great to sell shoes an' the other stuff the ladies were making, while they were waiting for a kitchen to cook in. Stuff like tablecovers and flowerpots and fans with dancing people on them.

"An' when they died, the people who *weren't* dead took them to the very top of the mountain and made them nice places to lie down and rest in peace after all their hard work. They took them to the very *top*, so's they'd be a bit near to God, if they wanted a little chat to Him.

"Oh, yeah, I nearly forgot, *before* the people died, they had their photos taken. Yesterday, me and Grandad saw all these pictures. On their lovely white graves. It was tremendously cool… well, actually it was swelterin' hot – that's why Granny didn't climb all the way up an' had a nice cup of coffee instead – but it was cool, too… seein' it…"

"Did *you* tell him all that, Gordon?" Mary muttered, when Charlie returned to his meal.

"Not in so many words, darling, although, as usual, he did ask lots of questions." Gordon laughed softly. "You *have* to admit, his version is a lot more entertaining that anything you'd find in a guide book!"

"Wow, I am really really full," Charlie announced, minutes later. "I feel like a Teletubby. I *would* like to have a good swim, but you can't swim if your tummy's full up, can you?

"Cos you'd sink to the very bottom, like a ginormous rock and that wouldn't be very nice, would it? So shall we all go for a long walk, first?"

Mary groaned inwardly. All these steps, yesterday. The relentless heat. In spite of comfy shoes, her feet had felt as though they were on fire. And still hadn't completely recovered.

Gordon gave her a sympathetic smile. "Don't worry, love, you take it easy. I've got a plan.

"Charlie, Granny's got some things to do. How about if you and I go and visit the sandman?" he suggested, referring to the talented young Spaniard, Alberto, who constructed intricately-detailed sand sculptures on the main beach.

The little boy rose and punched the air. "Brill! Alberto told me he was gonna start on a new one. A horse, with a cowboy on its back. Can we go right now, please, cos I can't wait… an' can I take some of my money, my pesetas, to buy presents to take home for everyone?"

Dashing round the table, he planted a kiss on Mary's cheek.

"See you later, Granny, to go swimmin'. I'll give you a race if you like. We can practise for tomorrow, when we're goin' to that ginormous water park, where there's the biggest swimming pool in the whole world.

"It's got well high slides and scary whirly, twirly things that spin you round and round and round.

"You and me and Grandad are gonna go on *absolutely* every single thing, aren't we, Granny? Won't that be great. Can you hardly wait?"

* * *

Martin had been right. The gelled spikes *had* disappeared. Besides seeming to have grown another couple of inches, Charlie looked his old self again.

Tessa hugged her son hard.

"I've missed you, sweetheart," she murmured. "We've *all* missed you, so much. Dad, the girls, Sam, Grandma and Grandad Harper, Hector-next-door, Daisy…"

Then, realising she might be making her sensitive child feel guilty about being away, added, brightly, "But I bet you had a really wonderful time. We can't wait to hear *all* about it.

"The exciting things you did. The brilliant people you met. The places you visited. What you liked the *very* best, although I suppose you'll have to think mega hard about that. Having done so *many* cool things."

Charlie shook his head. "No I can tell you what was *really* tremendously excellent, Mum. I can tell you *right* now…"

In bed, that night, a giggling Tessa snuggled into Martin.

"Never, in my wildest dreams, did I imagine he'd come up with that!" she spluttered.

Martin's chuckle was deep and rumbly. "Oh, I don't know! He is *your* son, after all. When *you* were asked about the best moment of our wedding day, which, I would say, was well cool from start to finish, *you* said it was when you were able to take your satin shoes off and wriggle your toes!"

His arms tightened round her.

"So why you are even *remotely* amazed that your Charlie's choice was the loo in the aeroplane – because it was all made of real silver and you only had to close the lid to make it flush and *he* did it three whole times – I can't begin to imagine…"

Broken Bones, Broken Hearts

One minute, Tessa had been stacking the dishwater and making plans for the rest of the day; the next, she'd been speeding towards the hospital, her heart in her mouth.

Thank heavens for families and friends, she thought now, back in the comfort of her own home.

Caroline, her new neighbour, in spite of having three lively children of her own, had more than willingly held the fort until the two grandmothers had arrived to care for the younger members of the Harper family.

And it seemed that a lot more than wiping runny noses and changing soggy nappies had been going on.

Tessa sniffed. Mouth-watering smells were wafting through from the kitchen. As though on cue, Mary Allen, wiping her hands on a towel, came into the living room.

"Right, that's tonight's dinner seen to, dear, and Sheila's putting together a casserole for tomorrow, with some chicken and bacon she found in the fridge. Just in case Charlie needs – well, you know – an extra bit of attention? We hope you don't mind, that you don't think we're interfering…"

Tessa raised her eyes, comically. "Mum, without the pair of you, I often think my life would be one major disaster area! You and Sheila, you're—"

"Constantly filled with amazement at how you cope with this wonderful lot! The way you never lose your temper or come out with daft remarks like 'Because I said so!' How you always talk things through with them – even the twins, although I doubt that Georgia takes a lot of notice. What a girl!

"Anyway," Mary carried on, "how's our wounded soldier?"

Her elder son's face, Tessa thought, fixing her gaze on the eight-year-old, sprawled on the settee, accompanied by his adoring sisters, was exactly the colour of the plaster on his right arm.

In spite of that, and the ordeal of six hours waiting in the Accident and Emergency department, where he had seen sights she'd rather he hadn't had to witness, Charlie seemed quite cheerful.

"I'm okay, now, Granny. Thanks a lot for askin'."

"And my little poppets?" Mary enquired of her twin granddaughters.

"Poor Charlie. His one arm got well broke." Gentle Beth patted Charlie's chestnut hair. Her mischievous identical sister Georgia put her hands on her hips.

"*Was* not me to break it! *Not* today!" the three-year-old firmly announced.

Charlie chuckled.

"'Course it wasn't you, Georgia. *You* weren't even in next door's garden when it happened. I was playin' football with Tristan an' when I was going to score a mega-tremendous goal, I tripped over.

"Anyway," he carried on, "I gotta wriggle my fingers, every single day. Like this. To stop my arm falling off an' to keep my blood swishin' round and round my body. I *think* that's what the nurse said…"

"Swish," Beth echoed, softly, mimicking the action.

"Swish! Swish! Swish!" Georgia shrieked, waving both arms in the air.

Charlie's grin was followed by a long wistful sigh.

"I wish my darling Daisy Pollock was *here* and not in Gateshead visiting her nan and grandad. I miss her, an' Daisy knows loads of great stuff about broken things an' blood.

"She'll think it's *excellent* when she hears about the girl with the lovely green hair an' silver knobs an' rings all over her face. Remember, Mum, the one who had that picture thing on her leg an' we couldn't see what it was a picture of, cos it was all swelled up an' bleeding well bad?

"What was that picture thing called again?"

"A tattoo," Tessa supplied, wincing at the memory of the gory sight.

"Yeah, so it was." Charlie nodded. "An' I'd *really* like to tell Daisy about that man whose head fell off and then got put back on again. She'll likely say it's amazin'."

Sheila Harper, bringing her newly-fed baby grandson to his mother, had caught the last of Charlie's disclosures. Placing chubby six-month-old Sam on Tessa's lap, she whispered into her daughter-in-law's ear.

"*I* think it's amazin', too!"

Sharp-eared Charlie picked up the remark.

"You *should*, Grandma. Cos it was." He shifted position. "This man, you see, was lying on a bed thing with some wheels on it. His shirt was *covered* with blood. Tons of it. An' some of it was all over his face an' he was holding on to the top of his head with one hand and the special collar thing with the other.

"I 'spect that was to keep his head from falling off again. Until the glue got nice and hard. Or," Charlie's mouth twisted thoughtfully, "maybe he'd had it *sewed* back on, with strong string. Or even wire.

"I don't really know. I wanted to go and talk to him, to find out, but Mum said she thought he might not be feeling very well."

Tessa could see both her mother and mother-in-law battling furiously to keep their faces straight, their cheeks crimson with effort.

"Charlie," she said quickly, "tell Grandma and Granny about your X-ray. You thought that was magic, didn't you?"

"I did and it was. I put my arm, the broken one, on this metal tray and a lady in a white coat took a picture of it. But it wasn't a picture of my *real* arm. It was a picture of my skelington arm!

"Then the lady showed me 'zactly where my bone was broke. She was a well happy lady – she laughed all the time she was talkin' to me."

"What a surprise," Sheila murmured as her grandson suddenly sprang up from the settee and headed for the door, calling over his shoulder that he was going to get his pen, so he could practise writing and drawing with his other hand.

"Exactly what *did* Charlie say to the radiographer?" Mary asked.

Tessa giggled and cradled baby Sam, who was nodding off in her arms.

"Well... among other things, when she said it was a nice clean break, Charlie said 'Thank goodness for that. It must be pants having an ugly dirty one.'

"Then he asked her if, in the olden days, before X-rays were invented, did people have to get held up to the light while an artist drew a picture of their bones...'"

* * *

The following morning, at breakfast, Charlie looked his usual, pink-cheeked, healthy self.

"Does you arm hurt?" Martin asked, watching the contortions as his right-handed son, refusing any offers of help, struggled to spread peanut butter on his toast with his left.

"Not really, Dad. But I 'spect it would if I punched a wall with it."

"Must *not* punch walls!" Georgia waved an admonishing finger at Charlie.

"Must not punch *Bef!*" Beth said.

"I wouldn't punch you, Beth," her brother assured her. "That wouldn't be a nice thing to do."

"Georgie punches me!"

"Do not!"

"Do!"

"Do *not*, Bef!"

"*Do*, Georgie!"

"Was a raccident, Bef."

"Was *not* a raccident."

"Enough, girls! Eat your breakfast." Tessa turned away, hiding a smile, as Georgia, the one who always had to have the last word, muttered, "*Was* so a raccident."

"Mum," Charlie's voice rang out. "When I've finished, can I go next door to see Tristan? And Sacha? And Piers? I 'spect they'll *all* want to draw something great on my plaster.

"Yesterday, the nurse said it would be okay for people to write on it tomorrow. An' that's today, now. When I phoned my darling Daisy, last night, she said I had to keep a space on it for her to write me somethin' tremendously excellent when she comes home the day after tomorrow.

"Tomorrow, Charlie," Martin corrected.

"No, Dad. Daisy def'nitly said the day *after* tomorrow."

"Ah, but that was *last* night!"

In the brief silence while Charlie digested the information along with his toast, Tessa checked the calendar, to make sure she'd given the milkman the correct information.

"Daisy *will* be back tomorrow, Charlie," she confirmed and was rewarded with an ear to ear grin.

"Oh, wow, that is tremendous news! I 'spect she'll put a kiss on my plaster. An' a heart thing, with a arrow through it.

"I can't wait! I can't wait to see Tristan either. To tell him about the man with the joined-on head, even though you told me that it hadn't *really* fallen off, that he needed to wear that collar thing to stop it hurting his other bones.

"But it *looked* like it had fallen off, so can I go, Mum? Please…?"

As Charlie's voice tailed away, Tessa recalled the conversation she'd had with Martin earlier this morning.

"You can't wrap him up in cotton wool, love," he had warned, when she'd voiced her concerns. "You've got to let him carry on as normal. I mean Charlie's *not* exactly invalid material, is he?"

"Of course you can, sweetheart," she responded now, unable to resist adding, "but you *will* be careful, won't you?"

Charlie's greeny-blue eyes met her own concerned grey ones.

"I certainly will, Mum. Please do not worry for a single minute. I don't want to break my other arm. I mean how can you... use a computer... or eat your dinner... or... go to the loo if you don't have any arms that work?"

"With great difficulty," Martin chuckled. "Especially going to the loo!"

"Yeah, Dad. You'd need to take a *very* good friend with you, wouldn't you? To give you a bit of help pulling your pants down. And then, when you've finished, your friend would have to—"

"Enough, boys!" Tessa interrupted. "Eat your breakfast. Oh, and Charlie, tell Caroline that Piers can come round and play with the girls, if he wants to."

"Piers. Cool! He's my *boyf'end*," Beth said, softly, her emerald eyes sparkling. Then, "Ow!" she shrieked. "Georgie punched me a bit. In my tummy."

There was no denial. Only a fierce scowl and rosebud lips pressed tightly together. Tessa adopted her no-nonsense face.

"Say sorry to your sister, Georgia," she instructed. "And promise you won't do it again. Or... you'll have to go upstairs to your room and have a little think about how being naughty isn't a good idea. And that means you won't be able to play with Piers."

"Sorry, Bef. Won't do it again. Was just a little m'stake." Smiling sweetly, Georgia slid off her chair, kissed her sister on the cheek, picked up her empty cereal bowl and carried it over to Tessa, muttering under her breath, "Piers is *my* boyf'end. My boyf'end…"

* * *

Half an hour later, four-year-old Piers was unceremoniously shoved through the gap in the hedge, which divided the Warren-Smith's garden from the Harpers, by his elder sister, Sacha.

"He's such a little pest," she declared, as she joined her brother, Tristan, and Charlie, who were sitting, cross-legged on the grass, under the apple tree, deep in conversation, an unopened packet of coloured pens at their side.

Charlie glanced up. "Piers isn't a pest. He's nice and kind and gentle. Like Beth. *Georgia's* a bit of a pest… but she's okay most of the time. I 'spect it must be a bit difficult being a twin person. Like when you look at someone else and see *you* looking back at *you*… or something…"

"Even more difficult," nine-year-old Tristan stretched out his long thin legs, "must be if you're a quadruplet, or a quintuplet, or a sextuplet." His solemn face broke into a wide smile. "Imagine *six* little Piers running around, Sacha. Or six Georgias, Charlie!"

Sacha shuddered. "I think that would drive *me* mad."

Charlie chuckled. "I think that would drive *Mum* mad! But I wouldn't mind if there were two of my darling Daisy. Then one of them could go and visit her nan in Gateshead and the other could stay here with me. That would be great."

Tristan nodded. "Daisy's tremendously cool. I like her!"

Sacha's large dark eyes widened. The seven-year-old flicked back her long black hair. She smoothed her ankle-length, floral cotton dress.

"Do you think Daisy is *pretty*, Charlie?" she asked slowly and thoughtfully. "Is that why *you* like her?"

"I don't jus' like her – I *love* her, Sacha. I'm going to *marry* her when I'm twenty-five."

"But what if you met another girl… one who was very very beautiful and didn't wear glasses, but wore lovely clothes, and who could play the piano… like me. Would you not love *her* instead?"

"No, Sacha. I would not! Daisy is *very* special, you see. She's all nice an' soft, like yummy marshmallows. Her glasses are really cool, too. She says when she's older, like fifteen or something, she'll get glass things to put inside her eyes, instead, but I hope she doesn't do that.

"Cos when the sun shines on Daisy's glasses, her eyes sparkle like real diamonds." Charlie drew up his knees and rested his plastered arm on them.

"I think her clothes are great, too," he carried on, "but what I love most about my darling Daisy is that she is clever an' interestin an' that, if she had an X-ray, her insides would be just as nice as her outsides.

"My Granny says that's the most important thing in the whole universe. Bein' nice inside. And," he finished, loyally, "I 'spect Daisy *could* play the piano. *If* she really wanted to."

"A gorilla could play the piano," Tristan murmured, pulling a purple pen from the pack. He glanced, sideways at his sister. "Probably better than you can, Sash."

"I play beautifully. Mummy says so. And don't call me Sash! I don't like it one bit. *Tristy!*"

"Oh, yeah, cool! I love being called Tristy, Sash. Call me it always. Pleeese…"

Sacha sprang to her feet, cheeks crimson and stomped off up the garden, towards the back door. Tristan raised his fair head from his artwork.

"She'll never call me Tristy, again, Charlie."

"Of course she will… now she knows you like it."

"But I *don't* like it. That's the point."

Charlie scratched his head. "So why did you say you did?"

Tristan sighed. "I think I'm going to have to teach you a few things about girls. I'm older than you, remember…

nearly ten... so I've learned a few things and... oh, tell you later... hi, Sash... stopped sulking?"

His question was ignored. The pretty little girl sat down on Charlie's other side.

"I've been thinking, Charlie," she said, "about Daisy going to see her family. She goes quite a lot, doesn't she? And you miss her when she's not here, don't you?"

"She goes away a bit. Not every week or anything, but I always miss her. I'm *always* a bit sad when she's away."

Sacha smiled. "Well, I've had a tremendous idea. When Daisy's away, *I'll* be your girlfriend. And if she goes away for ever, *I'll* marry you when you're twenty-five.

"You'll never need to be sad ever again and we—"

"That would be two-timing!" Tristan's interruption was swift. "Two-timing is horrible. Charlie, don't even think about it."

Charlie hadn't a clue what to think. Two-timing? What did it mean? Something mega-horrible, judging by Tristan's angry face. And since Tristan knew a lot more about girls than he did, Charlie decided that he thought it was mega-horrible, too.

Besides that, his arm was beginning to hurt a bit. And he fancied going home and having a bit of a chat with his mum...

* * *

Next door, Tessa put the telephone down and flopped beside Martin on the settee. He had been only half-listening to her one-sided conversation, but it hadn't been difficult to work out that someone was in trouble and that someone was Daisy's mum, Susie Pollock.

And, judging by the expression on his wife's face, it wasn't anything as simple as forgetting to restart the milkman's delivery of a couple of pints of semi-skimmed.

He pulled Tessa close. She snuggled against him.

"Susie's in a real flap," she said. "Steve's company want him to move back North again. *She* doesn't want to go."

Charlie's face swam into Martin's mind. "And Daisy?" he asked hoarsely.

"Daisy hasn't been told, yet, Martin. But Susie wonders if she *might* have got wind of it. That's why she telephoned... to forewarn us..."

Off With Their Heads

Because his son, Charlie, had to be at the school gates by eight o'clock, instead of the usual nine, and also because it was on his way to work, Martin Harper was chauffeur to the excited little boy, the love of his life Daisy, and his great chum Chloe.

The racket inside the car made Martin wince. Heaven help the coach driver and the teachers whose tasks, today, were to keep thirty over-excited eight-year-olds under control.

Pulling into the kerb, he had to raise his own voice to make himself heard over the din.

"Does everyone have everything they should have? Packed lunch? Tissues? Money?"

His right arm still in plaster from his football accident, Charlie carefully undid his seatbelt. Using his undamaged left arm, he scooped his backpack off the floor and on to his lap.

"Yeah, Dad. Thanks for askin'. I've got loads of brown bread peanut butter and marmalade sandwiches, two packets of prawn cocktail crisps, a toffee yoghurt, a banana and an apple, and loads of juice.

"I've got a whole packet of tissues and tons of money," he continued. "An' the camera Grandad Allen gave me. It's *his* old one, but *my* brand new one. It's got a film in it."

"Wouldn't be much point in bringin' a camera if it didn't have a film in it, would it, pet?" matter-of-fact Daisy asked from the back seat. "I've got cheese and pickle sandwiches, Mr Harper, salt and vinegar crisps, some rice stuff that you mix with the fruit stuff 'til it's really scrummy, an' three of me mam's home-made coconut buns. One for each of us.

"Oh, yeah, an' diet cola, tissues, and... my mobile phone!"

"Uncle Martin, I've got salmon and cucumber – don't tell fibs, Daisy Pollock. You do *not* have a mobile phone with you!"

"Actually, Chloe, I do."

"So where is it then?"

Daisy fished in her pocket. "Here! It's well cool, isn't it?"

Glancing over his shoulder at the small silver oblong being held aloft, Martin groaned inwardly. Chloe's round blue eyes were filled with envy. No doubt Charlie would soon be stating his own case as to why he, too, ought to be the proud owner of a portable piece of modern technology.

Honest Daisy's next words came as a bit of a relief.

"Really, it's me mam's. But I was the one who taught her what buttons to press. I'm good with things like this, me. That's why Mam let me bring it today. In case I fell into a dungeon at the Tower of London an' no one knew I was down there, cos they were too busy lookin' at other interesting stuff, like the place where people got their heads cut off.

"She didn't want me to starve, see. Or get haunted by a scary ghost. So I said 'Why don't I take the mobile, then I can phone the police and ask 'em to get me out?' and Mam said 'What a great idea!'"

"It certainly is," Charlie agreed cheerfully.

Chloe tsked. "Nobody's going to fall down any dungeons. It would be against the law to let them do that. And," her mouth twisted, "my gran says there are no such things as ghosts."

"There are so, Chloe. Millions of 'em."

"There are *not*, Daisy!"

"I think there are some..." Charlie said, thoughtfully, "in that tower with the rude name."

"What tower with the rude name, pet?"

"Er... the... Bloody Tower!"

"Charlie!" Chloe looked primly appalled.

"But that's what it's really called," a pink-cheeked Charlie insisted. "And Grandad Harper told me a song about a man with his head tucked underneath his arm and walking around the... Bloody Tower. Or maybe it was a lady. But it didn't have a head on its shoulders, did it, Dad?"

Through the window, a grinning Martin could see more and more children being dropped off.

"It certainly didn't, Charlie. And now, it's time you were off. Look the coach is coming. Have a great time, all of you..."

* * *

On the journey to London, the children had been arranged into small groups and given colour-coded name tags. Charlie, Daisy and Chloe's were a zingy lime green; the teacher in charge of them – Brent Herring – was new to the school.

"You'll have an entertaining time with *that* trio," he'd been assured by his colleagues, and moments after they had entered the precincts of the ancient building, he was given a sample of what lay ahead.

Her speckled hazel eyes solemn behind her glasses, the small plump girl with the mane of wild brown curls, gazed curiously up at the tall young man. "I'm Daisy. Daisy Pollock. D'you like being called the same name as a fish, Mr Herring?"

The petite blonde by her side nudged her sharply in the ribs. "Don't be so rude!" she hissed.

"I'm *not* bein' rude, Chloe. I'm just interested. You can't help having your name, you know. It's something you get when you're born and then it's yours for ever and ever."

Charlie, who'd been standing a few feet away, engrossed in the small guide booklet which each child had been given, suddenly looked up.

"Not if you're a girl, Daisy. I mean, when you and me get married, you won't be Miss Pollock any more. You'll be Mrs Harper. For ever and ever and ever. Have *you* got a wife, Mr Herring? A nice lady called Mrs Herring?"

Brent smiled at the earnest little boy with the greeny-blue eyes and the thick chestnut hair, "I do, Charlie."

"Well, that's great news," Charlie declared, returning his attention to the map on the pamphlet. "The man who built the White Tower, which is number 43 on the list, had a well cool name, too. William the Conker!"

Chloe's nose wrinkled. "I wouldn't like to marry anybody with a name like that. Chloe Conker! Yuk."

Brent took the opportunity to deliver a brief history lesson.

"The king's name was William the *Conqueror* and he was the first Norman King of England. He reigned a very long time ago... in the year 1066 and he was called the 'Conqueror' because—"

"I know about 1066," Daisy interrupted, her voice high-pitched with excitement. "Me grandad and me, we watched a programme on the telly, a few weeks ago when I was in Gateshead, and it was about a lot of lads havin' a fight.

"One of them got shot in the eye... with a bow and arrow... in a place called Hastings... wherever that is! Near Bradford, I think. Or it might be in Canada... anyway, it doesn't matter, Mr Herring, cos I want to see the place where that other king – Henry – had all his wives heads cut off, cos he kept fancying the woman who lived next door—"

"And *I* want to see the Queen's beautiful jewels. And the men who don't eat chicken or fish or lamb, only steaks and burgers, the ones who wear red and black dresses over their trousers and funny hats. The ones who walk around with blackbirds on their shoulders," Chloe butted in.

"They're called Beefeaters, although their correct title is Yeoman Warders and the black birds are ravens," Brent explained, struggling valiantly not to laugh.

"And King Henry the Eighth didn't have *all* his wives beheaded, Daisy. Only two went to the block. He divorced two others, one died, and the last one was still alive when—"

"So what you're tellin' us, Mr Herring," Charlie put in, frowning, "is that he wasn't a very kind king…"

"More than not kind, Charlie!" Daisy raised her eyes. "He was a tremendously pants sort of person. Not decent. It's not right to cut people's heads off… and I don't think it's right to get a divorce neither! Do you, Mr Herring?"

Dodgy ground, Brent decided. He turned to Charlie. "And what would *you* like to see?"

"I would like to find a place where I can take a photograph of some real live ghosts… then, in about an hour, a place where we can eat our lunch.

"I've got some *brilliant* peanut butter and marmalade sandwiches. My Grandma made the marmalade. All by herself. With her own hands. An' some oranges.

"You could have one if you wanted to, Mr Herring… in case Mrs Herring was too busy to make you something delicious… then you could write your name on my plaster, if you like." Charlie held up his well-decorated arm. "There's still a little space left. Next to my darling Daisy's heart… where it says I LOVE YOU PET. FOR EVER AND EVER…"

* * *

While their school-age children were enjoying the fascinating sights and sounds of the Tower of London, in Tessa Harper's kitchen were her oldest friend, Molly Young, Chloe's mother, cradling her ten-week-old son, Jake. Also Tessa's identical twin daughters, three-year-olds Beth and Georgia, with their other brother, seven-month-old baby Sam.

And an ashen-faced Susie Pollock, who had only picked at her lunch.

"What's the latest, Susie?" Molly asked.

Tessa shook her head and slid a sideways glance at her little girls.

"Hang on a minute – these two can eavesdrop for Britain and always feel it necessary to broadcast *every* detail! Beth, Georgia, have you had enough to eat?"

"Full up to mine own chin," Beth stated.

"Yeah, thanks a lot for askin', Mum," Georgia said, sounding exactly like big brother Charlie.

"Right then," Tessa said, "you can watch television for a little while…"

Moments later, with both babies contentedly snoozing in their little chairs, she refilled the coffee cups and sat down. "Susie…?"

"It looks like…" the pretty little blonde's blue eyes filled with tears, "it looks like we're going. Steve can't see any other way round the problem.

"The local guy who *was* going to take over as senior branch manager, in Gateshead, has changed his mind. Got a better offer from his old company, from what I can gather. There's no one else who can handle the workload, no one who knows the area and the customers quite like Steve does. And the company has just landed a major contract, so that means…"

Pulling a tissue from her sleeve, she dabbed at her eyes.

"…He wants me to put the house on the market, straight away, he told me yesterday. Then he texted me, late last night, on my mobile, to say that he'd seen a lovely bungalow and…"

"Surely," Molly said, briskly, putting her arm round Susie's shaking shoulders, "there's no need for that. I know it's not ideal, Steve up there and you and Daisy down here. But you've got friends and Daisy's nicely settled in school and doing really well.

"He could come home for weekends. You and Daisy could visit in the school holidays. I can't imagine that Steve would want to uproot the pair of you, again."

"He doesn't," Susie sniffed. "He loves living down here, too. Working in head office in London. Steve says the North, South divide thing is a load of nonsense.

"But he *also* says it could be months before they find a suitable candidate for the job in Gateshead and that he can't be doing with all this toing and froing, in the meantime.

"Steve reckons that'll be even more traumatic for Daisy. That she might begin to imagine – well, all sorts of things! You *know* what she's like…"

* * *

Charlie's camera had been going non-stop. The grisly Scaffold Site had been shot from every angle. But inside the infamous Bloody Tower, he'd taken picture after picture of, in Brent Herring's opinion, nothing in particular.

But when he'd gently questioned the enthusiastic little boy, Charlie had an explanation, delivered in a hushed tone.

"You know ghosts, Mr Herring, well, they don't want to frighten people – they're not bad, or anything – so they sort of hide. Become invisible. In walls and things.

"But they like having their picture taken. *Everybody* likes havin' their picture taken. So when I get my film developed, I might have a tremendously brilliant photo of one. Or even two! That would be great, wouldn't it?"

Who, Brent asked himself, could even begin to argue with that kind of logic?

Now, on the way to a designated area, where packed lunches could be consumed, Traitor's Gate caught Charlie's attention. After a quick check in his WHAT TO SEE guide, he scratched his head.

"Mr Herring, if *you* were *you*, hundreds of years ago, would *you* invite people you knew very well, your friends, or p'rhaps your next-door neighbours, to come for a nice little sail down the river and to have tea in *your* house, then lock them away in a very cold room, without a telly or a Gameboy, for another hundred years and, after that, cut their heads off?"

Daisy tutted. "'Course he wouldn't. Mr Herring's decent, aren't you, Mr Herring? Me nan says you can always tell what people are decent. They're the ones with the shiny hair and the shiny shoes and clean underwear.

"An' some other things, too, but I can't remember what they are. I 'spect I will later, then I'll tell you."

"Decent people don't like hurting other people," Charlie said, thoughtfully "but they might not *always* be shiny, Daisy. They might have fallen in a muddy puddle or work at digging big holes in the road or be a brave fire-fighter and get covered in smoke and soot, saving people's lives.

"And," Charlie hesitated, briefly, "how can you tell what their underwear's like? It's not as if you can see *underwear*. It's very private!"

Daisy pushed her glasses up her snub little nose.

"D'you know, I never thought of that, pet. Neither did me nan. So I'll tell her when I next talk to her. She'll be well interested. Me nan likes to hear what I've got to say. She misses me, me nan does. Says she wishes I still lived in Gateshead."

Chloe was nervously twisting a long strand of pale hair round her finger.

"I don't like it here," she stammered. "It's horrible! And it smells, too. Like drains. Can we go somewhere else, please, Mr Herring. Can we—"

"Eat our lunch, now, cos I'm mega-starving..." Charlie suggested.

* * *

If anything, the noise inside the coach was several decibels higher on the return journey than it had been on the way to the capital as the children discussed the highlights of their day.

Without doubt, an exhausted Brent reckoned, the Scaffold Site had been a main attraction, closely followed by the Crown Jewels, the Bloody Tower and Traitor's Gate.

But, he realised, listening to the excited chatter, the trio he had been in charge of were now involved in an in-depth discussion on another matter...

"You didn't use your mobile phone, did you, Daisy? Not even once!"

"I couldn't, Chloe, cos it said in the book that you couldn't eat or drink or use 'em in historic areas. An' everywhere was dead historic! B'sides, I didn't fall into any dungeons or get chased by a man with a axe, so it didn't really matter."

"I'm glad you didn't, Daisy. Get chased by a man with a axe or fall into a dungeon, I mean."

"I am too, Charlie, pet."

"So... that means that mobiles aren't a lot of use... doesn't it, Daisy?"

"They *are* a lot of use, Chloe. You can do all kinds of things with 'em."

"What kind of things?" Charlie queried.

"Well, you can send messages. Without talkin'. 'Texts', they're called. Hang on, I'll show you. I press this button... and this arrow... that's it... incoming messages... oh, look, here's one from me dad to me mam. Last night."

Daisy grinned wickedly.

"He's in Gateshead, right now. Doin' a bit of work. I 'spect he's tellin' her he loves her. He's a dead soppy lad, me dad! Bet there's loads of kisses at the end.

"Listen, it says..." A sudden wail of anguish made the weary teacher sit bolt upright. Unclipping his seatbelt, he crossed the aisle to the distressed little girl, hunkering down at her side.

"What on earth is wrong, Daisy?"

"It's me dad, Mr Herring. He says he's found a nice bungalow in Gateshead. That means he must be gettin' a divorce from me mam… an' I'm not standing for that!

"Me dad's not that evil King Henry and I'm goin' to tell him. Right this minute. On me mobile…"

Desperate Measures

The cat was well and truly out of the bag. The love of Charlie Harper's life, his darling Daisy Pollock, was moving back to the north of England. Already, a FOR SALE sign was on display at her house.

Like it had been a few months back, when his dear old friend, his elderly next-door neighbour Hector Smythe, had died, suddenly, in his sleep, Charlie's usually lively face was pinched and drawn.

His mother, Tessa, had tried everything she could to assure him that it wasn't the end of the world. That he and Daisy would still be friends, even though she wouldn't be living in Eddingfield, any longer.

That good friends stayed good friends. For ever and ever…

"Don't be *too* sad, sweetheart. You can phone each other, and write to each other, and visit in the school holidays," she reminded him, this morning. "That would be great, wouldn't it?"

The response to her question was a long time coming. His chestnut coloured head bent, Charlie continued twiddling his thumbs. Eventually he looked up.

"No, Mum, that would not even be a *tiny* bit great. Daisy isn't just a *ord'nary* good friend – she's my very important girlfriend! We're gettin' married, remember." Greeny-blue eyes narrowed, he carried on, "*You* wouldn't like it if Dad went to live in Gateshead, would you? Or… America or Germany?

"*You* wouldn't think it was tremendously excellent if you could just write to him... or talk to him on the phone... or hardly ever see him... you would think it was *well* bad..."

Further explanations about how it was all to do with Daisy's dad's work, that the family had to go back or they wouldn't be able to afford to enjoy a nice life, were met with a stubborn silence.

Charlie suddenly stood up.

"I'm goin' next door to talk to Tristan, Mum," he said, digging his hands into the pockets of his jeans. "Tristan's a bit of a genius. Tristan knows loads of brilliant words that other people don't. Some words that haven't even been *invented* yet!

"An' I bet he'll be able to think of something to keep my darling Daisy here with me. I bet you – seventeen pounds, fifty pence he can.

"Oh, yeah, an' Daisy said she'll prob'ly be round this morning. Tell her to come through the hole in the hedge. Tell her I'll be waitin' for her..."

As Charlie stomped out of the back door, slamming it behind him, Martin, a giggling twin hanging on each arm, their knees bent and their small feet several inches off the ground, staggered into the kitchen.

"My arms are breaking," he groaned, trying to shake off the identical three-year-olds. Gentle Beth immediately released her grip.

"Oh, dear, Charlie's one arm got well broke on Tuesday."

Still clinging on, Georgia shook her bright copper head. "Wasn't Tuesday, Bef, it was Friday or Monday. Or when Father Chris'mas came down the chimley!"

"Was not Father Chris'mas. Was Tuesday."

"Was Monday!"

Georgia's voice had risen by several decibels. Tessa was not in the mood for any further dramatics. Besides that, the gurgles coming from the baby intercom revealed that little Sam had wakened from his nap.

Soon, she knew, the contented coos would turn to demanding shrieks as the tot realised his tummy was on the empty side.

"Charlie broke his arm on a Saturday, six weeks ago, and it's all better now. Let go of Daddy, please, sweetheart," she said.

In spite of the endearment, her tone must have been sharper than she'd intended, because the more determined of her daughters, the one who never gave in without a struggle, immediately obliged, landed on her small bottom, then scuttled the floor on all fours.

"Sorry, Mummy. I'll be a ex'lent good girl now." Georgia clutched Tessa's leg and gazed up, her bright green eyes full of concern.

"Charlie's 'mendously sad. Cos Daisy's goin' away. I'm 'mendously sad. Don't want Daisy to go 'way. Love Daisy. She's well cool."

A large tear trickled down Beth's face and plopped onto the floor.

"Mine own self does not want Daisy to go 'way. Mine own self loves Daisy, too. An' Charlie loves Daisy well good."

A few long strides and Martin Harper was holding tightly on to a Tessa whose own eyes were suddenly moist.

"Sometimes, darling, I think we underestimate the power of children's emotions," he murmured into his wife's soft tawny hair...

* * *

Tristan was the only one of the Warren-Smith children at home. Little Piers was at a birthday party and Sacha had gone shopping with her Mum.

"For *more* clothes!" Tristan said, his lip curling. "Boring! That's why I decided to stay with Dad. To get a bit of peace and quiet. But," he quickly carried on, "I'm glad you came round, Charlie. About Daisy... I've had a bit of an idea... we'll go inside and discuss it, since the weather is looking inclement."

Inclement, Charlie decided, looking up at a sky heaped up with fat clouds, must mean 'grey'. He made a mental note to remind his mum that his inclement school trousers were getting too tight and that he needed a new pair.

In the living room that used to belong to Hector Smythe, perched on the chair he had hauled over to the window, overlooking the garden, Charlie heaved a loud sigh.

"If my friend Hector hadn't gone and died... if Hector had still been alive, he'd have made everything all right. He *always* did that. But I don't mean," Charlie glanced, worriedly, over his shoulder at the tall fair boy, "that I'm not pleased you're livin' here, now, Tristan. I bet you've got a *tremendous* idea, but... we're just children. It's grown-ups that say what's gonna happen next.

"Like... well... I asked Dad if we could adopt my darling Daisy – there's a boy in my class, Jarred, who got adopted. He says it's great – but my dad said we couldn't adopt Daisy, cos she's got a mum and dad who love her an' that even if she didn't then I wouldn't like it either. Cos then she'd be my sister and you can't marry your sister. It's against the law!"

Tristan clutched his stomach and made loud, dramatic 'being sick' noises.

"Thank goodness for that! It's gross enough having to live under the same roof as Sacha. She's the biggest pair of pants in the universe."

Tristan's younger sister wasn't that bad. Not *all* the time. Charlie smiled shakily. "Sacha's okay... well, sometimes... when she's not being—"

"Abominable!" Tristan interrupted fiercely.

This time, Charlie spun his whole body round.

"Like that ginormous snowman thing? The one who hides on mountains or in forests... in Greenland or Iceland... and scares people by leaving mega-huge footprints?"

Tristan raised his eyes.

"Compared with my creepy sister, the Abominable *Snowman*, the Yeti of *Tibet*, is okay. Sacha is just *abominable*. A pain in the you know what!

"Unlike Daisy, who's… oh, look, she's coming… I'll go and let her in. Then I'll make Dad a fresh pot of coffee – he drinks gallons of the stuff when he's writing – and get us some cola and biscuits."

Tristan pushed his floppy fair hair off his forehead.

"See if you can cheer Daisy up a bit, Charlie. She looks really miserable…

* * *

Charlie was trying to think of a tremendously excellent joke which would make his sweetheart laugh when Daisy walked slowly into the room. Seeing her sad face and the pink bits round her eyes, he thought even harder.

Flopping into a chair, Daisy drew up her plump jeans-clad knees and rested her chin on them. "How are you, pet?" she asked, peering at him from behind her glasses.

Charlie shook his head.

"Not very okay, but thanks for askin'. I'm tryin' to think of a joke that'll make us a bit happy. Oh, yeah, I remember a great one. My Grandad Allen told me it. It's about a ogre an' you love ogres, don't you?"

Daisy nodded. "They're pretty cool."

"Right," Charlie agreed. "So, the great joke is, on what day does a ogre eat people?"

"Ogres are *always* hungry." Daisy shrugged. "So the answer is everyday, an', Charlie, I don't think that is a great joke!"

"That's cos you got the answer wrong. Ogres eat people on Tuesdays. Get it? *Tuesday*? *Chews*… with his mouth… day?"

Daisy sighed. "I wish a humungous, ginormous ogre would eat me dad! All up."

Charlie sat bolt upright.

"No, you do *not* wish that, Daisy! If a ogre did eat your dad, you'd be well sad. So would your mum. You ask her. I bet she'll say 'Yeah!'"

Her lower lip jutting out, Daisy stared at the ceiling.

"I can't ask her. I can't ask me mam *anything*. I'm not talkin' to her. Or me dad. Cos it's *their* fault, all this. It's their fault we won't be gettin' married, now. It's *their* fault that when I'm gone you'll be bloomin' Sacha's boyfriend and—"

"No," Charlie interrupted, fiercely, "I don't love Sacha. I love you! For ever an' ever. Cross my heart. Honest!"

Daisy pulled a tissue from the sleeve of her purple jumper, removed her glasses and wiped her eyes. Charlie dashed to her side.

"Don't cry. Please don't cry, Daisy. It makes me well sad. We'll think of something brilliant. In fact I think Tristan's already done that."

"I 'spect," Daisy hiccupped, "he'll say I ought to run away, cos that's what *I've* been thinking. Then, once me mam and dad have moved, I can come back again and—"

"That's probably the dumbest idea known to modern mankind. It's not even logical." Returning to his friends, Tristan dumped the heaped tray on the floor.

Daisy's confused eyes met Charlie's equally puzzled ones.

"What's he on about, pet?"

"Don't know. What are you on about, Tristan?"

"I'm not on about anything. You know what logical means, don't you, Charlie?"

He'd *definitely* heard the word before. Charlie searched his memory. Eventually he held one thumb up.

"Yeah. I do know. It's what my dad says my mum's not, but my mum says she is and my dad's not!

"Like… like… when the washing machine broke down and Mum chose this really tremendous one, with loads of buttons and flashing lights an' stuff, that could do *abs'lutely* everything.

"An' Dad said it wouldn't be *logical* to buy it, cos Mum would never need to press all the buttons, but Mum said she might an' anyway, it wasn't very logical of Dad to wear his good T-shirts to clean out the garage," Charlie finished, nodding.

Daisy looked thoughtful. "So, logical means gettin' the washing machine you want – cos your mum got it, didn't she, Charlie? Is that right, Tristan?"

"Mm, in a way. Charlie's mum was thinking things through in an organised way. Like I'm trying to do, right now." Tristan brows met in a straight line. "Daisy, if you ran away, where would you live? In a cardboard box in a falling down building, like some of the people who sell the *Big Issue*?"

"Like Matthew," Charlie suggested. "He's nice. My mum always gives him a pound when she buys the magazine, an' at Christmas she gave him *five* pounds, some tins of food, an' a nice warm scarf."

"An' there's Winston," Daisy murmured. "He's Matthew's friend an' he's got a beautiful curly dog called Dog."

Tristan poured three glasses of cola and ripped open a packet of chocolate biscuits.

"I know Matthew and Winston. I talk to them a lot. But, Daisy, they're men. You're just a little girl."

"I'm gettin' bigger every single day."

"Yes, you are. But how would you feel if you didn't have a nice bath to get clean in? Or a soft bed to sleep in? A great meal on the table? Someone to *really* care about what happens to you?"

Daisy's lower lip wobbled again. "I don't think I'd like bein' smelly an' tired an' hungry an'… I'd miss me mam and dad…"

Tristan looked satisfied. "Logical thinking, Daisy! So here's the plan. You and your mum are staying here until your house is sold… correct?"

"Yeah, Dad's lookin' for a new one in Gateshead – that bungalow he liked, Mam said the lady that lives in it changed her mind – but that Dad needs the money from *this* house so's he can pay for the other one.

"Or," Daisy's mouth twisted, "I don't know what he'll do…"

As her voice tailed away, Tristan picked up a biscuit and snapped it in half. "Tell me, Daisy, are there any parties interested in *your* property?"

"Don't know about a party, but there's some people comin' round to take a look tomorrow. *P'rhaps* they'll be wearing paper hats an' wavin' streamers."

"Right, well here's what *you* do…"

* * *

As she checked for the umpteenth time that the house was spotless, that there were bowls of fragrant *pot pourris* in all the rooms, and that the coffee machine was switched on, Susie Pollock was also feeling happier.

Well, as happy as she could be under the circumstances.

In spite of agreeing with Steve that there really was no alternative but to move back north, every time she thought about leaving her dream home and her terrific friends – Tessa and Molly – to start all over again, tears sprang to her eyes.

But at least Daisy's three-day silence was over. After visiting Charlie, yesterday, she was her old chatterbox self again. Obviously her adored boyfriend had said something to cheer her up. She'd even seemed extremely eager to welcome this morning's visitors.

"I'll dress up smart, Mam, and I'll help you show 'em around."

As the clock in the hall struck eleven, there was a crunch of tyres on gravel and the sound of footsteps thundering down the stairs. Heading for the front door, Susie's jaw dropped at the sight of her daughter.

Daisy had plaited her wild curls into two fat pigtails, a style she had always referred to as 'well pants'.

Instead of her usual jeans and sweat shirts, the little girl was attired in a demure pink candy stripe dress – a gift from her grandmother, which had been greeted with a curled lip and pronounced 'tremendously gross'. To complete the look, were prim white ankle socks and the outgrown black patent shoes which Susie had put aside to go to the charity shop.

"Go on, then, Mam. Let the party in," Daisy said softly as the doorbell jangled. "A very good morning," she simpered to the couple on the doorstep, a Mr and Mrs Carruthers. "Welcome to our beautiful house."

Susie felt a distinct sense of unease. Something was going on. But finding out what would have to wait until later, because Mrs Carruthers was already peering into the living room.

"How lovely," she murmured. "So light and airy. And such a lovely view of the garden."

Daisy skipped over to the pleasant-looking woman's side and clutched her hand.

"Yeah. An' there're *loads* of dead things buried in that garden. Even a horse, called, er, Albert, an'a—"

Susie's shoulders shot up to ear tip level. "Daisy," she interrupted firmly, "there are *no* horses buried in our garden."

The little girl shrugged and flashed her eyes at the tall man, standing behind her mother.

"I think there might be, Mr Carruthers. Mam's just forgot. But I know 'zactly where it is. I'll show you later, if you like. After you've seen the rest of the house.

"You'll like my room." Her eyes shining with excitement, her voice hushed, Daisy carried on. "There's a ghost in it! Sometimes, late at night, he comes and sits on my bed. Or it might be a girl ghost. I can't tell, cos it doesn't have a head or anything. But it's well cool."

Susie considered interjecting again, but knew, deep down, that it would be a waste of breath. Besides, *too* many protests…

But she couldn't help cringing as her daughter confided, "An' when we go outside, so's I can show you my cemetery, don't mind the drain under the kitchen window. Me dad's got another bloke comin' to have a look at it. We've had *seven* already! Or p'rhaps it was eight.

"But I'm thinkin' you prob'ly won't even notice it, today… the toilet smell… not with that strong coffee me mam's made and all them bowls of dead flower petals…"

Half an hour later, Daisy having disappeared to make what she had declared to be a mega-urgent telephone call, Susie bade her visitors farewell.

"'I'm so sorry about—" she began her apologies.

Mrs Carruthers interrupted, giggling. "Please, don't worry. We've got one just like her at home. A male version. Jake doesn't want to move, either.

"He told our last viewers that the house was overrun with mice and that the woman next door liked dancing around the front lawn without any clothes on!

"But they're *still* extremely keen on our property and we're *very* interested in yours, Mrs Pollock…"

Friends in High Places

"They were at the cemetery looking for *what*?" Sheila Harper stared at her lunchtime visitor, Tessa, who was spooning the last of the jar of creamed haddock into baby Sam's mouth.

"Yummy strawberry yoghurt next," Tessa told her gurgling six-month-old son.

"Guardian angels," she repeated to her mother-in-law. "When Charlie asked Martin to take him and Daisy and Chloe to Hector's grave, we presumed it was just one of their usual visits. You know, when they take flowers – or interesting vegetables – and tell him all their news, but, apparently, Chloe heard a story about how everyone had a guardian angel and—"

"Charlie decided," Sheila interrupted, thoughtfully, "that the cemetery was the right place to find his and Daisy's?"

"Exactly! They've even got it all worked out what these angels can do, Sheila. It seems that a few flicks of magical wings, and a word with God, will conjure up someone to take over Steve Pollock's job in Gateshead and make that couple, the Carruthers, who are after Daisy's house, change their mind and move to Greece or Japan instead!"

Sheila couldn't help grinning. "Greece or Japan! Charlie's or Daisy's suggestions?"

Tessa chuckled. "Daisy's. She also came up with a grisly plan involving runaway tractors flattening the Carruthers' car, and another about rare fatal diseases, for which there was no known cure. Then she changed her mind and said she wasn't being decent thinking like that!"

Tessa's smile suddenly faded. She sighed. "I honestly thought that, by now, she and Charlie might have come to terms with the situation. You know how resilient children usually are?

"But, if anything, it's getting worse… and I'm at my wits end trying to come up with, if not a solution, then something to distract their attention…"

The two women sat in silence for several moments, each lost in their thoughts. Then Sheila stooped and picked up the bundle of creamy fur, who had been sleeping at her feet.

"Here's another little soul who could do with a guardian angel," she murmured, stroking the small dog's long silky coat.

"Still not settled down with Bouncer and Ben?" Tessa wiped pink dribble from Sam's chubby chin.

Sheila shook her head, sadly, and gazed out of the kitchen window into the garden, where the two energetic retriever brothers, who she and Jim had adopted the year before, were enjoying a boisterous game, which involved a lot of tail wagging, and good-natured sparring over a collapsed football.

"They're mad as hatters, but they're lovely lads," she said. "They've tried everything to make friends, but she's terrified of them. The problem is that this gentle little girl has never learned *how* to play. She's not much more than six months old, but she's far too well-mannered for her age.

"And she still doesn't have a *proper* name. Jim wants to call her Lady." Sheila pulled a face. "Talk about a lack of imagination! Mind you, *she* doesn't seem to care. Answers to anything, really. Honey. Blondie. Poppet."

Poppet seemed to fit the bill perfectly, Tessa thought, her grey gaze meeting a pair of melting-chocolate coloured eyes. Then the dog dropped her head, as though embarrassed. Or, perhaps, Tessa wondered, aware of what might lie ahead of her. She felt her throat go dry.

"What are you going to do with her, Sheila?"

"Well... Jim thinks the fairest thing would be to take her back to the rescue people. He feels she might get on better in a house where she's the only dog. Maybe one with children – she seems comfortable with children – you've seen her with Charlie and the twins and Sam. Gentle as a lamb..."

* * *

Another little accident! Martin had been right when he'd declared that they needed a dog like they needed all the ceilings to fall down, the central heating boiler to give up the ghost, and Tessa to decide that she was going backpacking, to Kathmandu, for six months, to find her inner self, with the help of a yogi mystic!

And yet, as she mopped up the small puddle from the kitchen floor, a smile lifted the corners of Tessa's mouth.

The change in the timid little animal was remarkable. In less than a week, she had not only stopped trembling, but could chase a ball along with the best of them. And had revealed a comic talent of being able to dance, uninvited, on her stocky hind legs!

Also, her devotion to all the children was patently clear.

Charlie seemed to be her favourite. Wherever he went, she went. Like a little bouncing shadow. Hardly surprising, Tessa supposed, considering the welcome the little boy had given her.

Dropping to his knees, his arms filled with champagne-coloured silky hair, flurries of damp kisses landing on his bare arms and his scarlet cheeks, Charlie's delight had been almost tangible.

"You mean... she's ours, now, Mum? Ours? To keep for ever and ever? Oh, wow! How fabulously, tremendously excellent! Mega-cool! I've wanted a dog all of my life. Every second of my life, actually..."

Then again, she was devoted to the twins, spreading herself equally across both laps, snuffling with pleasure at their, occasionally, not so tender gestures of love.

Like being put in a doll's pram and being pushed, at high speed, round the garden... until Tessa had firmly pointed out that dolls were dolls and dogs were dogs! And that no, dogs did *not* like being dressed up in hats, socks and Barbie sunglasses.

"Does so like it," had been Georgia's defiant response, delivered with a fierce glare. "Thinks it's ex'lent."

"P'raps puppy'd like a pretty dress?" Beth had suggested. "Pink one. Or a lallow one."

Puppy! Tessa glanced over her shoulder to where Sam was sleeping in his little bouncy chair. At his feet, was a creamy bundle who was gazing at Tessa with anxious, guilty eyes. Washing her hands, she picked up the small creature.

"Don't worry, sweetheart," she soothed, dropping a light kiss on the silky head, "I'd probably wet myself, too, if anyone hugged me as hard as Georgia hugged you. But don't worry, I've explained to her that she must be more gentle.

"And it's also high time we decided what your name is. We can't go on calling you Puppy..."

* * *

Martin's suggestions of 'Bitsa' or 'Hearthrug' were met with a storm of protest. Tessa curled her lip.

"I know she's not exactly a pedigree, but that's just downright corny. Bitsa this and bitsa that – honestly! Besides, it's a lad's name. And, you must admit, this little poppet is very cute and feminine."

She grinned, slyly, recalling the evening before when she'd come into the living room to find her husband and dog, snuggled together on the sofa, sharing a packet of chocolate buttons, while he explained the offside rules of the football match he was half-watching.

"In spite of what you said, Martin, you're hooked, darling."

Hearthrug, Charlie pointed out, wasn't a *proper* name.

"You wouldn't like it if Grandma and Grandad had called you Hearthrug Harper, would you, Dad?" he queried.

"Probably not. So, what would you christen her, Charlie?"

Charlie went through his entire repertoire of facial gymnastics: nose wrinkling, eyebrow wiggling, mouth twisting. Then the eight-year-old shrugged.

"I need to have a bit of a think. My darling Daisy says names are brilliantly important and that you should *think* about them well hard. So we did.

"When we get married and have some girls, we're going to call 'em Tulip, Poppy and Lily, cos then we'll have a bit of a garden all the time – even in the winter!

"That's a great idea, isn't it?" Charlie's bluey-green eyes shone with enthusiasm. "An' then, I 'spect if we have *more* girls, we'll call these ones... Buttercup and Pansy. Yeah, that's what we'll do. I'll tell Daisy later."

"What are you going to call your little boys, sweetheart?" Tessa asked, flashing a warning glance at Martin, who looked as though he was about to burst out laughing.

"Daisy thinks it might be mega cool to call boys things like River and Moon and Sky. River Harper – that's tremendously excellent. What do you think?"

"It's certainly different," Tessa said carefully, while a scarlet-faced Martin pulled his handkerchief from his pocket and blew his nose hard.

"Gotta bad cold, Dad?" Beth, sitting on the floor, stroking the contented small dog, gave her father a sympathetic smile.

"Must *not* use your sleeve to wipe your nose or Mum'll tell you off," Georgia advised. "An' I wanna call my nice new puppy Cheesie."

Martin managed to turn his snort of laughter into a convincing cough.

"An' I wanna call mine own new puppy... er... er... San'wich!" said Beth.

"Good job Sam's not old enough to have his say," Martin spluttered, dabbing at his eyes, "otherwise the poor scrap could end up being saddled with Banana Custard! Tess, you got any thoughts on the matter?"

"One or two, but I'd rather wait and see what Charlie thinks might be mega cool," she declared, turning her attention to her elder son. "What are you going to do this afternoon, sweetheart?"

"Daisy and me are going to Chloe's. Remember, Mum? That Auntie Molly said we could stay for tea an' Uncle Adam would bring us home later?

"Remember, Mum... about Chloe knowing a real live angel, who lives right across the road from her? And that we're gonna visit her?"

Tessa remembered her friend Molly's invite, but the angel thing...

"You didn't tell me about visiting anyone *else*, Charlie."

"I absolutely did, Mum. Cross my heart. I said there was this lady, who did amazin' good work for people in hospitals, an' readin' to ones who can't see very well, an' bakes great cakes so the church can get a brill new hall, an'... oh, tons of stuff.

"Auntie Molly always says she's a absolute angel. Remember now?"

The penny dropped. Tessa smiled.

"Okay, but don't make a nuisance of yourselves, will you? Miss Button'll be pleased to see you, I'm sure, but she is a *very* busy lady, you know, and she's not exactly... well... young."

Charlie rose.

"Actually, that doesn't matter if you're an angel. You can be any age you like if you're one of them. An' Miss Button *is* well looking forward to seein' us. Auntie Molly told her all about me an' Daisy and she said we can come round and talk to her an' have a cup of tea. It'll be great. Can I go now, please, Mum?"

Tessa nodded. "Have a lovely time."

Saying his goodbyes to the fluffy little dog took a long time. At the back door, Charlie turned.

"Miss Button's got a tremendously interestin' first name. An' I bet she'd be pleased if I told her we were gonna call our new puppy the same thing! I'll think about it – see what Daisy and Chloe say."

"What *is* her first name, Charlie?"

"It's Gutsy, Dad. See you later…"

Tessa had to wait a good five minutes before her almost hysterical husband, head in his hands, shoulders shaking and repeating 'Gutsy Button', over and over again, recovered enough to hear her say, "It's not *Gutsy*, Martin, it's *Dulcie!*"

* * *

"For me? Oh, thank you, Charlie, dear. What a beautiful picture. And, Daisy, what a splendid bunch of flowers. How kind of you."

"Angels always say things like 'dear' an' 'beautiful' an' 'splendid' and 'wonderful'," Daisy murmured to Charlie, as Chloe proffered a small box of chocolate.

"My very favourites. Absolutely wonderful."

"See!" Daisy whispered. "An' when d'you think I should ask her to show us her wings, pet?"

Charlie didn't answer. His eyes were fixed on the laden tea-table. Some fat yellow scones with currants in them. Tons of chocolate biscuits. And angel cakes!

A ginormous plate of them. Like the kind his Grandma Allen made, except these ones had little *real* gold balls stuck into the cream.

Daisy dug him in the ribs.

"Come on, she wants us to sit down while she goes and makes herself a nice cup of tea an' gets us some cola and juice."

"Don't call her *she*, Daisy, call her Miss Button," Chloe hissed, sinking into a chair. "*She's* the cat's mother, my Gran says."

"Who – Miss Button?" Charlie's jaw dropped as he joined Daisy on the settee.

"No, silly." Chloe narrowed her blue eyes. "*She's* the cat's mother?"

"Who?" Charlie persisted.

"Chloe'll tell us later, pet," Daisy patted his hand, "cos I don't really understand what it's all about, neither. When me Bradford Nan says it. I mean, your little puppy – Whasername – must have had a woman dog for a mother and *she* would be the dog's mother, wouldn't she?

"An' me mam had me, so *she's* Daisy mother. Your mam had you, so *she's*..."

* * *

Charlie was in a state of high excitement when he returned home, at half past seven. Cross-legged on the carpet, the dog practically glued to his side, he revealed the events of the afternoon.

"Great news, Mum! Dad! I had *two* teas, today. One at Miss Button's – it was well excellent, we ate loads – then another one at Auntie Molly's.

"*She* made..." Charlie stopped. "Oh, I can't say that even if Auntie Molly is def'nitely *not* the cat's mother. Chloe can't even have a *kitten*, cos it would make Auntie Molly sneeze and sneeze. She gets straw fever, you see."

"*Hay* fever, Charlie." Over his son's head, Martin met Tessa's eyes. He raised a questioning eyebrow. Tessa gave a barely perceptible shrug.

"Oh, right, thanks for telling me, Dad. Anyway," Charlie rattled on, "at Chloe's house, we had lasagne and chips. An' look what I've got."

He fished around in his pocket, pulled out a clenched fist and slowly uncurled his fingers, revealing three, small, sugar-coated golden balls.

"These," he announced, in a hushed voice, "were on Miss Button's angel cakes. A present from God, Daisy says. She's got some, too. So has Chloe.

"Miss Button didn't show us her wings, or anything, an' she said she couldn't cross her heart about bein' able to help Daisy stay here, but we think she'll be able to. We *know* she's a real angel, cos... well, it was rainin' today, wasn't it?"

"It certainly was," Tessa agreed. "Cats and dogs!"

Charlie nodded. "Yeah, or it might have been their mothers. But when we left Miss Button's house, she came out with us... to make sure we looked right, left and right, again... an' all of a sudden, the sun came out.

"When we got to the other side of the road, we turned round to say 'Thank you for havin' us', again, an' also 'thank you for makin' sure we got over the road, nice and safe.' An' guess what?"

"She flew across and said 'Don't mention it'?" Martin suggested, dryly.

Charlie tutted.

"Don't be silly, Dad. She was wearin' one of these things that baby Jesus and his mum and dad wore in the stable. A hello, I think it's called."

"A *halo*, Charlie," Tessa gently corrected.

"That's right. One of them. The sun shone on her nice white hair and, suddenly, Miss Button had a halo! That's well brilliant, isn't it? An' then," Charlie continued, barely pausing for breath, "when we went into Auntie Molly's, Uncle Adam was home from work. With a miracle. In his pocket! Guess what it was..."

Martin had *that* look on his face! Tessa jumped in quickly before he could come out with a wisecrack. "I really can't imagine what it might be. You tell us, sweetheart. Hurry up. I can't wait."

"Neither can I," Charlie said, breathlessly. "Neither can *I* wait to go to London an' see all these wax people, who look just like *real* people, but aren't.

"Uncle Adam's got tickets. One for Chloe. One for Daisy. One for me and one for him. It'll be great to go to Madame... Too... er, Tootsies... er..."

"Tussauds," Tessa supplied. "It's a wonderful place. You'll love it. I can remember going there when I was just a little girl. I remember—"

"Was it *invented* then, Mum?" Charlie interrupted, his eyes wide, then, without waiting for an answer, yawned widely and scrambled to his feet.

"I'm really tired, now. I think I'll go to bed an' do a bit of readin'. Come on, Gutsy." He opened his arms wide; the puppy sprang into them, pushing her damp nose under Charlie's chin.

"Is that – is that what you've decided to call her?" Martin asked, weakly.

"Yeah, Dad. Gutsy Angel Harper. It's great, isn't it? Daisy thinks so. Chloe does, too. Miss Button says it shows a lot of, er, 'magination and that Gutsy means brave.

"An' Miss Button should know, shouldn't she? Bein' an angel..."

Waxing Lyrical

Originally, the trip to Madame Tussaud's had been for himself, his daughter, Chloe, and her friends Daisy Pollock and Charlie Harper. But when his wife, Molly, had pointed out that it would be the children's other close friend's, Li's, ninth birthday the following week, Adam Young had swiftly acquired a fifth ticket for the delightful Chinese lad.

"Are you sure you'll be able to handle them? On your own?" Molly had queried anxiously, earlier this morning.

"No problem. They're good kids. Bright as they come. In fact I reckon that I'll return home tonight a *much* wiser man! Can you imagine what they'll have to say about the Chamber of Horrors, Moll? The mind boggles…"

Cradling her baby son, Jake, she pulled a face.

"Actually, Adam, I've been thinking… perhaps they're a bit *young* to be exposed to that kind of thing. I mean it's not exactly—"

"Darling, they'll *love* it. Kids adore being scared in a safe environment. Gruesome fairy tales when they're tucked up in bed. Tom and Jerry knocking the stuffings out of each other on the telly.

"Stop worrying. They'll have a ball…"

* * *

Adam herded his excited charges towards the lift, "Our first stop-off will be at the Garden Party, where we'll see… oh… film stars… people from the television… Eric Cantona and—"

"The Queen, I suppose," Daisy interrupted. "She's gotta be there, cos she's dead good at doin' garden parties. Every year, in the summer, she bakes tons of iced cakes and makes loads of sandwiches and ginormous pots of tea, then millions of really posh people come along for a bit of a chat. In tents, cos it's usually raining and they don't want to get their good hats wet!"

"What – all at the same time? *Millions* of them?"

Daisy nodded. "Yes, Charlie, pet. She's got a bloomin' big garden, you know, the Queen. With lakes an' rivers an' big pink birds with long thin legs."

Li solemnly shook his glossy dark head.

"I don't think it's millions, Daisy. Thousands, perhaps. But she does have long-legged birds called flamingos in her lake."

The lift had stopped. Chloe was the last of the children to step out.

"Flamingos are pink. They're pink because of what they eat," she stated. "Things like shrimps and prawns. And – wow, look at all these famous people!"

"*Well* famous! This is tremendously excellent. Mega amazin'!" Charlie spluttered, jiggling from one foot to the other. "Over there – that's whatsisname… from the telly… he digs gardens an' stuff."

"You were right, Mr Young. There's *Eric Cantona*." Li pointed. "He's my favourite footballer in the universe. He's French, you know? From France!"

Charlie nodded, enthusiastically. "Yeah. From France."

"If he's French, he's not likely to come from South Africa, is he, pet?" Daisy rolled her hazel eyes behind her glasses. "Oh, look, Chloe… there's that lady from *Absolutely Fabulous*! Her name's Patsy. She's cool, isn't she, in her nice red clothes and lipstick."

Chloe pouted. "Mummy won't let me watch that programme. She says it's for grown-ups."

"Oh it is," Daisy agreed, cheerfully. "Me mam won't let me watch it neither, but when I was stayin' at me Auntie Lucy's, in Leeds, me cousin, Saffron, she had a video of Ab Fab. I saw it then."

"Was it great, Daisy?" Charlie asked his sweetheart, who twisted her mouth, thoughtfully.

"Actually it was a bit silly. There are these two women, see – Patsy an' the other one. They like to get drunk an' then fall over. That's all really... 'cept they smoke a lot, as well."

"Smoking is crazy. It kills you, before you're ready to die. And getting drunk is stupid, too," Li declared. "Some of the people who come into my Dad's restaurant get drunk, then they shout and say silly things. I'm *never* going to do that," he finished, fiercely.

"Do Chinese people get drunk, too, Li?" Charlie queried.

"'Course they do, pet." Daisy answered the question. "An' people from Japan, an' America, an' Holland."

Chloe tossed her blonde ponytail, disdainfully.

"Well, I'm never going to do it, either, Li. Or smoke, cos it's smelly and disgusting and – oh, Daisy, look. That's Naomi Campbell. She's a supermodel.

"I think *I* might like to be a supermodel when I'm older. You get tons of money for just walking around wearing great dresses and designer jeans and T-shirts. I'd like to get a good job, so I can put money in the bank and not worry about paying my bills."

Adam, who often thought that Molly was a shade overprotective of their daughter, almost paranoid about her television viewing, snatching away newspapers when a particularly awful crime had hit the headlines, made a mental note to have a word with his wife about what he'd just overheard.

Point out that youngster weren't quite as gullible as some adults believed them to be.

He was still thinking along these lines as the party headed for the Sporting Greats hall, where Torvill and Dean (in their world famous Bolero costumes), Linford Christie, Tim Henman and many other heroes and heroines were oohed and aahed over.

Then it was on to Superstars and Legends…

"Who's James Dean, Daddy?" Chloe asked, frowning.

"I've never heard of him," Li said, almost apologetically.

Before Adam had time to explain, Charlie's voice rang out.

"And I've never heard about that man." He pointed. "Humphrey Bogart. What did he do, Uncle Adam? And that one, over there – Alfred Hitchcock? Was he tremendously famous?"

Again, Adam got no chance to answer.

"See that woman," Daisy nodded her curly head to where a curvy figure, wearing the famous 'blown by the subway air vent' white dress, from the *Seven Year Itch* movie, stood in all her incandescent blonde beauty, "well, if you ask me, she should have bunged her jeans on if she was goin' out on such a windy day.

"It's not decent dressin' like that. Nearly showin' her knickers. Who's Marilyn Monroe, anyway?"

Aware of muffled laughter surrounding the irrepressible Daisy, Adam hurriedly nudged the children forward. To more recognisable subjects…

"That's the *real* James Bond." Charlie's voice was high-pitched with excitement.

"And that's Indiana Jones," Li whooped.

"That man there," this time, Daisy's voice was hushed, "eats people!"

Chloe's jaw dropped.

"*Who* eats people?"

"Him! Sir Anthony Hopkins isn't his *proper* name, see. His proper name is Hannibal the Cannibal. I haven't seen the film – me mam won't let me watch that one, neither – but I know someone who has seen it. And he told me *all* about it."

Chloe's blue eyes were cloudy with confusion.

"*Why* does he eat people, Daisy?"

Plump shoulders shrugged. "Cos he's a bit mad?"

Chloe nodded. "That's okay, then. Oh, I can see Michael Jackson. He's a really cool dancer. And I think he can sing…"

As they approached the Great Hall, filled with modern and historic public figures – kings, queens, heads of states – Adam thought, not for the first time, that children were marvellous levellers!

How, in their honest innocence, they frequently managed to hit the proverbial nail, slap, bang, on the head.

"How many of them folk are dead?" Daisy asked, eyeing up Henry the VIII and his assorted wives, Kings Charles and Richard I.

"All of them," Adam supplied.

"An' this lot?" Hands on hips, Charlie's darling surveyed Gladstone, Churchill, Lloyd George and Margaret Thatcher.

"Lady Thatcher is still alive, Daisy."

"So the others are all dead, then?"

"Yes, Charlie, but if we go over there, we'll see people who are still alive. Wonderful characters like Nelson Mandela, who cares desperately about the world and even went to prison, for a long, long time, just because he believes that each and every one of us is equal. No matter what colour our skins are…"

Just his luck, Adam thought as they strolled towards the Modern Royals and Creative Arts, their last ports of call before stopping for lunch, that all his charges had focused their attentions on Gandhi, John F Kennedy and Abraham Lincoln, resulting in a comment from Chloe: "It's a bit like a plastic cemetery in here, isn't it, Li?"

The royals, bar one, did not stand up to scrutiny. Only the late Diana, Princess of Wales, was declared to be perfect.

"There's the Queen. I wondered where she'd got to. But that's *not* the Queen Mum!" Hands on hips, Daisy shook her head. "*That* woman looks more like me Gateshead's nan's next-door neighbour, Maud Jessop."

"The Queen's hair's the wrong colour. It's brown. Hers is white," Li murmured.

"Prince Charles is a bit bald now," Charlie offered. "You can see pink bits on his head when the wind blows. *This* Prince Charles has got loads of hair."

"Perhaps he was a bit embarrassed, so he wore a nice wig when they made his model," Chloe suggested.

Adam was still chuckling as the small quartet came face to face with the Beatles. To his amazement, all four children immediately recognised the 'Fab Four' and were clued up regarding the groups long string of hits.

A good-natured disagreement followed over which was the *best* song, then dance-crazy Chloe broke away from the others and pirouetted across the floor towards the model of ballerina Darcey Bussell.

"I don't think," she said after several moments, "that I'll be a supermodel after all. I think I'll be a ballet dancer, instead."

"You should, Chloe," Li said, earnestly. "You're very talented, my mum said, when she saw you in the school concert. I'm going to run a restaurant… like my dad does. Or I might be a lawyer."

Daisy's gaze was locked onto Luciano Pavarotti.

"Yeah, an' I'll be a singer like this nice big fat man, with the twinkly eyes.

Mr… Loo… Pavra… something Italian, like pasta, but with more letters in it."

Charlie's greeny-blue eyes lit up. "Pasta! Can we have our lunch now, please, Uncle Adam, cos I'm well starving. Then can we go down to the Chamber of Horrors. I can't wait to go there… it's gonna be tremendously scary an' creepy! Loads of blood an' stuff. It'll be great, won't it?"

Nodding, Adam offered up a silent prayer that Charlie wouldn't decide that when *he* grew up, he fancied being Vlad the Impaler, mark two…

* * *

On the spur of the moment, Susie Pollock had invited her friends, Tessa and Molly, for lunch. She had so much to tell them. Things she didn't want to mention when Daisy was around.

"You look harassed." Leaving her three-year-old twin daughters to play in the garden with Gutsy, their much adored new little dog, Tessa hugged the small blonde woman.

"Worn out," Molly agreed. "But then there's nothing quite like moving house to frazzle the nerves. Got a completion date yet?

"Oh, no, Susie," she gasped, minutes later, "*when* did you find out?"

"Last night. Quite late. Mrs Carruthers came round to tell me. She's gutted, poor woman. She really had her heart set on this place. Of course she fully understands that Steve and I can't wait 'til they find another buyer… that we'll have to take the first offer that comes along."

"It's awful when this happens. You think you're home and dry, then, someone along the line breaks the chain." Tessa sighed. "What has Steve said about it?"

Susie took a deep breath. "He doesn't know. His mobile seems to be playing up and I couldn't get hold of him at the hotel. I rang the office, as soon as Daisy left, this morning, only to find out that things are pretty chaotic in Gateshead, too.

"Apparently, last night, there were meetings going on well into the small hours. I've left a message for him to ring me as soon as he's got a minute." She shrugged. "I can't think of anything else to do. Except wait and see…"

"Have you rung the agents? Told them to get cracking?" Tessa asked.

Susie's pale cheeks flushed. "Not yet."

* * *

"Am I just being mean-minded and spiteful, Tess, or did it cross your mind that Susie isn't exactly breaking her heart about this setback?" Molly queried, later that afternoon.

Finishing strapping the last of her three small children into their car safety seats, Tessa turned. Her grey eyes were serious.

"She's never wanted to move back north, again. *Steve's* only insisting because he can't see an alternative. *We* don't want to lose them. *Charlie and Daisy* are miserable about the prospect of being separated. So would *you* be heartbroken – in Susie's situation?"

Molly grinned. "Absolutely not!"

* * *

None of the children seemed disturbed by the gruesome sights in the Chamber of Horrors. But they *were* curious and had plenty of opinions…

"Did anybody *like* anybody in the olden days, Uncle Adam?"

"Of course they did, Charlie. The people you see here are the *very* wicked ones."

"Not that Joan of Arc woman," Daisy pointed out. "The one standin' on top of the bonfire. She was a saint, it said. A good friend of God's."

"And I feel sorry for Guy Fawkes," Chloe said, "cos if we hadn't had him, then there wouldn't be any beautiful fireworks."

"Yes, Chloe, but you mustn't forget that he tried to do a very wicked thing. He tried to blow up the Houses of Parliament," Li said.

"Well, they could have built another one, couldn't they?"

The main attraction, Adam decided, the one which brought forth the most gleeful groans, was, without doubt, the French Revolution exhibits.

Especially Madame Tussaud herself... portrayed by lamplight, sorting through decapitated bodies, searching for the severed head of Marie Antoinette in order to make a death mask...

"That is disgusting!" Chloe giggled, hands over her face, fingers widely splayed to allow a good view.

"I agree. Not a very nice way to earn a living." Li frowned.

Daisy took off her glasses, cleaned them on the hem of her skirt, then replaced them, thoughtfully.

"Well, don't worry about it, Li, cos it would be against the law, now. Mr Blair says it isn't decent to chop people's heads off and that we should all work in supermarkets or offices or hospitals, instead. What do you think, Charlie, pet?"

"I'm thinking... I don't know zactly what I'm thinking... so I'll have a bit longer think, then p'r'aps I'll tell you what I think then! If I think anything!

"But," Charlie grinned, "it is great, isn't it? An' I know something well interesting. Tristan next door told me. He knows tons of things about words. Great big long words. Like abominable and shenanigans – that means 'getting up to tricks' – equiv'lent, which means—"

"Charlie! Get to the well interesting bit," Daisy butted in, impatiently. "Tristan knows zillions of words an' if you're gonna tell us every single one, then we'll still be standin' here when this place closes!"

She peered around. "I mean it is mega-amazin' but I don't fancy bein' here all night. In the dark. Near that man gettin' hung—"

"Hanged!" Charlie interrupted. "That's the interestin' word I was talking about. You see, you *hang* your coat up and when your mum says 'Where's your coat?' you tell her you *hung* it up."

"That's not very interesting," Chloe said quickly, when Charlie paused. "In fact it's quite boring, actually."

"That's because I had *not* finished. The *interestin'* thing is that when you hang up a *person*, you don't say you hung them. You say you *hanged* them."

Adam's head was spinning. And he could see from the expression on both Chloe and Daisy's faces that they were still unimpressed. Li saved the moment.

"Mmm," he murmured, "that could be useful to know. If you were writing an essay on... history, perhaps. Or one called My Visit to the Chamber of Horrors. Thanks, Charlie, for telling me that."

Charlie grinned. "Don't mention it."

"He already did, pet, so there's no point in tellin' him not to, is there?"

"I was being *polite*, Daisy."

"Oh, right! Well, that's okay then. Polite's good."

"Come on, gang," Adam instructed, "we've still got more to see, before we go home. The Spirit of London's next – where we all get into little taxis and learn how life was for people hundreds of years ago."

He studied his guidebook.

"William Shakespeare, the famous playwright; Admiral Lord Nelson, who fought the battle of Trafalgar; Queen Victoria and another great writer, Charles Dickens.

"And," he carried on, "some of these models actually move and talk!"

"Wow!" Chloe gasped.

"Amazing!" Li said.

"Tremendously excellent," Charlie declared. "I could stay here for ever and ever."

"I don't want to go home, either." Daisy face was a mask of misery, "Cos I reckon me mam'll have signed some papers while I've been away and that'll mean our house isn't our house any more…"

Celebrations

It was Charlie Harper's great friend, Li Chang's ninth birthday. The celebration was taking part in the Golden Bridge restaurant, one of Eddingfield's most popular eating places and owned by the Chinese lad's parents.

Dressed in his new cream chino trousers and trendy ginger-coloured shirt, Charlie's gaze took in his exotic surroundings.

"Your mum and dad are well-clever, Li. This is tremendously excellent. A mega-amazin' place to eat your dinner in."

Seated beside Charlie, the love of his life, his darling Daisy Pollock, wearing a dress in her favourite bright orange, sighed her own approval.

"You're right, pet. All them beautiful lanterns! An' pictures of lovely bridges an' birds. I've not ever, in me whole life, been anywhere so nice and posh. Have you, Chloe?"

The petite blonde's mouth twisted. "I once went to a *quite* posh place, in London, with my gran and grandpa. It had real velvet chairs and a ginormous glittery light thing hanging from the ceiling.

"But I was a bit worried that would fall down on my head. And it was in the *daytime*." Chloe looked at her watch. "Eight o'clock. At night! On a Saturday. This is much, *much* better. Well grown-up." Her blue eyes, the same shade as her strappy T-shirt, sparkled. "I'm really glad you're Chinese, Li."

"Thanks a lot." Soft colour swept across the shy lad's handsome face.

"So am I really glad, Li. It wouldn't be nearly as cool if your mam and dad had a burger bar. Not that I don't like burgers. I do." Daisy picked up the menu and studied it, briefly.

"But I like this kind of stuff better," she declared. "'Specially sweet an' sour an' them crispy pancake rolls. An' I'm also well pleased you had your birthday before I had to go back to…" Daisy stopped. Her lip trembled. Under the table, Charlie caught hold of her hand and gently squeezed it.

"P'raps you *won't* have to go to Gateshead, Daisy," Chloe put in quickly. "I mean your house isn't sold, yet, and there's still a chance that a guardian angel'll help you out. You're praying, aren't you? Every single minute? Tremendously hard? I am."

Daisy's wild curls wobbled as she nodded frantically.

"I'm doin' it right now. You can't see me lips move, cos I'm prayin' inside me head."

"So am I," Charlie declared. "An' all my family are, too. Well, not Sam, he's a baby. But Beth and Georgia are, 'though they're only three. I told them about God and his angel friend, Miss Button, who helps *everybody*, and Georgia said that was cool an' began to pray.

"Beth does everythin' Georgia does – 'cept for some of the naughty things – so she's talking to God as well, now."

Li tilted his glossy dark head, thoughtfully. "I've been praying for you, too, Daisy. To God and to Buddha."

Chloe and Daisy exchanged a confused look. Charlie's face lit up.

"I know about Buddha. Tristan, Sacha and Piers, next door, in my friend Hector's house, have a beautiful statue of him in their garden. Not of Hector. I wish it was. I miss him well much, now he's dead."

"We all do, pet," Daisy said. "But tell us about this Buddha person."

Charlie's thoughtful look vanished. "Well, he's a lovely fat man, a God from another country, I think. He's got bare feet, not many clothes, an' a brilliant smile. He's got a big round tummy, too!

"Tristan says if you rub it, the Buddha will be mega-happy and bring you good luck. Oodles of it, Tristan said. He likes interestin' words. 'Oodles' means tons an' heaps an' loads.

"Tell you what," Charlie rattled on, "I'll go round there, tomorrow, soon as Tristan, Sacha and Piers come back from their holidays, an' I'll give Buddha's tummy a well good rub. You can come, too, Daisy. In fact we could *all* go."

"If Buddha's not wearin' many clothes, won't he mind if we all touch him, pet? I mean won't he think we're not bein' decent?" The plump little girl looked anxious.

"'Course he won't," she was assured by her boyfriend. "He's a very kind person an' he'll be pleased we're thinkin' about him."

"Okay, then. We'll go. Do you pray in Chinese, Li?"

"No, Daisy, in English. But my mum and dad are probably doing it in Chinese. I don't think it matters what language people use when they pray… as long as they believe something good in their hearts."

Li's dark eyes narrowed, suddenly. "I wonder what the Fortune Cookies will have to say. My mum's made some extra special ones. Just for us. Instead of a cake."

"What're Fortune Cookies?" Chloe frowned. "I've never heard of *them*, before."

"Neither have I," Charlie said.

"Nor me," Daisy said.

Li smiled. "You'll see. At the end of our meal… oh, it's coming, now. Dad thought it we be good if he brought us all sorts of different things. A real birthday feast… with chopsticks…"

* * *

"Wow, that was tremendously excellent! I am fuller than I've ever been in all of my life," Charlie announced an hour later. "My favourite was prawn chop suey. Or p'rhaps it was that chicken chow mein. Noodles are cool. I never knew I liked 'em, before. Now I'm gonna eat tons of them. An' I'm gonna practise usin' chopsticks, too."

"D'you think *your* mam would tell *my* mam how to make proper rice, Li?" Daisy asked. "Me mam's tastes like it's stuck together with glue, me dad always says."

Chloe, who had proved most efficient with the chopsticks, giggled as the empty plates were removed by a smiling waiter who had just said, 'Excuse me, Madam,' to her. "Egg Foo Yung's a funny name, but it's brill. And I never knew, Charlie, 'til tonight, that mushrooms are so scrummy."

Satisfied, by the food and his friend's reactions, Li relaxed back in his seat. Over Charlie's head, he could see his father approaching. "Our Fortune Cookies – now it's time to find out what's going to happen to us all," Li said.

After thanking a beaming Mr Chang for a mega-brilliant dinner – the best in the entire universe – Charlie, Daisy and Chloe turned their attention to the four plain pastry twists, on an oval silver tray.

"Er… is there toffee or chocolate or something inside?" Chloe queried.

"Do we eat 'em with cream?" Daisy asked. "An' them chopsticks?"

"No," Li said.

Leaning forward, Charlie put his elbows on the table and rested his chin in his cupped palms. "So what *do* we do with them, Li?"

"We take it in turn to choose one, we break it open, and then we read the very special—"

"Hang on a minute," Daisy interrupted, "we haven't sung Happy Birthday, yet. We've gotta do that. So you know you're really nine, Li."

As the rest of the diners joined in, Li's face turned the same scarlet as the tie he was wearing with his smart grey suit and crisp white shirt.

"Don't be embarrassed, pet," Daisy soothed. "That was well nice... everyone singin' to you. Now... let's see about them Fortune Cookies. You go first, Li, since it's your birthday."

"No, *you* go first, Daisy. Go on," he persisted as she looked dubious, "take a big breath and then pick up the one which you feel holds a very special message, just for you."

"But how will know if I'm takin' the right one?"

"You just will, Daisy. You just will..."

Daisy took a long time making her mind up, but, minutes later, all four children had a cookie in front of them.

"*Now* what do we do?" Chloe asked.

"This!" Li snapped the pastry shell and removed the tiny paper scroll. The others did the same.

Charlie was the first to begin to untwist his coil. His mouth twisted. "Er, this is in... real Chinese, I think, an' I can't read real Chinese."

Li grinned. "Keep going, Charlie. It's in English, too."

"Yeah, you're right... it says 'SUN SHINES ON YOUR LIFE, BECAUSE YOU ARE SUNSHINE'." He frowned. "What 'zactly does that mean?"

The children hadn't noticed that Mr Chang was standing nearby.

"It means, Charlie," he explained, "that you are a good and warm person, who brings much happiness to others and, because of that, people around you become warm and caring, too."

"It means you're well cool, pet," Daisy stated.

"Does it? Wow! Thanks a lot for tellin' me, Daisy. Thanks a lot, Mr Chang." Charlie's gaze settled on Chloe, who had completed her task and was staring at the scrap of crisp paper. "What does it say?"

"It says... 'LIKE THISTLEDOWN YOU WILL LIGHTLY FLOAT, TO BEAUTIFUL MUSIC FOR A WATCHING AND LISTENING WORLD'." She looked up at Mr Chang. "This is true. I'm a dancer. And my teacher says I sometimes look like I'm floating. This is amazing! Daisy, what does your one say?"

The curly head was bent. Daisy's fist was tightly clenched. "Don't know yet. I'm a bit scared to look at it, in case it says I'm horrible an' bad an' evil, cos I don't want to go back to Gateshead even though me nan and grandad want me to."

"You're *not* evil, Daisy," Li said, firmly.

"Not even a *tiny* bit horrible," Chloe consoled.

"An' if *I'm* not bad, *you* can't be," Charlie said, "cos I don't want you to go, either!"

A small smile lifted Daisy's mouth, but she still seemed reluctant to reveal her fortune.

"Tell you what," Li offered, "I'll do mine, next. Mine says 'YOU HAVE BEEN GRANTED LIFE'S PRECIOUS GIFT OF BEING ABLE TO WORK HARD AND TAKE THE RIGHT PATH TO FIND YOUR OWN FORTUNE'."

Charlie sat bolt upright. "My grandad's always saying somethin' like that. About it bein' okay to have a bit of good luck, but you need to work hard, because not many people get everythin' they want for doin' nothing!"

"They might if they won the lottery, pet."

"I know that, Daisy, but if you won the lottery an' had nothing interestin' to do, you'd be well bored. Just watchin' telly all day long and eatin' cream cakes.

"An' now," Charlie continued, "we all want to hear about the really great thing that's gonna happen to you."

Very, very, slowly, the little girl opened her palm and, equally slowly, unrolled the paper. Several seconds passed in silence, before she looked up at her friends.

"There's somethin' goin' on, again!"

"Is that *all* it says, Daisy?"

"No, Chloe! It doesn't say that, at all. That's just me thinkin'. What it says is 'THE HEAVENS SMILE ON YOU. LOVE PROTECTS YOU. LUCK WILL ALWAYS BE YOUR COMPANION'."

Daisy's brows drew together. "D'you think that means that me lucky guardian angel has had a word with God, and p'rhaps that Buddha, as well – to be on the safe side, like – and they've said they love me, so it's okay for me to live here? For ever and ever…?"

* * *

Tessa's plans for a quiet evening of catching up on neglected chores, once the little ones were in bed, had gone right out of the window. The Harper household was bedlam, everyone talking at once and Gutsy, the new puppy, yelping in excitement and prancing around on her short hind legs.

Steve and Susie Pollock had been the first to arrive. Hand in hand. Giggling like teenagers.

"*We're staying!*" Susie shrieked. "It's all been sorted out. They've finally got someone for the Gateshead office and, even if that doesn't work out, they've promised Steve they won't mess him around again.

"I know we should have phoned first, Tessa," she'd apologised, half-heartedly, waving a huge bottle of champagne, "but we were just too… oh, all sorts of things! I did think to ring Molly, though. Before she settled baby Jake down for the night and—"

"What she's trying to say," a grinning Steve had interrupted, "is that the Youngs are on their way here, too. Hope you and Martin don't mind. We just thought that, well, with you having *three* tots, it would be easier if we broke our good news here, rather than invite you all round to our place. At such short notice…"

Tessa hadn't minded in the least. Not even that her hair needed washing, she wasn't wearing a scrap of make-up and that her jeans bore the remnants of teatime tomato ketchup and a blob of dried chocolate pudding.

The Pollock's excitement was infectious. Susie had lost that worryingly drawn look, although she still looked rather pale. But, uppermost in Tessa's mind were Charlie and Daisy.

She waited until little Jake had been settled upstairs, in Sam's room, with the benefit of a baby alarm, and all six adults had a glass in their hand, before raising that subject.

"You've only just had the call... so Daisy doesn't know yet?"

Susie pushed back her thick blonde curls from her flushed face.

"We thought about it, didn't we, darling?" she said. Steve nodded. "And we decided," Susie continued, "not to telephone the Golden Bridge. It's *Li's* special occasion. *His* birthday. And he's such a sweetheart. We didn't want to jump in and spoil anything."

Molly, sprawled in an armchair, stretched out her long legs.

"Then it's a good job one of us still has her feet on the ground!" she stated, grinning.

"Feet on the ground?" Martin echoed.

Molly nodded.

"The children? Mr Chang was going to drop each of them off at their *own* houses? Around ten o'clock? Remember?"

Susie clapped a guilty hand against her mouth. "Oh, heavens," she spluttered.

"No sweat!" Molly chuckled. "I've spoken to Mrs Chang. Arranged for them *all* to be dropped off here... in about fifteen minutes." She rose and picked up the champagne bottle. "Time for a top-up, I think. Especially you, Susie. We need to get a bit of healthy colour back in those cheeks, now everything's nicely settled."

Susie placed a hand over the glass from which she had taken only a tiny sip.

"Actually, there's something I haven't told you." Gnawing on her lower lip, she glanced sideways at her husband. "Not even you, Steve. I didn't want to worry you… being away and all that… and with everything up in the air… another reason why I wanted to stay here among our friends… the *best* reason in, as Charlie would likely say, the entire universe…"

* * *

The following afternoon, the children gathered together in the Warren-Smith's garden, sitting around the statue of the smiling Buddha.

In one of his open hands sat a red rosebud.

"A lovely thought," said Li, who had just announced that because the Warren-Smiths had still been away on his birthday, his parents were planning a special Chinese barbecue for everyone, including all the parents.

"I pinched it out of the big bunch me dad sent me mam," Daisy said. "She won't mind that Buddha havin' it. Nor will me dad. They're well happy, see. Cuddlin' each other. And kissin'."

Tristan, his face golden brown from two weeks in the sun, grinned.

"More than just that, Daisy. They've been doing a spot of procreating, too."

Charlie's greeny-blue eyes widened. "Have they? My goodness!"

"Absolutely! No doubt about it."

"What's procky… that thing you just said?"

Sacha's lip curled. "It probably doesn't mean anything, Chloe. Tristan's just showing off. He's *always* showing off. Even in Portugal, when he was pretending he could speak to the shopkeepers in… in… whatever language they talk in!"

"Portuguese, you pleb!" Tristan smiled lazily at his younger sister.

"Pleb! What's a pleb?" Daisy peered over the top of the glasses.

"Hold on," Chloe said, "we don't know about the procky thing, yet?"

"*Procreation*," Tristan sounded out the word, "is how the human race is carried on. Your mum's having a baby, isn't she, Daisy?"

"Yeah. She and me dad must have been doin' that stuff some people do in Blackpool, but not, Charlie's mam says, in supermarkets or buses, cos it's dead private."

"Exactly. They've been procreating! Making a new human being."

"That is *well* interestin'," Charlie said. "How do you know all these brill words, Tristan?"

Sacha answered the question.

"Because he eats dictionaries for breakfast, instead of cereal, Mummy says," she accused, sniffily.

Charlie chuckled. "That's not true. You're havin' a joke, Sacha. But jokes are great. *Everythin's* great, cos my darling Daisy's stayin' here, with me, and Sam and Jake'll soon have a new friend to play with."

"I'm mega-glad you're not going away, Daisy," Chloe said.

"So am I," Li said.

"And me," Sacha said, in a small voice, her brown eyes momentarily settling on her secret hero, Charlie.

There was a hiss and a fizz as Tristan filled plastic beakers with sparkling cola.

"Time for a toast," he announced. "To Daisy."

Charlie took a sip. Then, "Tristan, what are the very best words you know to say how happy you are that Daisy's not goin' to Gateshead."

The response to the question was immediate. Tristan raised his beaker. He did a backward somersault, without spilling a drop.

"*Tremendously excellent!*" he shrieked.

It's Magic! - Christmas Special

"Oooh, lots an' lots an' lots! Pretty! Do more, Georgie. Do more an' more an' more!"

At the shrill sound of his little sister's voice, Charlie Harper, curled in a chair and engrossed in his new electronic game – his most tremendously excellent present ever – glanced up.

Russet-coloured eyebrows drew into a straight line as he glared at the tot.

"Stop *tellin'* her to do it, Beth!" He turned his attention to the bolder of his identical twin siblings.

"Georgia, stop playin' with that Christmas tree! You're making all the needle things fall off. Again. You *know* what Mum said about them gettin' stuck in the hoover? No, don't shake your head. You do know. Mum's told you a zillion, trillion times!

"I got one stuck in my bare foot, this morning, cos *you've* hid my new slippers. It well hurt! Serves you right if you get a ginormous Christmas needle stuck in your bottom!"

Exasperated, Charlie switched off his game.

"Where *are* my slippers, anyway, Georgia. I know it was *you* who hid them, cos you did it to my old ones, last week, and Mum found them in the cupboard under the sink.

"I know it was you, cos *you* said 'Sorry, Charlie,' when Mum told you that Father Christmas only brought loads of tremendously excellent presents to good girls' houses. So where are they, this time?"

"Don' know!" Georgia exchanged a secretive sideways glance with her now silent sister.

Charlie sighed. "You're a lot of a pest at times, Georgia. Look at the mess you've made on the carpet."

"Am not a pest! Had a raccident." The defiant three-year-old snaked her arm behind her. The tree shuddered. Her bright red ponytail quivering, Beth whooped with delight.

"Lots an' lots an' lots again! Clever girl. Ex'lent!"

"'S'not excellent, Beth! That was *not* an accident, Georgia! You did it d'liberately. I'm gonna tell Mum if you don't pack it in," Charlie threatened.

"Tell Mum what?" Alerted by the shrieks, Tessa hurried into the living room.

Her grey eyes immediately settled on the usual cause of minor domestic disturbances in the Harper household. Georgia's innocent round green ones met her enquiring gaze.

"'Lo, Mummy. Bein' good girls," she declared sweetly, sliding back a few inches and spreading the skirt of her blue velvet dress over the evidence of her antics.

But not before Tessa had spotted the piles of dry pine needles.

"Georgia, have you been shaking the tree again?" Her question was met by the sight of a small index finger pointing upwards, towards the sparklingly-dressed white fairy, perched on the topmost branch.

"Was a raccident. Twinklebell did it!"

"Twinklebell's a well bad girl," Beth said solemnly.

"Is she? Oh dear!" Tessa attempted what she hoped was a suitably sombre expression. "Well, if *Tinkerbell* is a very bad girl, she won't be at the pantomime, this afternoon, and if *Tinkerbell* isn't there," she turned briefly to wink at a suddenly concerned-looking Charlie, "there won't *be* any pantomime."

Georgia's creamy cheeks became an angry scarlet.

"Will so be a pantomine for mine own self! Want to clap for Twinklebell. Want to make lights shine for Twinklebell."

Beth's lower lip trembled. "Want to see Peter Pam flyin', for mine own self, too."

Tessa nodded, calmly. "We *all* want to see Peter Pan flying, we *all* want the whole world to light up for Tinkerbell, so we *all* have to hope that she has no more little accidents, don't we?"

"That was well brilliant of you to say that, Mum," Charlie congratulated when he'd followed his mother into the hall to help get the vacuum cleaner out of the cupboard.

"I bet it works. It worked when you told Georgia that Father Christmas wouldn't come to bad girls who told big fibs, so I bet she won't touch the tree again. Well, not today.

"She really wants to go to the pantomime. She's always playin' the *Peter Pan* video. Tell you what, Mum, I'll go and put it on for them, and maybe Georgia will be so tremendously happy that she'll tell me where she's hidden my brand new Pokemon slippers.

"Oh, yeah, and can my darling Daisy Pollock sit beside me at the pantomime? She says she might get a bit scared when she sees the crocodile and Captain Hook. She says she *might* need to hold my hand…"

* * *

Charlie had been to the splendidly ornate old town theatre on several occasions, as had his friend, Chloe, seated on his other side. For his sweetheart, Daisy, having moved to the area from the north-east of England, it was her first visit.

For several minutes, the plump, pretty little girl silently surveyed her spectacular surroundings, her hazel eyes enormous behind scarlet-framed glasses, around which she had twisted slim strands of sparkling silver thread.

"I'm twinkling cos it's still *sort* of Christmas," she'd explained when the party – the Harpers, the Pollocks (Daisy's parents) – and the Youngs – Tessa's closest friend,

Molly, her husband, Adam, with their daughter Chloe, had met in the foyer.

"I'm thinking, Charlie, that I'm sittin' inside a cake!" Daisy said now. "Not one of them posh birthday cakes. Not a Christmas cake. I *hate* Christmas cake – all hard nuts and chewy red bits. Yuk!

"No, this is a beautiful bride and groom's one. With frills and lacy stuff and white and golden bits. An' *real* angels!"

She turned to Chloe. "D'you think it's like bein' in one of them?"

Chloe tilted her head. "Mmm… it is a bit!" She giggled. "It would be magic to be *inside* a cake, wouldn't it? We could eat loads, then, when we were full up, we could dig a hole in the icing and shout 'Hello' to everyone."

Daisy held both thumbs up.

"Yeah, magic! The beautiful bride would likely faint – cos she'd be well scared! Her handsome husband would have to lift her up and put her to bed and kiss her all better, so's they could live happily ever after."

Her expression became momentarily dreamy as she carried on.

"Like the pantomime I went to with me nan and grandad. In Gateshead. *The Sleeping Beauty* it was called. There was this girl, see, a princess with very long yellow hair – a bit like yours, Chloe – and when she was a baby she got a christenin'.

"Her mam and dad, that was the Queen and the King, forgot to invite her auntie… or something like that… maybe it was their next-door-neighbour. I forget.

"But *she* heard about the party and came anyway. A bit late, so she missed the sandwiches an' the sausage rolls an' the wine an' the cake.

"She was well angry. She thought it was pants. Then," Daisy lowered her voice to a hiss, "she did something mega wicked! Guess what?"

Engrossed in the girls' conversation, Charlie's chestnut-coloured head had been swivelling from side to side. "As if he was sitting centre court at Wimbledon," Martin, in the row behind the threesome, a wriggling, impatient twin on either side of him, commented to Tessa.

"What did the bad auntie – or the next-door neighbour – do, Daisy?" Charlie asked, breathlessly, only to have to turn again as Chloe took up the story.

"Well... she wasn't really a *proper* auntie... or a neighbour... she was a *wicked witch*, so she put a tremendously bad spell on the little princess. She said that when she was... sixteen... or eighteen... or twenty... she would prick her finger on a evil needle, when she was making herself a new dress, and she would go to sleep for—"

"Ever and ever an ever!" Daisy interrupted, dramatically.

Chloe tsked.

"She did *not* say for ever. She said *a hundred years*. And that did happen, Charlie! The beautiful princess went to sleep for a whole hundred years and so did every single person in the palace. Even a cat and some mice and a spider in its web. Honest!"

"Oh, dear!" Charlie frowned. "That wasn't very nice was it?"

"No," Daisy cheerfully agreed, "but it had a happy ending. Pantomimes *always* have happy endings.

"This one's was that, one day, a handsome brave prince was ridin' through the forest and he saw this ginormous castle with weeds growin' all over it.

"He was a bit nosey. He got his sword out... some of his friends had axes an' shovels... and they cut all the weeds down. Then the prince went into the palace and saw the Sleeping Beauty. He fell in love with her, so he couldn't help givin' her a kiss, and—"

"She wakened up!" Chloe butted in. "Everyone in the palace wakened up and went to the prince and princess's wedding. *Everyone* lived happily ever after."

Charlie slid down on his red plush seat. He rested his chin, thoughtfully, on his chest.

"Why," he asked, after a lengthy silence, "did the handsome prince want to kiss a well thin old lady with no teeth and white hair?"

"What old lady?" Daisy and Chloe responded in unison.

"The sleepin' one! You said she was more than a hundred years old, so she must have had white hair and no teeth. An' if she hadn't ever wakened up for her dinner – or a pizza – she must have been mega thin. Like a skelington! Yuk!"

"No, she was still 'zactly the same as when she fell asleep," Chloe assured him. "*Everyone* was the same. Like… they'd just gone to bed the night before. Like… when they turned the telly on to watch *Neighbours*, after being on holiday for two weeks, they felt like they hadn't missed a single bit of it!"

"That's what happens in fairy tales, Charlie." Nodding, Daisy patted her sweetheart's hand. "You're a boy, see. An' boys don't like a lot of kissin' stuff. That's why you didn't know about what happened to the beautiful princess.

"But," she carried on, "you know about magic. There's tons of magic in every single pantomime… like boys changin' into girls and girls changin' into boys. When I saw the *Sleeping Beauty*, the handsome prince was *really* a girl!"

Charlie's tone was hesitant as he looked from one friend to the other. "So… was the beautiful princess… a boy?"

Chloe raised her bright blue eyes to an intricately painted ceiling, where heavenly hosts of gilded, pink-cheeked cherubs snuggled together, beaming down on the layers of audience.

"'Course not. Don't be so silly! The princess was – oh, we'll tell you 'bout that later – the curtain's going up. The pantomime's starting. Good! It's been ever so boring sitting here with nothing to do and nothing much to talk about."

"Bet Nana the dog isn't a real dog. Bet it's a bit of fur with two lads inside it. An' bet Peter Pan's a *girl*," Daisy whispered in Charlie's ear as the house lights dimmed.

"Me dad'll like that," she confided. "Bet yours will, too. Later, me mam'll say, 'Steve, you were looking at her legs!' But me mam won't be annoyed, or anythin'. Cos she knows it's only magic. And it's Christmas. Sort of!"

Daisy's fingers closed round Charlie's. "Don't forget to cheer the brave people and shout 'Boo' at the bad ones, pet. Like Captain Hook and the crocodile who ate the clock... an' the bad pirate's hand... I think... or p'rhaps it was his head..."

* * *

The following morning, only Charlie and Martin were in the kitchen. Fired up by all they had seen, the over-excited twins had wakened in the very early hours.

"Look, Mummy, we can fly," they had squealed, using their beds as trampolines. "Like Peter Pam an' Twinklebell an' John an' Wendy an' Michael!"

It had taken Tessa a long time to settle them down again and all three were still asleep.

"My voice well hurts, Dad," Charlie declared, after demolishing two bowls of crunchy cereal and a couple of slices of toast. "I think it must have been cos I cheered an' hissed and shouted 'Boo' a hundred thousand times!

"An' I clapped, so hard, that my hands felt all hot and sizzly. My darling Daisy's did, too. She said her fingers looked like a pound of the best pork sausages her grandad always buys from his favourite butcherman.

"The butcherman's name is Felix. That's interesting, isn't it? A butcher called Felix? Pantomimes are also tremendously interesting, aren't they? Thanks a lot for taking me."

Martin poured himself a second cup of tea and topped up Charlie's orange juice. "I enjoyed it, too," he said. "We all enjoyed it."

"I liked the *real* dog best. The real *Nana*," Charlie said. "It would be great to have a ginormous dog like that, wouldn't it? An' it didn't do a wee on the stage, did it? Daisy was worried that it might, cos the men playing the music in their smart black suits would get all wet!

"What bit did you like best, Dad? Was it Peter Pan's legs? Daisy said *her* dad would like that bit best. Peter Pan was really a girl, you know? Just pretendin' she was a flying boy…"

Martin couldn't meet his son's innocent eyes. Remembering Tessa's murmured comment as she'd dug him in the ribs: "Not a wobble. Not a stretchmark. No wonder you're goggle-eyed. *She* clearly hasn't given birth to four kids!" He pushed his hand, several times, through his dark hair, until it stood up in sharp spikes.

Then cleared his throat.

"It's hard to say *which* bit I liked best, Charlie. I thought the whole thing was great." Swiftly, he changed the subject away from long slender legs and potentially incontinent canines.

"Did you know that the man who wrote *Peter Pan* made up the name Wendy? That no little girl had ever been called it before?"

Charlie's jaw dropped.

"Why did he have to make a name up? Didn't he like any of the other ones? Were girls all called well horrible names before the man wrote *Peter Pan*? Were they called things like…" he glanced round him, "Microwave… or… Rubbish Bin?"

"No, sweetheart, they were called beautiful names like Beth and Georgia and Charlotte," a shadowy-eyed Tessa offered, walking into the kitchen. She ruffled Charlie's hair.

"I think the writer – his name was J M Barrie, by the way – just wanted to be a little bit different."

Charlie's mouth twisted.

"*He* had a bit of a funny name, didn't he? I don't know a boy called Jayem. Still," he shrugged, "he was a well good writer. *Brilliant* at magic.

"An' you know that glittery fairy dust that looked like silver clouds and always came when Tinkerbell was around – well, Chloe says a little bit of it got stuck on every single person in the theatre.

"Today, she says, we'll all be a bit more magic than we were yesterday. Today, I 'spect, tremendously wonderful things might happen. Georgia might pack in shakin' the Christmas tree and—"

Charlie stopped as his giggling sisters charged through the door.

"Got a ex'lent present for you, Charlie!" Beth shrieked, taking her hands from behind her pink-dressing gowned back.

"My Pokemon slippers! Wow! Thanks. Where did Georgia hide them? Tell me, please, so's I can look there the *next* time she does it."

Beth stuck her thumb in her mouth. Beside her, Georgia shook her head indignantly until her fiery curls spun out like miniature chairoplanes.

"Did not *hide* 'em. S'magic! *Twinklebell* brought 'em. Left 'em in mine own toy box. At the bottom. Under all my dollies an' my cuddlies an' my puzzles… an' my books…"